Magic AND Mocktails

a cozy fantasy romance

AMBER L. WERNER

Contents

FAIRVALE
Crater Gorge
CARRAN
Maudwin
Wile Basin
FAIRVALE
Rubble Mines
Halwin Lake
Veil Ruins
Larkinge
Jade River
Everpass
Peloith
Pelo Lake
Avalon Shallows
Paradise Plains
Faversham
Windswept Woods
Southhold
Tempest Isle
Seahaven
Sunken Cove

You Hear That

Nora

"Put down the imp!" In a quaint little tavern within a picturesque town nestled in the shadow of the Savurios Mountains, Nora planted her hands on the bar and stared down a red-faced orc while wondering how her life had come to this.

Sure, it wasn't all bad. In her teens and twenties, she'd endured the horrid pinching of travelers' fingers on her bum while slaving away as a barmaid in the only tavern in Everpass, always with a smile on her face and an amused twinkle in her golden-brown eyes—so she could pocket their tips, of course.

After years of scraping and saving, she'd achieved her lifelong dream of business ownership—finally working up the courage to take out a lease on an old, run-down potion store on Main. She'd worked endless hours cleaning it and invested most of her savings into stocking the shelves with unique liquors and cordials. Now, at thirty, she was exactly where she'd always pictured—working for herself and loving every moment.

Well, almost every moment... As the orc continued to fume, his nostrils flaring and limbs quivering more with each second, she reminded herself that by welcoming all patrons—even temperamental giants—she'd begun earning a small profit six months in.

By dubbing her bar as the opposite of her former workplace, she attracted a different sort of clientele. The pompous owner of the Golden Lark Inn had a strict code of conduct for all employees and customers, though he was content to look the other way when travelers got handsy with the waitstaff.

At Stellar Spirits, all races could mingle any day of the week and relax without having to dress up or be on their best behavior. But it didn't come without its own set of headaches. Like the one staring back at her right now, looking livid enough to explode.

"Ivan, please." Summoning her coolest demeanor, Nora met the furious gaze of one of her regulars.

Like most orcs, Ivan's head nearly brushed the ceiling, his muscled frame twitching with barely restrained rage beneath his homespun shirt and trousers. But she couldn't let his size faze her. Not if she wanted to escape this encounter without seeing one of her customers' blood spilled on the freshly mopped tile floor.

"When I agreed to let you host your weekly card game here, you promised not to let things get out of hand. Remember?" She glared pointedly at the wooden bench he'd spent all morning seated on. The same one he'd likely cracked when he shoved it on its side beside a table scattered with cards and coins.

Ivan's hands trembled, one clenched tightly over Yolti's mouth, his other arm banded around the bristling imp's torso, plastering the poor guy to his chest. "You didn't hear what he said about—"

"Words, Ivan. That's all they were." Nora spoke soothingly, the knowledge well-honed from decades of dealing with an orc at home. Well, half-orc. Her brother, Seth, was five years her senior, but she'd always been the one who reacted best when things went sideways. And she'd learned calmness was the key to talking orcs out of their mercurial shifts of temper. "Let him down. Please."

Ivan's heaving chest gradually settled. "I did make a promise."

"That's right! You did." Nora flashed a smile. "Just let him go."

"All right." Slowly, Ivan set Yolti back into the chair he'd plucked him out of. The imp's boots clunked on the wood, his eyes narrowed to tiny slits. "I'll let him go. So long as he takes back what he said."

"Perfect. No harm done." Nora held Yolti's gaze as Ivan's hand began to unclamp from his mouth. "Go ahead, Yolti. Time to make nice." But the instant his hand fell away, revealing a grotesque sneer that made Yolti's wrinkled face even uglier than usual, Nora's stomach sank.

Yolti glared up at Ivan, the tips of his wiry hair barely reaching Ivan's nipples even while he stood on a chair. "You hear that? It's the sound of me not caring."

"Take. It. Back!" Ivan's hands curled into fists.

Nora blanched. "Fellas, please—"

"Why would I take back the truth?" Yolti hissed.

Ivan roared, "If you don't, then I'll crush your puny skull into dust."

"Fine. I take it back."

Nora's breath escaped in a huge, relieved whoosh.

Then Yolti's sneer melted away, an evil grin rising to replace it. "I was too generous earlier. Truth be told, your mother's so damn ugly she could scare the shit out of an outhouse."

Oh no. Nora had a single fleeting moment to wonder where she went wrong before all hell broke loose.

"I'll kill you!" Spittle flew out of Ivan's mouth as he lurched forward, face crimson, arms swinging.

Yolti ducked and swiped at his boots, avoiding the first wild blow.

Her brows pinched together, and she yelled, "Stop! Take it outside before you—"

Ivan swung again as Yolti bounced into the air, leaping far higher than any imp had the right to. But it wasn't quite high enough. Ivan's fist clipped Yolti's foot in midair.

"Ahhhh!" Yolti spun, rolling end over end and barreling straight for—her!

Gasping, Nora ducked beneath the bar just in time to avoid having her head lopped off by Yolti's flailing limbs.

Crash!

Eyes wide, she whipped around, staring in horror as the shelves wobbled on the wall. Dozens of bottles had smashed when Yolti landed on the top shelf. Liquids in a myriad of colors pooled on the tile.

She jolted to her feet. "Yolti, for the goddess's sake. Don't mo—"

The top shelf buckled and, with a final groan, cracked down the middle, spilling every bottle to the floor as that shelf crashed into the next. And the next.

No. No, no, no! Nora sank to the tile, her hands tangling in her long dark-brown hair.

The liquid creeped closer, drenching her plain black dress in its sticky embrace. And yet, she couldn't find it in herself to care. She couldn't move. Not while her stock lay destroyed, the shattered jars a reflection of her hopes and dreams.

There was no way she could fix this... Those bottles represented a lifetime of labor and love. Many of the ingredients she'd grown herself over the course of *years*.

Sobs echoed, the only sound in a room that had fallen eerily silent. It wasn't until Ivan planted an enormous beefy hand on her shoulder that she realized the cries were emanating from her. "Nora, I'm so sorry. If I'd known his boots were charmed, I'd have never..." He trailed off, as if his words sounded wrong even to him.

Fact was, Ivan would've probably blown up at Yolti either way.

"Yolti." She blinked, belatedly seeking the imp amid the mayhem.

"I'm all right." The idiot finally had the sense to look chagrined as he picked his way out of the broken mess of glass and ruined liquor. "I'm really sorry about this. You can keep my winnings, to offset the loss."

The damn game... That was what had gotten them into this in the first place. An argument over who had won the last hand.

Ivan dug into his pocket. "Mine too." Coins clattered on the bar.

"Fine. Just go." Nora's voice escaped in a breathy whisper she hardly recognized.

"You sure?" Ivan asked. "We oughta help you clean up."

Her hand shot out, pointing at the door. "Just, please, go. I can't look at you two right now." Burying her head in her arms, she closed her eyes. Maybe if she pinched them tight enough, when she chanced another glance, everything would be back the way it was.

Please, just let this be a horrible nightmare...

The front door's hinges creaked before a slam echoed in her ears.

She wasn't sure how long she sat there, alone, stewing in the wet puddle behind the bar. It wasn't until the door groaned again that she finally lifted her head.

"Nora?" the familiar voice of her dearest friend called out. "Ivan told me I needed to—" Her words cut off on a gasp. "My goddess! Nora, where are you?"

"Here," she said, only managing to dredge up a tired whimper of a reply.

Alsira Mikelli, whom everyone called Ali, kneeled beside her. "What fresh hell is this?" She cocked her head at the wreckage, making her coal-black bob cut bounce against her neck. "All my beauties... I can't believe this."

With a sob, Nora tugged her into a tight hug. Along with being her best friend, Ali also happened to be Everpass's resident glassblower. Since she'd handcrafted all the bottles currently smashed to pieces, she was bound to be a little emotional too.

"This is... crazy." Ali rubbed Nora's back soothingly. "I'm so sorry, Nora."

With a deep sigh, she shook off the embrace. "I don't know what I'm going to do."

Ali twisted her lips as she stood. "Well, that's easy. You'll rebuild. I'll get started on some replacement bottles right away. Sure, this isn't ideal, but you'll get through it. I know you will." She toed at a large shard with her boot, causing her typical garb—a long-sleeved tunic over tight-fitted trousers—to pull taut against her tall frame.

"What if I can't?"

"Of course you can." Ali spun back, her dark-brown eyes flashing. "You'll just have to dig into your savings."

Nora winced, dropping her gaze to the floor.

"Nora..." Ali's hard tone made her head snap up. She suspected if Ali's skin wasn't so dark that her emotions rarely showed on it, her entire face would be flushed. "You *do* still have your savings, don't you?"

When she first leased Stellar Spirits, she'd purposely kept a modest amount of funds in the bank, knowing something like this might happen. But it wasn't long before that nest egg disappeared. "Well..."

"Goddess, no! Why, Nor?"

"You know why," she grumbled.

With a sigh, Ali thrust her hand down, twiddling her fingers in Nora's face. "Get up."

Nora huffed. "Must you be so bossy?" She snagged Ali's hand.

"I think so, yeah." Ali chuckled humorlessly. "Gross, you're dripping."

"Guess I should get changed..." But Nora didn't move. She just stood there, staring at the mess she'd likely never bounce back from.

Then Ali grabbed her shoulders and twisted, propelling Nora away from the bar. "Nope. I am not gonna stand here and watch you wallow. Go upstairs. Clean up. Then pull your head out of your ass and figure out what comes next."

Nora's shoulders stiffened. "You know what? You're right. I refuse to abandon my dream over a little spill." She looked back, instantly regretting it. *Who am I kidding? That's not little at all.*

Ali clapped her hands. "That's more like it! Nora Rowen is no quitter."

A tentative smile graced her lips. "Damn right I'm not."

"You'll work your ass off like you always have and come out on top of this."

"I will." Hope bloomed in Nora's heart. "Thank you, Ali."

Ali grinned. "Of course. Now get moving. And if you need any help, you know where to find me."

With her friend's advice ringing in her ears, Nora climbed the steps to her tiny loft two at a time. Ali was right. This was her dream, and she'd be damned if she was gonna let anything stand in the way of keeping it.

About an hour later, freshly showered and wearing a navy-blue dress that hadn't soaked in the ruined fruits of her labor, Nora marched through the streets of Everpass with a familiar destination in mind. A cool autumn breeze followed her, whirling her long skirt with each step.

Her boots clattered on the cobblestones as she made her way past dozens of homes and storefronts, each unique in its own way. The buildings here were as varied as the people. As a last stop before the mountain pass leading to the capital, Fairvale, Everpass had become a hodgepodge town, attracting all manner of species.

Not just orcs and imps, but nymphs—like Ali—elves, trolls, and humans—like herself. They'd all brought their unique styles and architecture with them. Few other towns could boast that the tiny wooden cottages of imps sat side by side with massive stone dwellings of orcs.

Soon, she'd left Main Street behind, emerging on a side street in the less savory east half of town. She'd overheard a traveler or two complain about feeling unsafe here after they'd downed a few drinks at her bar, but for Nora, this was home.

They'd never had much when she was a kid. Certainly not enough to live in one of the opulent manors in Westpass. The hoity-toity folk who called that neighborhood home might look down on her for her humble origins, but Nora never minded them much. What she had with her family was much more important than material wealth.

Her mother *never*—not for a shadow of a second—ever let her forget she was loved. And for a girl who learned at an early age that she'd been abandoned as an infant, dropped on her mother's doorstep like a forgotten parcel, that meant more than words could say.

Nora drew a deep breath as she approached a small brick cottage perched on the end of a dead-end road. She eyed the thatched roof warily, wondering, like she always did, if it would cave in while she was inside. Somehow, despite sagging in the middle for decades, it always held, but she hardly trusted her luck after today's events.

A crooked handwritten sign hung in the front window, dubbing the humble building Rowen's Tinctures and Tonics. With a weary sigh, Nora twisted the knob.

"Hello? Ma? Are you home?" She certainly hoped so. Her mother had a bad habit of leaving the front door unlocked, whether she stayed home or went out.

Luckily, Moira Rowen's warm voice preceded her into the front room. "Nora, dear! I wasn't expecting you." With her full skirt swirling across the wooden floor, Moira hustled forward, a delighted smile stretching across her full lips, and dimples denting her freckled cheeks. She'd tied the long red hair that made Nora endlessly envious up into a loose bun, leaving a few curls to dangle against the shoulders of her knitted shawl. "Come in, love. Take a load off. You must be tired after that long walk across town."

Nora resisted the urge to wrinkle her nose at the upholstered settee her mother gestured to. "I'd love a drink, actually. Can we sit in the kitchen?"

Despite living there most of her life, Nora had never enjoyed sitting in the living room. Her mother didn't just use it for entertaining, but for seeing her clients as well. Hundreds of bottles and jars filled with her mother's concoctions lined the many shelves. She couldn't help feeling uneasy among them. Like she might catch some curious side effects if she remained in their presence too long.

"Of course, dear," Moira replied smoothly.

Truth be told, her mother wasn't the most successful at her craft. Her potions and tonics had gained quite the reputation among the townsfolk for being a gamble most were wary to take. Occasionally, she'd have a streak of good luck and heal an ailment or two, which saw her business increasing, but it was never long before a failure inevitably occurred and wrecked all her momentum. Selling duds that did nothing—or worse, increased flatulence—wasn't exactly the best way to win repeat customers.

Of course, that hadn't made life easy for them. Moira was frequently riddled with debts. Throughout Nora's childhood, she'd always bounced back. When the potion business was slow, she'd supplemented her income selling vegetables she grew in the enormous garden out back. Nora had always been happy to help. Her brother, Seth, had as well until he left for Fairvale.

Then Nora moved out, chasing her dream of business ownership. Without her children to help tend the fields, Moira's vegetable garden dwindled. Nora hated to leave her, but when she'd offered to stay, her mother wouldn't hear of it. She'd shoved her out the door and made her promise not to come back—unless it was for a visit, of course.

As she sank into one of the hard wooden chairs ringed around the modest kitchen table, Nora's hands tangled in her lap. "How's business?"

"Slow. But it will pick up. It always does." Moira grabbed a pitcher off the table. "Water all right?"

"Sure, thanks." Water trickled into a wooden mug. The kitchen, painted a soft blue, had always been one of Nora's favorite rooms in the cottage. So many wonderful memories had happened at that little table. Namedays by the dozen. Meals full of laughter and endless love.

The chair across from her creaked with Moira's weight. Nora frowned. That chair had always creaked as long as she could remember. It was likely why she sensed something was off... The creak wasn't quite as loud as it should be.

Peering closely, she noticed something she'd missed with her mother sheathed in a poofy dress and wrapped in a shawl. As Moira set the cup down, flexing a bony wrist, Nora choked down a gasp. "You've lost weight. Are you eating, Ma?"

Moira folded her hands in her lap. "Oh, you know how forgetful I can be. I miss my fair share of meals now that you're not here cooking every day. I'll try to do better remembering, dear, if it'll wipe that frown off your pretty face."

"You better." She hoped her memory was the culprit, and not a lack of funds. "Do you need anything while I'm here?"

"Now that you mention it." Moira rose and tugged open the cupboard she kept her important documents in. "I can't seem to find my reading glasses. Can you read this for me, love?"

The parchment crinkled as her gaze traced the page. "Ma! You took out a loan on the house?"

Her lips thinned. "On second thought, I'll have Mrs. Kepler read it."

Nora jumped out of her chair when Moira reached for the loan statement. "If you don't pay the remainder in ninety days, you'll be in default. Oh my goddess. How did this happen?"

Moira caught up to her at the back door. "Times were tight. I didn't want to bother you. Especially after—"

Nora handed the page back. "You're never a bother."

Tears welled in Moira's eyes. "I'm happy to hear that, love." She folded the parchment crisply before stuffing it into her pocket. "Don't you worry about this. Everything will work out fine, you'll see."

"Mother, how can you say that? This is serious."

"I know it is. But the goddess will send a solution my way. She always does."

"You don't really believe that, do you?" Sure, she liked to invoke the goddess's name as much as anyone, but Moira took it a step too far.

Moira squeezed her shoulders. "She sent you to me, didn't she?"

"Well, I wish I could bail you out. I truly do. But I'm afraid I can't. Not after the day I had."

Moira led her back to the table. "Oh dear. That doesn't sound good. What happened?"

With a sigh, Nora spilled the entire twisted tale, sparing no detail. "And that's when I decided to walk here, so I could scour the garden for ingredients," she finished. "But it sounds like you need them more than me."

"Don't be silly. You're welcome to take anything you need." Moira grabbed her hand, tugging her away from the table again. "Come on. Let's see what's left."

Nora held her breath as the back door swung open. As she gazed outside, her heart sank. The formally lush fields were mostly brown. A few scraggly plants dotted the space, but she could tell at a glance there was nothing close to what she needed to replace everything that'd been destroyed. She should've known. With it so close to the first frost, there wasn't much left that hadn't already been harvested.

"Not what you were hoping for?" Moira asked softly.

"No, but it's a start."

Her mother patted her arm. "I can tell you're still stressed. Why don't you let me draw you a bath? It'll be like old times. I'll even polish your necklace while you soak."

Nora's fingers absentmindedly rose to trace the lone piece of jewelry she owned. A striking white opal set into a crescent moon pendant hung off a delicate chain around her neck. It was the only clue to her past she'd ever owned. It had been looped twice around her neck while she lay in the basket on Moira's stoop, and came with a letter, asking that she wear it always.

Her hand fell to her side. "I'll skip the bath, but thank you."

Moira's smile faded a little around the edges. "You sure I can't tempt you? You know you always feel better after a good long soak."

"I just showered. And besides, I better get to work out here if I want to harvest what's left."

Moira sighed. "All right, love. Let me gather some supplies for you, at least."

"Sure. Thank you." She followed her mother to an old, rickety shed that looked like it might blow over in a strong breeze. "You could always come live with me, Ma."

Moira scoffed. "In that little shoebox apartment of yours? No thanks."

"We could manage."

"I don't want you to manage, love. I want you to *thrive.* Then you can find a nice fellow to marry and finally give me some grandchildren to spoil."

Nora nearly rolled her eyes. "Don't hold your breath. Trust me, no man in his right mind would sign up for a role in my disaster of a life."

Moira turned to Nora with a coy grin. "I wouldn't be so sure of that, dear. Life is full of surprises."

That's the understatement of the century...

Pretty Boy

Kieran

The sun sank over the rooftops of Kieran's hometown as he trudged down the final stretch of the mountain pass. The wind whipped at his back, his wrists firmly wedged inside the jacket pockets of his sensible traveler's attire—blue pants lined with a multitude of pockets, topped with a long waterproof cloak to ward off the chill.

Seth, his best friend and loyal assistant, glanced sideways with a wide grin. "Feels good to be back, doesn't it?" He was dressed much the same, only he'd wrapped his cloak around his waist, revealing a tan long-sleeved tunic.

"Maybe for you," Kieran grumbled. "I don't expect a hero's welcome." Not this time, at least.

"I'm sure your parents will be delighted to see you." Seth winked, one big blue eye closing. "And the ladies too, I wager."

Kieran lifted a brow. "I doubt they'll be too eager after they discover what happened last month."

"Woe is me." Seth laid an arm across his forehead, palm out, adopting a ridiculous high-pitched voice like he was the world's unlikeliest lady in distress. "I was injured in service to the Crown. I'm a pitiful, useless old washed-up—"

"Shut up." Kieran used his good hand to punch Seth's shoulder.

Of course, the bastard didn't budge. As a half-orc, Seth was built like a brick outhouse. Luckily, his human side had taken center stage when it came to his appearance. At thirty-five, he still sported a full head of auburn hair and boyish good looks that had plenty of ladies swooning—despite the fact that his skin was far greener than any human's.

"I've had about enough of your self-pitying nonsense. You're the same man you were before the accident. I wish you'd get that through your pretty little head."

Seth was always giving him shit for being a "pretty boy," and he couldn't even deny it. Like Seth, he was a halfling, part-human, part-elf. His elvish ancestry had ensured he'd be attractive, with sparkling blue eyes, flawless tan skin, and dark-blond hair that always fell perfectly no matter how many times he dragged his fingers through it. And of course, the increased nimbleness elves possessed had been a boon to his work as a spy for the Crown.

Former spy, now. "If you say so."

Seth halted outside Everpass and heaved a heavy sigh. "Look, I probably shouldn't even mention this. It's just... I thought you'd be out of your funk by now."

"Excuse me for being a little upset that my life was completely upended." After that snarky comeback earned him a scowl, Kieran forced a smile. "Well, what is it?"

"A couple weeks back, I wrote Ma to tell her to expect me." Seth's brow furrowed, and he tugged on the back of his neck. "I told her why we were coming, and when she wrote back, she claimed to have just the thing for you."

A startled chuckle escaped Kieran. "Did she now?" It shouldn't have come as a surprise. Moira Rowen was no stranger to peddling potions around town. But for every villager who swore by her iffy cure-alls, she had just as many unsatisfied customers.

"I wouldn't have suggested it if you'd stop pouting." Seth shrugged. "Who knows? Maybe she'll be right this time. Sometimes she gets lucky."

"I suppose it wouldn't hurt to stop by and say hello." Kieran's heart raced. Was this the answer? Then again... "What about your sister? Will she be there?"

"I doubt it. From what I hear, she spends every waking minute at that tavern of hers. I wish she'd hire some help, but Nora's determined to work herself to the bone."

"Oh." A pang of something that felt an awful lot like disappointment stabbed Kieran's chest. "Good for her. It's a step up from working for that old grump down at the Golden Lark."

"I might offer her my services, now that I have the time. I hate the thought of her behind that bar, where any riffraff off the road might decide to drink away his troubles and get fresh with her."

"So your plan is to become her hired muscle?" Suppose it made sense. Dealing with drunken idiots could be dangerous. Yet, the idea made something in Kieran's gut rankle. *No way we'll remain as close if Seth is constantly around* her.

"Yep, that's the plan. If she'll let me."

He clasped Seth's shoulder. "She'd be a fool not to."

He and Seth went way back, all the way to grade school. As two of the only halflings in Everpass, they'd shared an instant bond. It helped to have a friend who innately understood the challenges that came with living a life between two worlds.

As they'd grown, they'd stayed close. So close that he became friends with Seth's little sister. Nora was five years younger, but that hadn't stopped her from tagging along wherever they went. Seth would always try to chase her off. And yeah, Kieran might have laughed at her attempts to drag a fishing pole twice her size down to the lake, but he always ended up carrying it for her in the end. Being an only child, he loved having a couple friends who were almost like family.

That all changed when he started dating. Despite the stigma of being a halfling, he and Seth never had trouble finding willing women to bed. Unfortunately, by then, little Nora had developed something of a crush. She'd never said as much out loud, but it was pretty obvious from the blush staining her cheeks whenever he entered a room. He'd distanced himself, not that he'd had much choice in the matter. He'd have earned dirty looks from the entire town if he'd attempted to date a twelve-year-old while he was seventeen—and rightfully so.

Shortly after, he'd graduated and set off for life in the big city. Seth had been delighted when he'd invited him to tag along. Together, they'd taken Fairvale by storm. Him as the spy, Seth as his trusty right-hand man. He hadn't seen Nora again until that fateful night a decade later.

He shook the memory out of his mind. It wouldn't do to think about that night now. Not unless he wanted to enter town with his trousers bulging awkwardly.

"Off to the east end, then," he announced as they marched toward town. He eyed the setting sun. "Sure your mother won't mind visitors this late?"

"Course not. You know you're welcome anytime."

Kieran wished he could say the same to Seth. Unfortunately, his father had only accepted his friendship with the half-orc grudgingly. It was always the same story with his folks. Their life wouldn't be complete until he found a nice group of elves to call his own—and don't forget the elvish wife, too.

Thanks, but no thanks. Elves might be attractive and nimble, but they were huge snobs. Surely there were exceptions out there somewhere, but he'd yet to encounter any. And he'd met plenty during his time in Fairvale. The capital boasted the largest population of elves in the realm.

The woman he settled down with had to be a special sort. He refused to marry a bully after enduring endless taunts as a child. No way would he shackle himself to anyone who looked down their nose at their "lessers." She needed to be hardworking, too. And beautiful—inside and out. Wouldn't hurt if she had long brown curls, golden-brown eyes, and sinful lips that could bring a man to his knees.

"Ah ha!" Seth exclaimed. "That's where your smile's been hiding. What were you just thinking about?"

Kieran ducked his head. "Oh... nothing important." Couldn't exactly tell his best friend he'd been reminiscing about the one slipup he could never forget, no matter how hard he tried. Not when it involved his sister.

"Fine. Keep your secrets. Whatever it is, if it made you beam like a fool just from thinking about it, then you should go after it." Seth smirked. "Or should I say... her?"

"Oh, look at that. We've made it." Kieran didn't miss Seth's snicker as his boots slapped the cobblestone road. But changing the subject was better than having his head lopped off.

Seth was *very* protective of Nora. And he wasn't shy about complaining about the few boyfriends she'd had over the years. To hear him tell it, she deserved nothing less than the perfect man.

Kieran certainly wasn't anything close to perfect. Especially not now. Honestly, though, it didn't matter. After the way things ended when he saw her last, Nora was probably itching to slap him rather than rekindle their old friendship.

"Come on." Seth shivered and unwrapped his jacket from his waist. "Let's get out of this wind."

Autumn evenings in Everpass tended to be chilly, and that night was no exception. Still, Kieran was thankful the sun had finally set. Less chance of being spotted and waylaid by some kindly villager while they strode through town.

It seemed luck was on their side. They arrived at Moira's ramshackle cottage with no one noticing. "Think you might want to do something about that roof while you're here."

Seth chuckled. "Already on the agenda." He pushed the front door open without knocking. "Hey, Ma! You home?"

"My baby's home!" Moira rushed out of the kitchen, a blur of swirling skirts and flashing dimples.

Seth grunted as her arms wrapped around him like a vise. "It's good to see you, Ma."

"I missed you so much. My big city boy." Moira didn't let the fact that she only reached her son's elbows stop her from hugging him like her life depended on it.

Kieran hung back, gazing warily at the walls. Dozens of bottles and jars stared back at him, and he couldn't help wondering if one was meant for him.

Finally, Moira released her death grip, only to throw her arms out wide again. "Come here, son. I've missed you too."

He went with a smile, soaking up her unconditional love like a fiend as her arms closed around him. "Thanks for letting me visit, Ms. Rowen."

She pulled away, lightly slapping his chest. "Stop that this instant. I'm not Ms. Rowen to you. Either call me Moira or Ma. I'll settle for nothing else."

Kieran flashed a grin. "All right, Ma."

"That's more like it." Moira's eyes narrowed. "Now. Let's see it."

His grin vanished. "Sure you don't want to chat first? Or grill your son about who he's been courting?"

Seth shot him a glare that could melt lead.

Moira pursed her lips. "I think not. Go on. I can't help if you won't show me."

With a sigh, Kieran tugged his wrists out of his pockets one at a time. The right came easily. Thank the goddess it was his dominant hand, or everything would be so much worse. Then came the hard part.

As he pulled, he swore he felt fabric ghosting across the back of his hand. He hadn't. Not truly.

He lifted his left wrist slowly, showing Moira the ugly stump where his hand used to be. He sucked in a deep breath and held it, dreading what came next. First, she'd apologize—nearly everyone did. Goddess knew why. It wasn't like their "I'm sorry" would make his hand grow back. Then would come the question he was absolutely *sick* of answering. How did it happen?

Wasn't that just the worst joke of all?

Much to his surprise, Moira did none of that. Instead, she tilted her head, examining the scarred flesh on his wrist with a scrutinizing gaze. Then a bright grin spread across her cheeks, leaving dimples in its wake. "I can help you."

"You can?"

"Of course. I know exactly what you need."

Kieran's gaze sought Seth's across the room. He sank onto the fluffy sofa, making the poor furnishing groan under his weight. "You sure this one's gonna work, Ma? I know you think you've got witches way back in your lineage... but surely your lack of successes says otherwise."

Moira huffed and crossed her arms. "Why'd you bring him here if you were so sure I couldn't help? I'll have you know, I succeeded in something similar while you two were away." She turned to Kieran. "A servant that works for your father hacked off a few fingers while tending to the garden. Ask him if you don't believe me."

That did sound promising... "Was it Edgar?"

"It was," Moira answered. "Have him show you his hands. They're perfectly normal, you'll see."

"Guess I'll ask him." Edgar had been in his family's employ for decades. He took care of the grounds and all the odd jobs that might dirty Father's hands if he handled them himself.

"Course you will, dear." Moira smirked. "Once you talk to him, you can get started working on my payment."

Seth scoffed. "Really, Ma? You're gonna make him pay? Kieran's family."

"I know that, love. It's just that your sister paid me a visit this afternoon..." Her hands tangled in the hem of her woven shawl, and a tiny frown spread on her lips.

"What's wrong with Nora?" Seth demanded, sitting straight so fast the sofa groaned again.

"Seems she had a little trouble at work this morning. To put it bluntly, it's a colossal mess. She needs a couple strong men to help her set things to rights."

Kieran hoped the shock reverberating through his chest didn't show on his face. "I'm not so sure she'd want me helping her." Seth's eyes narrowed suspiciously, and he quickly added, "I hear she's a proud one. I'd hate to make her feel like a charity case."

"Well, you'll have to convince her you're helping whether she wants you there or not." Moira smiled sweetly. "You do that, and I'll make sure you get exactly what you need. No other payment necessary."

Kieran bit back a groan. It would've been so much easier if she'd charged him a fee. After his years of service, he wasn't hurting for funds. But from the hard clench of Moira's jaw, he suspected she wouldn't be swayed.

"I'll help Nora too." Seth leaned back. "You want to meet there in the morning? She's in the old potion shop on Main."

Kieren sent him a saucy wink. "It's a date."

Moira giggled. "You boys! I'm so blessed to have you in my life. And Nora's life too."

She might be singing a different tune if she knew the thoughts about her precious daughter that had been rattling around in his head earlier.

"Are you staying for dinner?" Moira asked.

"Better not. I really ought to head home. Say hello to my folks."

"Of course. Don't be a stranger, dear. I'm dying to hear more about your adventures. You know Seth won't breathe a word to his old mother."

Kieran chuckled as she led him to the door. "I'll remember that Ms—Ma. Good night."

He'd made it out the door and halfway to the road before Seth's voice halted him. "Kieran, wait."

"Forget something?" Kieran spun back to face him, stuffing his wrists in his pockets.

"Yeah. Just have a favor to ask."

He lifted a brow as Seth wandered closer, wearing a serious expression. "Of course. Whatever it is, count me in." He wasn't kidding, either. If what Moira was offering turned out to be real, then he owed Seth—big time. Healing his injury would mean he could return to the city. Back to his old life, where he felt useful.

Seth drew a breath through his nose and met Kieran's gaze directly. "It's about Nora."

"Oh?" Kieran asked casually, ignoring the way his stomach churned.

"She's not like the girls we run with in the city."

"I know that."

"Good. Just remember that, for my sake, yeah?" Seth flashed a relieved smile.

Kieran felt like the ultimate scoundrel. "Sure. Not a problem."

"See you tomorrow, then," Seth called with a wave, taking step after carefree step back to the warmth of his childhood home.

If only we could all be so lucky...

Bright morning sunshine woke Kieran the next day. "Someone really ought to draw those curtains," he grumbled, glaring at the window of his childhood bedroom like he had a vendetta against it.

Not much had changed in his room since he'd moved out as a teen, making him feel like he'd stepped back in time. He was swathed in the same blue-and-green-checkered bedding, the turquoise walls plastered with paintings of knights on horseback and tapestries depicting epic battles of old.

He'd been obsessed with taking part in adventures like those as a child, despite their realm being at peace for the last century or so. Too bad reality didn't match the old tales. Since working for the Crown, he'd never chanced on any witches using spells to subdue beasts and scores of men, like the scene on his favorite piece in his collection. More often than not, his work had been rather… dull. Long, tedious hours of watching and waiting. That part, at least, he wouldn't miss.

Tossing the blankets off, Kieran hopped out of bed and opened the wardrobe. He sifted through the old clothes he'd abandoned ages ago, hunting for something he could work in. "Did I really dress this… fancy?" Every shirt had a stiff starched collar or a long row of buttons that would be an absolute joy to fasten one-handed.

With a sigh, he gave up and snagged the bag he'd brought off the floor. Each article inside was far more casual than the things he'd left behind, despite being much newer. He settled for a pair of brown trousers and a black long-sleeved tunic. His parents could donate his old clothes. No sense holding on to things he'd never use.

Speaking of his parents, they'd been out when he'd arrived last night. He'd been forced to eat alone. Being the only person at the gargantuan table in the dining room never ceased to make him feel small.

"Can't even skip a dinner party on the night their wayward son returns," Kieran muttered under his breath as he threw open the door.

Keeping up appearances was the highest priority for his parents—his father especially. As one of the largest investors in Everpass, Tanyth Dornelis never missed an opportunity to hobnob with the village elite. And his mother always went along for the ride.

He strolled down the carpeted hall, shielding his eyes as he entered the grand foyer. A magnificent chandelier hung over the grand staircase, which, while guaranteed to earn a chorus of *oohs* and *ahs* from guests, had the nasty habit of reflecting morning sun from the skylights into his eyes.

His boots tapped loudly on the polished stairs. He paused at the bottom, drawing a steadying breath. Then, with his head held high, he strode into the dining room.

"Good morning, Kieran," Tanyth mumbled from his spot at the head of the table. He lifted his gaze from his ledger for a bare second before resuming his reading, his pale hand jotting notes in the pages. Dressed in his robe and pajamas, his father still managed to look every inch the polished businessman. His ice-blue eyes darted along his book, his short-blond locks perfectly coiffed despite the early hour.

"Morning, Father." He grabbed a plate off the buffet, heaping it high with rashers of bacon and two slices of Chef's famous egg pie. He avoided the sausage, not wanting to listen to his father's lecture on table manners as he struggled to cut it with his new limitations.

A twinge of disappointment hit him hard in the chest. How sad was it that the thing he missed most about home wasn't his parents, but the hired help's cooking?

His mother breezed in, her tan cheeks rosy, a cloud of floral perfume trailing in her wake. "Kieran, how lovely to see you, darling." She smiled widely, stopping short so quickly her robe tangled in the legs of her polka dot pajamas. As her green eyes slipped lower, her smile faded. "Let me help you with that." She rushed forward, reaching for his plate.

He sidestepped around her. "I've got it, Mother."

"If you're sure." Flicking her sleep-tousled brown hair off her shoulder, Courtney took her turn at the buffet table.

He wasted no time tucking into his meal. His father was content to let him eat in silence, but once his mother sat, he knew the inquisition would begin. While he'd love to take a moment to savor the delicious egg pie, which was filled with aromatic scallions and savory chunks of sugar-glazed ham, he'd shoveled about half down his throat before her chair scraped the porcelain-tiled floor.

"So, how are you settling in? I hope you slept well." Courtney gazed at him over the rim of a steaming teacup.

He swallowed. "I did."

"I was hoping you'd join me for lunch at the Golden Lark today. There's a delightful young elf I'd love for you to meet. Her family is—"

"Can't, I'm afraid." No sense letting her drone on. "I promised Seth I'd help him today."

The teacup clattered. "Oh. What does he need help with?"

Kieran glanced up from his plate, quickly returning his gaze to it after spotting both his parents frowning. "His sister could use a hand at her tavern. I believe it's called Stellar Spirits. She's taken over the old potion shop on Main."

Tanyth shut his ledger with a loud smack. "That's one of our properties, you know."

His pulse raced. "It is?"

"Indeed. Ms. Rowen is leasing the property from one of our holdings. I didn't have much to do with the contract, but I've been monitoring things from afar."

Kieran dropped his fork, his appetite completely wrecked in the face of that news.

"Do me a favor and tell me if anything is out of the norm while you're there. Can't be too careful with these first-time business owners."

He forced a grin. "Of course." *Fantastic. Not only does Father hold the key to Nora's success in his hand, he wants me to be his snitch.* That wouldn't be happening, but he didn't see a reason to let his father in on his plans. "Well, I ought to get going."

"Darling, do let me know when you're free. I'll set another date with that young lady I was telling you about." The smile his mother flashed was so earnest he couldn't bear to dash her dreams to smithereens.

"Of course. Another time." With a wave, he left the dining room, wishing he was back at Seth's. "Thanks for the hugs, guys. I love you so much too," he muttered under his breath as he strode out into another chilly autumn morning. Yet, after that icy welcome, being outside was a relief.

"Morning, Master Kieran," a voice called from the garden.

"Edgar. What luck! I was actually on my way to see you."

Edgar's bushy eyebrows dipped so low they nearly covered his dark-brown eyes. "You were? Whatever for?" Despite his surprise, Edgar set down the pair of hedge clippers he'd been using and dusted his bronze-hued fingers on his dirt-stained overalls. Then he thrust out a hand.

Kieran shook it, using the greeting to inspect Edgar's hand for defects. A few calluses dotted his palm, but the fingers were all intact. "I spoke to Moira Rowen last night. She claimed to have helped you with a little problem a while back. I wanted to ask you about your experience."

Edgar tugged his hand back like he'd scalded it. "Why in the world would she tell you that?"

Kieran blinked repeatedly, surprised at the venom in his tone. "Sorry? I assumed you wouldn't mind discussing it with me. And Moira was pleased enough to boast about it."

"Was she?" Edgar bristled. "That... That old witch swore she'd keep my performance issues with my wife to herself."

Kieran coughed, turning aside so Edgar didn't see the nervous smile he fought to hide. "Actually, this was about your fingers." He tugged his sleeve, and the chill breeze tickled his scarred wrist. "You see, she was only trying to convince me of her success."

"Oh." Edgar's face turned beet red, but the next words out of his mouth washed away all of Kieran's sympathy. "I'm so sorry, son. How did that happen?"

He gritted his teeth. "It's fine. I'd rather not say, if you don't mind."

"No, of course, I don't mind." Edgar held up his hands. "For what it's worth, Moira isn't lying to you." He wiggled the last three fingers on his left hand before pointing to them with his right. "I lost all of these about five years past. Got too close to the woodchipper. It was... awful."

"I'll bet."

Edgar winced. "The town healer told me I'd have to learn to live without them. They were far too mangled to reattach, you see."

A wave of nausea fought to overwhelm Kieran until he shoved the unwanted image out of his head.

"Luckily, Moira saw me the next day and asked me what I was hiding under the bandage. I know her elixirs don't always do what they claim to, but I took a chance. Figured, what else do I have to lose, ya know?"

Kieran nodded.

"I soaked my hand in the brew she gave me for hours that night, and—nothing happened. I'd made up my mind to return the next day to demand a refund, but when I woke in the morning, my fingers were back, good as new." With a grin, he thrust his hand closer. "Take a look. They're perfect, right? I could almost believe it was all just a terrible dream..."

He scrutinized Edgar's left hand. There was absolutely nothing different from the reformed fingers of his left hand and the original fingers on his right. "Wow. That's... incredible."

"Yep. That Moira knows a thing or two about healing." He leaned in, lowering his voice. "Some things, at least. Can't say she was too successful with the other matter I visited her for."

"Sorry to hear that." Forgetting for a moment that Edgar was pushing seventy, that might have something to do with Edgar's wife. He was married to their chef, and while she was a jolly enough lady, she wasn't exactly the type to encourage a man's lust. Her pale face was badly pockmarked, she frequently smelled of onions, and she enjoyed overindulging in the sweets she baked. He had a feeling Edgar's problem had more to do with a lack of attraction than his performance, but he wasn't about to make his opinion on the matter known.

Burying the urge to shudder, he backed away. "Well, thank you for your candor, Edgar. I'm afraid I'm expected elsewhere."

"You're most welcome, Master Kieran. Have a wonderful day."

As he walked down the road leading to Main, Kieran suspected wonderful might be a bit much to ask for. Who knew what might happen when he saw Nora again? "At least it will be an adventure," he told himself with a grin.

THROUGH THE BACK DOOR

Nora

Crouched on her hands and knees, Nora attacked the tiles behind the bar with a damp rag. *Stupid floor. I'd be better off tearing it up and starting over.* Served her right. She should've cleaned it yesterday, but after spending hours digging up the few remaining plants she could scrounge out of her mother's garden, she'd been exhausted.

Still, she regretted falling asleep after she'd finished brewing three replacement batches of spirits. Yeah, the work had kept her up well into the night, but if she'd just taken a break to wipe up the mess, it wouldn't have hardened into a substance so tough it might as well be shellac.

At least now she had something to sell besides mead. Or she would, after it finished aging. Making liquor wasn't a task you rushed. Not if you wanted it to taste good—which she insisted on. She refused to risk Stellar Spirit's reputation by serving subpar drinks.

Luckily, her mead and ale, which she stored under the bar, had survived the shelving collapse. After she cleaned up, the tavern would be back open for customers, albeit with a much smaller menu.

Her stomach churned. Would it be enough to keep the hounds at bay? She had suppliers to pay. Rent wasn't far off from being due. The meager amount of winnings Ivan and Yolti coughed up out of pity wouldn't come close to putting a dent in it.

And, of course, there were the repairs. The old shelves were a lost cause; the wood had splintered and cracked in so many places it couldn't be trusted. She'd need to hang new ones, and lumber wasn't exactly cheap.

Luckily, she'd found a note tacked to the front door when she woke. Ivan offered to drop by with some fresh boards later that morning. Ones he claimed were so hard and thick they'd hold up even if an orc smashed into them. So she'd left the door unlocked and hung the Closed sign in the window. Hopefully that would keep any customers out but allow Ivan to pop in when he arrived.

Chances were, she'd work her fingers to the bone before he got there. *Stupid stain.* Sweat poured down her brow. She'd forgone her usual demure dress today, knowing she'd spend most of her time cleaning. The tight shorts and tank top she'd opted for were supposed to keep her cool, but it seemed scrubbing utter destruction off of tile was quite the workout.

Her knees ached almost as bad as her wrists and shoulders. But there was no other choice. Someone had to fix this mess, and of course, *she* was that someone.

Nora often dreamed of hiring help. Yes, it was a ridiculous thing to dream about. While other women her age surely yearned to meet the man of their dreams, settle down, and raise a family, all she wanted was a barmaid to share the burden of running this place. Someone to pick up a shift here and there so she could have a break.

A few days ago, she'd have sworn she was almost there. Now it seemed just as unattainable as the prospect of meeting the man of her dreams.

Don't lie to yourself. You've met him already.

She brushed the wayward thought aside. It wouldn't do to dwell on the things she couldn't change. Dreams of love were for young girls with their heads in the sky. Nothing for it but to work on something realistic. She had to be practical and keep her hands busy if she wanted her business running smoothly. That, at least, was entirely under her control.

So she scrubbed. Nora scoured, wiped, and rubbed. As sweat pooled under her breasts and in every crease on her body, she promised herself a nice soak later. Certainly, before anyone saw her in such a state.

She winced at the thought of Ivan arriving...

The hell with it. He deserved to stew in her stink after the trouble he caused yesterday. At least he was happily married and such a sweetheart that he wouldn't dream of leering at her.

The creak of the door announced his arrival. "Oh, good, you finally made it." She continued to work as footsteps pounded the tile floor, merely pausing a second to call over her shoulder, "I hope you brought that hard wood for me, Ivan. I've been waiting all morning, so hurry up and get on with it. You can shove it through my back door."

Male chuckles rang out. Nora froze.

Goddess, that laugh. She'd recognize it anywhere. The heady sound lived in her dreams. It pulsed through her blood, leaving fire in its wake.

But before she could scramble to her feet and attempt to make herself decent, a shadow fell over her.

Abandoning the rag, she propelled her upper body off the floor. Then she spun on her knees, scowling at the devastatingly handsome man standing in front of her. "Kieran. What are you doing here?"

Leaning against the bar with his hands in his pants pockets, he made no attempt to disguise his blatant staring. Nora shivered as his gaze traced her body, before returning to linger on her breasts.

She followed his gaze, heat rising to her cheeks. The damn sweat-stained tank was practically translucent. Luckily, the bandeau she wore underneath it kept her from looking completely indecent. All the same, she had to swallow the urge to cover herself from his penetrating gaze.

"Excuse me? You planning to stand there and stare, or are you going to tell me what you're doing here?"

Kieran licked those delectable lips of his, making a rush of unwanted memories assail her. "Who's Ivan?"

"What?" She gaped at him before lowering her head in confusion. Unfortunately, since she was still crouched on her knees, that put her face-to-face with a very distracting bulge. She swallowed, her mouth suddenly dryer than a summer drought.

"You know," he drawled, "the guy you're waiting on so he can stuff your back door with his hard wood."

Her eyes widened so much it was a wonder they didn't fly out of her head and land in the sticky mess on the floor. She scrambled to her feet, swallowing a groan as her aching limbs protested. "None of your business, that's who."

She was proud of herself for that comeback. Honestly, she was surprised she even dredged up a coherent thought with Kieran standing in front of her.

He looked so insanely *good*. Ugh, it was criminal. Why did the one man who wanted absolutely nothing to do with her have to be the only one who made her bones turn into liquid and her skin tingle with a single glance?

Kieran had always been handsome, but the decade they'd spent apart had only enhanced his appeal. His long-sleeved tunic fit tight against his muscular upper body. Piercing blue eyes sparkled with mirth, even in the face of their less-than-welcoming conversation. And that smile... she wanted to bask in it forever.

Only she wouldn't. Not while he was standing there, looking good enough to gobble down whole, and she was drenched in sweat and caked-up muck.

"For the love of the goddess, would you just answer my question?" she spit out.

He stepped closer. The air between them crackled and hissed. Or maybe it was just the blood rushing through her veins. "I will when you answer mine." He twirled a loose curl that had escaped from her bun around his finger. "Who the hell is Ivan, and why are you inviting him in your... back door?"

Her cheeks burned. "Get your mind out of the ditch." She didn't owe him an answer. She should throw him out and let him keep assuming she was waiting on a strange man and his... wood. "Ivan's a *customer*. He's bringing me lumber to replace my broken shelves."

"Hm." His gaze rolled off the curl tangled around his finger and zeroed in on her eyes. "I heard about your mess. Thought I'd come by and help."

She smacked his hand away. "Oh really? And where did you hear that?"

"From your mother, of course."

She should've guessed. Moira was no stranger to meddling when she thought it would benefit her children. Only, this time, she really wished her mother had the sense to keep her mouth shut.

"Well, sorry to disappoint, but I don't need it. You can run back to your city and all your *fun*. Some of us are used to working hard for a living." She crossed her arms and pointedly glared at the door.

Kieran's answering chuckle nearly drew her gaze back to his hypnotic eyes, but at that instant, the door opened again.

"Seth?" Her jaw dropped. "What are you doing here?"

Kieran stepped back, widening the gap between them before Seth was through the door.

"Hey, Nora. Ma told me—" He stopped short, his eyes dragging over her and a frown pulling at his face. "What the hell are you wearing?"

"Nice to see you, too." She sighed wearily.

"Seriously, Sis. You shouldn't be out in *that*. It's... indecent."

"I'm not *out*. This is my tavern." She waved at the sign. "My *closed* tavern. If I want to be comfortable while cleaning, it's no one's business but my own."

"Fair enough, I guess." Seth strode closer, wrinkling his nose. "I would give you a hug, but I don't want to get... smelly."

"Forgive me for sweating in your presence." She sighed again. "Did Ma seriously send you to check up on me?"

"Not to check up. To help." Seth scanned the mess behind the bar. "Looks like you need it."

Well... that was certainly true. There was just one problem. "I can't pay you."

Seth grinned. "Good thing you have family who can pitch in for free, then, isn't it?" He slung an arm around Kieran's shoulders. "Just accept that you have two big brothers here who won't take no for an answer and tell us how we can help. Trust me, Sis, it'll save you a whole lot of trouble."

That was the biggest lie she'd ever heard. She'd stake her life on it.

Having Kieran there would definitely not add up to *less* trouble. She'd go crazy with his mesmerizing eyes watching her, that smile of his making her weak in the knees. And there was no way the feelings she had for him were anything close to *brotherly*.

"Seth, I won't keep you from your work. Your life is in the capital. You can't—"

"Nope. You're wrong again. We're home for good."

"You are?" Her brow furrowed. "But... why?"

Seth's gaze darted to Kieran, who'd returned to lounging against the bar, his hands stuffed in his pockets and a tight smile on his face. Seth shrugged. "Eh, you know how it goes. Can't serve the Crown forever. Aren't you lucky we returned at the perfect time to help you with this mess?"

She couldn't deny it would be nice to have help. Wasn't she just lamenting that her dream of hiring someone might never come true? Now here she was with two strong, fit men begging to help—for free.

Maybe her mother was right... The goddess *had* sent her the solution to her problems.

"All right. I guess I could use a couple more sets of hands." She flashed a tired grin as a knock sounded on the front door and an orc-sized shadow darkened the glass. "Don't suppose either of you learned how to work with wood while you were away?"

Kieran shoved off the bar with a chuckle. "Don't worry. I don't know about Seth, but I'm an expert at handling my wood."

As Nora's cheeks heated again, she cursed her luck. *It's going to be a long couple of days...*

Second Best

Kieran

Kieran winced as the words rang through his head for about the hundredth time since she'd uttered them that morning. *I guess I could use a couple more sets of hands.*

Nora still hadn't realized she was one shy of her request. He kept cursing himself for not jumping on the opportunity. He should've pulled out his arm and cracked a joke. It would've been an easy out that might have staved off the pity apology and inevitable questions. Now here he was, hours later, trying to figure out a way to spill the disappointing news.

He and Seth had moved into Stellar Spirit's backyard—a fenced-in grassy rectangle containing a few weather-worn picnic benches—to cut and sand the *hard wood* Ivan had dropped off. Guess it hadn't ended up being shoved through Nora's back door after all... He chuckled to himself.

"Something funny?" Seth asked.

"Just admiring you with that saw. We should invite some of the village ladies over to enjoy the show."

It hadn't been long before Seth stripped out of his shirt. Since he was still blessed with two working hands, he'd volunteered to cut the lumber down to size. Kieran still had his shirt on, though he was starting to wish he didn't. It might be late in the year, but the day was unseasonably warm. Bright sunshine beat down on his black tunic, and though he was only in charge of sanding, he'd worked up a decent sweat.

Hell... he couldn't even *think* the word sweat without flashing back to Nora in that ridiculous skimpy getup. The way it had molded to her every curve, so damp he couldn't help noticing the lacey fabric holding back her ample—

"Hardee har har." Seth's sarcastic laughter made Kieran's gut clench. "What do you think I should charge for the show?"

He shouldn't be lusting over Nora. He *couldn't*. "I bet you could fetch a silver or two. Maybe a gold, if you lost the pants."

Seth scoffed, lifting one big green arm and flexing it. "I'd earn way more than that with these babies."

The back door slammed shut. "I thought you two were here to help, not ogle each other." Nora bounced down the stairs, her tan skin glistening under the sunlight, and he choked down a groan as her curves bounced with her. At least she'd stopped sweating so much that her shirt left so little to his imagination, but he really wished she'd put him out of his misery and change into something less revealing.

He somehow kept his gaze glued to her face while slipping his arm under the wood he'd been sanding.

Seth narrowed his eyes at him before turning to his sister with a grin. "You need something?"

"Thought I'd see if you were hungry. It's about time for lunch."

"I thought you'd never ask." Seth patted his stomach, and if one were to judge from the gleeful look in his eyes, they might suspect his belly was far rounder than the washboard abs he was currently sporting. "What are you making?"

"Blackberry jam and pecan butter toasties." She rocked back on her heels. "You want one?"

"Make it two and you've got a deal."

Those gorgeous golden-brown orbs swung Kieran's way. "I suppose you'll be wanting two as well?"

He nodded lamely. "Sure. Thanks."

"Be back in a tick." She spun on her toes and disappeared inside.

"You can't keep hiding it forever."

Kieran's heart pounded so hard it practically leaped out of his chest. *Was I staring? Did he figure out how I'm dying to peel her out of those tight little shorts and—*

Seth waved at his arm. "She's going to spot it sooner or later." He cringed. "Or rather... spot it missing... You know what I mean."

"I know. I just don't want to hear it. The pity. The inquisition. I'm sick of talking about it. It was nice to feel like my old self for a change."

And he *had* felt like himself, all thanks to her. Nora hadn't looked at him with an ounce of pity. No, she'd done quite the opposite. Her eyes had flashed at him with ire. And her cheeks had pinked adorably when he'd wrapped that soft curl around his finger. He was dying to do it again—even though he shouldn't.

"You *are* the same. I don't know why you won't listen." Seth hacked at the wood, taking out his frustration on it, no doubt.

Kieran sighed. He wanted to get over it. Truly he did. But he just... couldn't. What's worse, every time he remembered what happened, embarrassment slammed into him—hard. It was impossible to feel anything less than an idiot when he remembered how senseless the loss was.

They worked in silence until the door creaked open. He hid his arm again, hating himself for it but unable to stop.

Nora strolled out, a loaded platter in her hands. "There's a pitcher of lemonade and some cups on the bar. Mind grabbing them, Kieran?"

How the hell am I meant to carry that?

He glanced at Seth, hoping he'd jump in to save him, but the ass kept sawing away like he hadn't heard the question.

"What are you waiting for?" Nora plunked the platter down on a picnic table and started setting out the plates and napkins.

Seth sighed heavily. "I'll get it."

"You're in the middle of something. Kieran can grab it." Nora pursed her lips and sent Kieran a glare. "Seth's not your assistant anymore. You need to stop acting like he is."

"I didn't. He offered." He nearly shot out his bad arm to emphasize the point, but stopped himself just in time.

Seth dropped the wood with a bang. "Hell with this." He turned to Nora. "Kieran lost his hand. No, he doesn't want your pity or to talk about it. Got it, Sis?"

A myriad of emotions washed over Nora's face in the space of a heartbeat. Surprise, sadness—empathy. Kieran's stomach sank. *Goddess, please don't let her cry...*

Then she blinked twice in quick succession and straightened her spine. "Okay." She aimed a curved brow at Kieran. "There's an extra tray under the bar. Oh, and grab some of the little paper umbrellas while you're under there. I'm feeling fancy." She turned back to the table and doled out the sandwiches.

Seth grinned arrogantly as Kieran passed him on his way inside.

That was it? He wasn't sure what he'd been expecting from Nora. Tears, maybe. Perhaps well-intentioned offers to *help* with every little thing, which honestly grated on him even more than the pity.

If this was his new normal—at least temporarily—then he had to get used to it. He refused to act like an invalid. Lots of people had it worse off than he did. Hell, he could be cursed with Edgar's performance problem. *Now, wouldn't that be a pity?*

So he bent behind the bar and pulled out a round tray. Then he stacked the pitcher, the cups, and the fancy little paper umbrellas atop it. With his good hand to hold it and his arm helping to keep balance, he drew in a deep breath, praying he wouldn't spill everything. *I can do this.* Balancing the tray carefully, he slowly strode back outside.

Kieran's pounding pulse almost drowned out the rhythmic scrape of the saw. Nora was perched on a bench, watching Seth. Yet there was nothing to stop her from looking up. She'd reacted well to the mention of it, but would seeing his missing hand be a different story?

"I'm hoping this won't become a habit of yours," she said softly, her gaze still rapt on her brother's work.

"What habit?"

"The staring." Slowly her head spun, those lovely eyes locking on to his.

That one look was enough to do dangerous things to his libido. *Yep. Definitely never having* that *problem with Nora around.* "Weren't you just saying I shouldn't ogle your brother? Thought I'd choose the lesser of two evils."

She clicked her tongue. "Staring *and* dubbing me evil. Are you sure you want to keep insulting the person who's feeding you?"

"Trust me, Nora. The last thing I want to do with you is trade insults."

Her eyes widened, and he could've sworn her breath caught, though he couldn't be sure since Seth's lumber chose that moment to finally split in two.

Guilt hit him at the same time the wood smacked into the ground. *Stop flirting, Kieran. She's not for you.* He set the tray on the table, grimacing as a bit of lemonade sloshed out of the pitcher.

He glanced up and caught Nora's gaze lingering on his scarred wrist. He held his breath, waiting for the wash of pity to cloud her features. Or worse, disgust.

But... it never came. A look of mild curiosity crossed her face before her gaze returned to his. "Better fill a glass for each of us before you spill the rest," she said cooly.

Seth gamboled over at the perfect time to snatch the first cup off the table. "Thanks. I needed this." He downed half in a single swig and smacked his lips. "Mm. Did you make this, Nor?"

She plucked a paper umbrella off the tray. "I did." The bright-pink paper top looked utterly ridiculous dangling out of Seth's cup, but he let her place it inside without complaint. "What do you think?"

"It's delicious. What's in it besides lemons?" Seth dropped onto the bench across from her, taking up three-quarters of it.

She took the second glass for herself and topped it with a red umbrella. "I make mine with honey. It gives it a more refined flavor than sugar."

The yellow liquid shimmered as it trickled down. Then a flash of purple landed in his glass as he carefully set down the half-empty pitcher.

He glanced up, catching Nora's eye. She smirked, and he couldn't help wondering if she was deliberately goading him. But he wouldn't be riled that easily. He slid onto the bench beside her—it was a perfectly understandable choice, what with Seth spread out on the other side—and lifted his glass.

The lemonade was tart and cool, with delicate floral notes he hadn't expected. And yeah, the stupid umbrella poked him in the nose, but he couldn't stop the smile that rose to his lips. "That has to be the second-best thing I've ever tasted."

Since Seth had just torn into his first sandwich, stuffing half of it into his mouth in one bite, his only reply was a lift of his brow.

"Second-best? Dare I ask what the best was?" Nora sipped her lemonade, nimbly avoiding any run-ins with the sharp paper top.

Kieran's gaze drifted to her lips before he forced himself to look away. "Better I don't say. I'm sure you'd have a strong opinion about it, and we're trying to enjoy a pleasant lunch."

Seth chuckled. "Nora always has to be right, that's for sure."

"Hey!" She shook her sandwich at her brother. "That's not true. There are plenty of things I'll admit to knowing nothing about."

"Sure, but not when it comes to cooking." Seth punctuated the statement with another enormous bite.

Buttery bread crunched under Kieran's fingers. "He has a point. You never let either of us take a turn in the kitchen when we were younger." He took his first bite, his eyes closing in bliss as the sweet, nutty concoction hit his taste buds.

Seth kicked him under the table. "Did you have to moan, you idiot? You might as well prove her point for her."

Kieran's eyes snapped open. Seth scowled, then gulped the rest of his lemonade. Nora smiled smugly, taking a small bite of her lunch.

"Sorry, man," he said after swallowing. "I couldn't help it. Your sister knows her way around a toastie."

"Only because she hogged all the practice." Seth grabbed his second sandwich and stood. "You should be ashamed, Nor. I had to spend a decade choking down Kieran's terrible cooking until he figured out what he was doing. I could've starved. Then who would be here, helping you build your shelves?"

She rolled her eyes. "If you expect me to apologize for not inflicting that torment on myself, you're going to be very disappointed."

Seth clutched the sandwich to his bare chest, leaving behind a dollop of purple jam above his nipple. "You wound me, Sis." He winked and waved the sandwich with a flourish. "But I'll forgive you since you're feeding me." Then he shoved the entire thing into his mouth and grabbed the next piece of lumber out of the pile.

"It's a wonder he hasn't choked yet," Kieran muttered.

"Not even on your cooking?" Nora tried to hide a not-so-sweet smile behind her glass, but he spotted it, wishing like hell she'd lay those lips on something other than the stupid cup.

"Not these days." He chuckled. "I've learned a thing or two in the kitchen since we first moved to the city."

"Is that right?"

"Yep. If you let me take a turn at cooking one day, I'll show you just how skilled I've become."

She bit into her bread and chewed thoughtfully before answering. He watched her lips, mesmerized and practically vibrating just from sitting beside her. "I don't know about that. What kind of host would that make me if I let you work for free and feed me too?"

He shrugged. "A happy one?"

"That's assuming it's a good meal."

"Oh, it will be. I wouldn't dream of making you swallow anything unless it was guaranteed to please you." As her cheeks flushed again, he cursed internally.

There you go again. Stop flirting. Just... stop. He couldn't seem to help it. Nora looked so beautiful flushed with her eyes flashing. And of course, he couldn't stop picturing her flushed for an entirely different reason...

"You done yet?" Seth called over his shoulder. "These boards aren't gonna sand themselves."

"Not all of us can unhinge our jaws and swallow our food whole," he replied.

Nora giggled before taking another bite.

He turned to her. "I noticed when I grabbed the drinks that you've finished cleaning. What's your plan for the rest of the day?"

She swallowed. "Once we're done eating, I'll open Stellar Spirits as usual. I can't offer half of what I normally do, but some sales are better than nothing."

Kieran frowned. "You sure you don't need some time off?"

"Can't afford it. Not if I want to stay in business. My landlords don't hand out extensions."

His stomach churned. Should he tell her that the property belonged to his family? Maybe it would take a bit of stress off her shoulders. Surely he could convince his father to bend the rules just this once...

Then again, it might not be so simple. Tanyth wasn't the type to forgive mistakes or hand out second chances. Kieran had learned that the hard way growing up. His father demanded perfection, and anything less was an excuse for a lecture—or more often than not, a screaming match. If he treated his own flesh and blood with so little compassion, why would he treat his business associates any better?

Probably best that he kept quiet about his family's involvement in Nora's lease. At least until he could get back in her good graces. She might have joked with him and Seth over lunch, but he sensed from the wary glances she kept shooting his way that she wasn't completely comfortable with their return yet.

She polished off her last bite and reached for his empty plate.

"I'll help you clean up."

Nora bit her lip and retracted her hand with another wary glance. "All right. Thanks."

Together, they loaded the trays and walked in through the back door. He settled his tray on the bar top and took a moment to really scrutinize the place. He'd been too shocked to find Nora crouched on her hands and knees at first, and too worried about dropping the tray the second time he'd ventured inside.

She'd clearly put a lot of effort into making the bar welcoming and unique. An L-shaped marble-topped bar ran along one wall, the cream counter contrasting nicely with the dark wooden base and thick-cushioned wooden stools perched alongside it. Black-and-white hexagon-patterned tiles covered the floor, every table neatly lined up and surrounded by enough benches and chairs to seat a few dozen people at a time.

"I really love what you've done with this place."

Glass clattered as Nora placed the cups into the sink. "You don't need to lay the compliments on so thick, Kieran."

"What? It's true."

She scoffed. "Sure. Just like my homemade lemonade is the second-best thing you've ever tasted."

He leaned against the bar. "Why would I lie about that?"

"You've lived in the capital for ages. I'm sure there was plenty there that'd put my drinks to shame."

"You'd be wrong. The best thing on my list isn't in the city either."

She wiped her hands on a towel. "Oh really? And where would I find this delightful delicacy?"

But she wasn't ready to hear the answer. Not yet.

His gaze dropped to her mouth again as he backed out the door. "Let's just say it's a lot closer than you'd think."

Kieran grinned as Nora's huff followed him outside. And as he stepped out back with a spring in his step, he realized something even more surprising than how much he'd enjoyed sparring with his best friend's little sister. *I haven't thought about my missing hand since we started eating.* That was certainly something to smile about...

STOP DREAMING

Nora

S he stood at the bar, staring off into space, scrubbing the same spot for about the thousandth time. Before opening the tavern for business, she'd slipped upstairs, washed up, and changed into a ruby-red dress, but she couldn't help wishing it'd been just as easy to shake off her strange mood.

She honestly wasn't sure what to make of Kieran's return. No matter how many times she replayed their interactions—both embarrassing and electrifying—she couldn't wrap her head around it. Why was Kieran here? Was it just his duty to Seth, and by extension, her, or was there more behind his motives?

A tiny part of her had wished he'd come back, intent on picking up where they'd left off the last time she saw him. But then a far louder voice drowned out the thought. *Why now, when he never wanted to before? It's been a decade, Nora. Stop dreaming.*

A gruff voice broke her out of the maddening circle of her thoughts. "I think you've cleaned it."

Her hand stilled as she peeked at her most loyal regular, his lips curved into a disapproving sneer before they disappeared behind his mug. Maalik was shorter than most, likely due to his troll lineage, and stouter too, which could probably be blamed on his habit of drinking his weight in ale every afternoon.

"Sorry. I'm sure I'm not the best company today. Just have a lot on my mind."

He leaned back on his stool, tugging at the front of his orange-and-red-checkered button-down. "I can see that. Probably have a headache as well with that racket out back."

"Thanks for putting up with it." She sighed. "They're making good progress. We won't need to deal with the noise much longer."

Maalik could be surly sometimes—scratch that, he was almost *always* surly—but at least he was loyal. Everyone else who'd stopped in that afternoon had only stayed for a single drink, or worse, left without ordering when the construction battered their ears.

"I've heard worse. Besides, it's better than that dreck they call music down at the Golden Lark." He shuddered, making the thinning brown hair on his pale freckled head quiver.

She chuckled. "You have a point."

Her old boss owned a charmed piano, and he kept it on constantly, playing soft instrumental music that, quite honestly, bored her to tears. He claimed it was necessary for ambiance, but she'd lost count of the times she'd nearly fallen asleep on her feet while working.

The front door slammed open, drawing both their attention.

"Ali." Nora smiled. "I didn't know you'd be by."

"Hey, Nor." Ali shuffled inside, carrying a box twice as big as her head.

Nora darted out from the bar, hands outstretched. "Can I help you with that?"

Ali dropped the box carefully atop a table and waved her off. "No, I got it. I brought you a few replacement bottles."

"I could've picked them up." Her gut twisted. "And you should know... I can't afford to pay you. Not until I sort out the rent."

Ali lifted her nose, sniffing deeply. "Dish me up some of whatever you have cooking as my interest payment. I'll wait for the rest. I know you're good for it."

"You sure?" Nora cooked a family-style meal every night for whoever wandered in hungry. Tonight's was baked chicken with black beans and rice. The hearty aroma was enough to make her stomach rumble, but it wasn't enough to repay Ali for all the help she was bound to need to save herself from eviction.

"Yep. Now I won't need to whip up something for Echo when I get home." Ali grinned. "She likes your cooking better than mine, anyway."

"Happy to help." She strode across the room to the attached kitchenette, which was walled off along the bottom only, allowing her to interact with her patrons even while cooking. It wasn't much, just a tiny cooktop and oven crammed in next to a sink and mini ice chest, but she made it work. "And I really appreciate the bottles. I certainly need the replacements. But I hate that I can't pay you right away."

"It's no trouble." Ali strode toward the back door. "Besides, I wanted to stop in after I heard the rumors floating around town."

She bit back a groan. "Oh, did you now? What are they saying?"

"Just that you managed to land a couple of hunky helpers." Ali eased the door open a crack, peeked out, then closed it with a whistle. "And they weren't kidding."

"Relax. It's only my brother, Seth." She scooped two generous portions into a paper box. "My mother goaded him into helping when he got home last night."

"That's your brother?" Ali had begun an apprenticeship with the old owner of Everpass's glassblowing shop when her daughter was a toddler. When he retired last year, she'd taken over the business. But learning her craft and running her own shop—not to mention handling everything that came with raising a child as a single mother with no support system—hadn't given her much time to socialize. "So... are you going to introduce me?"

"Sure. If you want." Nora returned to the table and set the to-go container next to the box of bottles. "Does it need to be now? I'd hate to interrupt Seth when he's in his workflow."

Ali grabbed the chair next to Nora and spun it around before perching on it backward. "I suppose that's fair. What about the other guy? Who's he?"

Nora pretended great interest in the bottles. Though they were lovely, each unique in its own way, her mind was too full of a certain man's distracting smile for her to notice the details. "Oh, him? He's just my brother's best friend."

"Hm. That so?" Ali tapped her chin. "Why do I feel like you're not telling me the whole truth?"

"What? Course I am." She winced when her voice escaped a few octaves higher than she'd intended. *Ugh, that doesn't sound suspicious at all...*

Maalik chimed in from his spot at the bar. "That's the Dornelis boy. Kieran, they call him."

Ali's eyes widened. "Ah… so *that's* the infamous Kieran."

"Yep." She was beginning to regret spilling the details of her old crush to Ali. Yeah, she'd told her about the first guy she ever fell for. What kind of friend would she be if she didn't dish about the guys who'd rejected her in the past?

Only now it was coming back to bite her. There was no way Ali would let Kieran's return slide without comment. Not after she'd confessed to being obsessed with him while growing up, while leaving out the much more embarrassing moment that happened when she visited Seth in the city. But how was she supposed to know he would bully his way back into her life?

"Well, well, well. Isn't that nice of him to come help you? I don't know a lot of guys who'd commit to hours of manual labor in the hot sun for their best friends' sisters, do you?" Ali smiled smugly.

She rolled her eyes. "I'm sure he's just being nice."

"Or he's angling for you to be nice back," Ali countered.

Maalik snickered.

Nora shot him a glare. "Don't you start now, too."

"She ain't wrong." He swigged from his mug and pushed it forward for a refill. "That boy's sniffing around for a reason. Mark my words."

"What are you two now, some kind of courtship experts?" She circled the bar and snagged Maalik's empty. "I bet he owes Seth a favor."

The back door swung open, and Nora froze, the slosh of ale filling the mug at war with the thrashing pulse in her ears. Then Seth strode in, and her shoulders relaxed as ale splashed her fingers.

"Shit," she whispered under her breath. Nora plunked the mug in front of Maalik, then grabbed a rag and wiped the spill.

"Hey, Sis. Sun's going down. Gonna call it a night. I was think-ing—" He halted mid-sentence as his gaze trailed over Ali. "Oh, hello there." He thrust out a big, sawdust-covered hand. "I'm Seth, Nora's brother."

Ali shot him a crooked grin and clasped his hand. "So I hear. I'm Alsira, but you can call me—"

"Ali!" Seth pumped her arm more enthusiastically than was merited. "Nora's told me so much about you."

Nora had to give her credit; Ali held her own, pumping back just as forcefully. "Same. Nice to finally meet you." She glanced at the back door. "Is your friend coming in too?"

Seth dropped her hand and spun to face Nora. "Not tonight. He left already but wanted me to tell you he'd be back tomorrow to finish sanding."

Nora shrugged, hoping the action disguised how much her belly fluttered. "Thanks for letting me know."

"Oh, and I was wondering..." Seth sank onto the stool next to Maalik's. "There's some extra boards. You mind if I take them back to Ma's? I've been meaning to fix that roof of hers."

"Please do." Nora tossed down the rag. "I'm bombarded with images of being crushed every time I visit."

Seth chuckled. "I know exactly what you mean." He slapped the bar cheerily. "Well, in that case, I hope you don't mind if I spend tomorrow shoring up Ma's roof."

"Not at all... But don't you need Kieran for that?"

He stood. "Naw. If we both go, it'll take us forever to finish your shelves. There's still plenty of sanding left since I finished cutting just now."

Ali grinned. "Divide and conquer. Makes sense to me."

"Exactly." Seth stepped toward the back door, but stopped short, whirling to face Nora. "Hey, before I forget, don't take Kieran too seriously, okay?"

She stiffened. "What do you mean?"

"Just that… he's used to flirting with every girl he meets. If he does the same with you, don't take it personally." Seth rubbed the back of his neck. "Normally I'd be the first to call him out for it, but he's going through a lot right now."

Way to make a girl feel special… Her lips thinned. "Sure. I understand. Don't worry about me."

"Thanks, Nor. Kieran shouldn't be in your hair too long. I know he's dying to get back to his life in the city as soon as he can." He resumed his path to the back door. "I better carry that lumber home before it gets dark. See you in a couple days to hang the shelves!"

The door swung closed behind him, and Nora's shoulders sagged.

"He seems nice." Ali pursed her lips. "So… did the flirting start already?"

Nora's gaze fell to the floor. "Ali, are you really asking me that now?"

Maalik stood, not missing a chance to grumble, "I know when I'm not wanted."

As he disappeared into the bathroom, Ali leaned closer with a devious smirk. "Don't spare the details. What happened?"

Nora dropped her head into her hands. "Ugh. I can't believe you're making me relive this…"

"It can't be that bad."

Lifting her head, she stared at Ali woodenly. "You have no idea how wrong you are, my friend." Then she launched into the whole embarrassing mess. Her lack of "decent" attire. The unfortunate wording she'd used to describe Ivan's delivery. Even the awkward way Seth had bombarded her with news of Kieran's injury.

"Huh. You really weren't kidding." Ali clapped her shoulder. "I think you handled yourself well, considering. I mean, he must not have been offended by you ordering him around if he kept flirting with you, even after lunch."

"I didn't know what else to do. Should I have been nicer?" She rubbed her temples. "Hell, what kind of person orders a guy around when he just lost a limb?"

"Don't second-guess yourself, Nor. Honestly, I bet he appreciated it. Everyone must be treating him differently now. But you didn't."

"Nope, I just turned him into an unpaid servant."

The bathroom door flew open. "What did I tell ya, girly? That boy's sniffing around for a reason. You ask me, he wouldn't have made such a fuss about Ivan's wood if he wasn't wanting to be the one supplying your... doorways."

"Oh my goddess! Maalik, did you hear everything?" Nora crossed her arms, her face heating.

He shrugged unapologetically. "Might want to tell those fellas to reinforce those thin walls when they're done with your shelves."

Ali lifted her to-go box with a laugh. "On that note, I better head home. Gotta feed my little gremlin. I'll swing by soon."

"Sure. See you later." Nora sighed and grabbed the rag again, taking comfort in the repetitive motion, even though the bar top was spotless. *Something tells me I'm going to need all the comfort I can get until my shelves are fixed...*

Six Feet Under

Kieran

He tugged the collar of his jacket higher as he strolled through the streets of Everpass. Little clouds of vapor coalesced in the air with every breath, only to be chased away by the morning sun. "I should've waited. She's probably not even up…"

He'd woken with the dawn, thanks to the wretched curtains he'd once again neglected to close. After bathing and snagging a slice of toast to go—avoiding another unwanted invitation from his mother—he'd hightailed it out of Westpass, into the quiet village streets.

It was so different here. After years of living in the bustling capital, it was strange to be alone, but for a few earlier risers.

And they were all so *friendly*. He'd lost count of the waves and smiles he'd returned before he'd even made it to Main, mostly from cheery workers headed into Westpass to cook and clean for the elite, and giggling rosy-cheeked children as they strolled into town for school.

You'd never see that in Fairvale. Sure, life in the capital had other benefits, like shops that sold anything and everything, open all hours of the night. But folk in Fairvale kept to themselves. Not like here, where everyone knew everything about everybody.

Then again, that had a certain benefit. It hadn't taken him long to realize his news had spread. Even if he weren't a former spy, the evidence was hard to miss. Practically everyone who'd sent him a merry wave or hollered hello that morning couldn't resist eyeing the arm he kept stuffed in his pocket.

That would save him from the endless round of questions... At least, one could hope.

Either way, it would be good to hide out in Stellar Spirits again. And today, he'd even get Nora alone.

Sweat prickled on his lower back, though it shouldn't with the cool breeze blowing. Only he knew his perspiration had nothing to do with the weather, and everything to do with her.

He'd spent half the night tossing and turning, plagued with images of her on her knees. Goddess, yesterday, when she'd spun around and stared up at him with that fire in her eyes, he'd almost lost it. He'd been about a second away from dragging her into his arms when Seth had shown up to snap him back to his senses.

You promised Seth, remember? Nora can't be a casual fling.

He planted the thought in the forefront of his mind as he stopped outside Nora's front door. Then he lifted a hand to knock, but the hushed rumble of voices in the backyard made him drop his fist at his side. He edged around the building, his ears perked.

"Are you sure you don't mind, Miss Nora?" a girl asked, the voice far too high-pitched to be anything other than a child's.

"Of course not," Nora answered, her familiar tone wrapping around him pleasantly, though he still couldn't see her from his spot in the alley. "You're doing me a favor. This would go to waste if I didn't find someone to take it off my hands."

The smell hit him next, the same delicious aroma that had lingered in the air last night. Finally, he popped out of the alley and spotted a girl wearing pigtails and a gap-toothed smile peeking into a paper box. "Burritos, yum! Thank you. Can I have another, please? For my little brother."

At the back gate, a skinny twig of a boy who couldn't have been over six peered in, his eyes wide.

Nora waved at him, smiling radiantly. "Sure you can." She pulled another box off a stack sitting on the picnic bench beside her and handed it to the girl. "Now, you two better run along and eat while you walk. You don't want to be late."

"We will. Thanks again!" The girl spun on her heel and took off, a spring in her step.

Nora watched them depart before lifting a steaming cup to her lips. Though she was dressed far more demurely this morning, in a deep-plum dress and a woven black shawl, his pulse still picked up speed at the sight of her.

"Good morning," Kieran announced softly.

Not softly enough. Nora gasped and pressed a splayed palm to her heart. "Goddess, Kieran! Are you trying to spook me?"

He chuckled. "I swear I'm not. I nearly knocked on the front door, but then I heard voices back here." He nodded to the boxes. "You do this every day with your leftovers?"

She stiffened. "On school days, yes."

"You know, you could make less if you don't want it to go to waste." He closed the space between them, taking a seat beside her.

"There were times growing up when I was one of those kids, heading to school on an empty stomach." She shrugged. "Just helping where I can."

He lifted a brow. "I'm not surprised. You're just like your mother."

"What's that supposed to mean?"

"I've seen her giving out moon tea to anyone who comes asking for it, whether or not they can afford to pay."

Moira might have a poor track record with her healing salves, but she'd perfected the contraceptive brew, and everyone knew it. Women from neighboring villages made the trek to her in-home shop each month, and she turned no one away.

Kieran had always admired her for it. Moira might be eccentric, but her kindness was palpable. Deep down, he often wondered if he'd have turned out differently without her influence in his life. Would he be cold like his father and mother if he hadn't spent every moment he could with Seth growing up?

"Oh... that." Nora's eyes narrowed. "Are you saying we're both too soft-hearted to run our own businesses?"

"Goddess, no. I'm trying to give you a compliment. The world would be a much worse place without people like you and your mother around." He nudged her gently with his shoulder, flashing a soft smile.

Pink stained Nora's cheeks. Too much to blame on the chilly morning. "Well... thanks, I suppose."

She met his gaze, and he lost track of time as he stared back at the most beautiful golden-brown eyes. Just like the honey in her lemonade, so incredibly sweet and full of unexpected secrets.

"Um... Miss Nora?" a voice called out. "Are you busy, or can I come in?"

Kieran blinked, flashing back to reality, only to realize he'd leaned in so close he was practically sitting in Nora's lap. He backed away, his pulse racing.

"Oh, hello, Oliver. I didn't notice you there." Nora chuckled, smoothing a hand down her skirt before she stood and snagged a box off the table. "Come in."

A lanky teen wearing ill-fitting pants that barely dusted his ankles ducked through the gate and grabbed the box with a big grin. "Da needed my help with the goats, so I missed breakfast. Thank you, Miss Nora."

"You're welcome. Now, hurry. You don't want to be late for class." She tousled his curly brown hair, then shooed him away.

Kieran waited for the lad's footsteps to fade before asking, "Do you really think it was the goats that made him miss breakfast?"

"Always an excuse with that one. His father's flock isn't doing well. Some illness tore through it and killed off more than half his stock. Of course, times are tight." She shrugged. "But I don't have the heart to destroy the boy's pride."

"Hm. Pride is a tricky thing, indeed. Ever wonder if you're holding too tightly to yours?"

She shot him a glare. "What's that supposed to mean?"

"It occurs to me that all your problems could be solved with an influx of funds."

"Really?" She huffed as she collected the last two boxes off the table. "Did you figure that out all on your own?"

"All you have to do is ask, and it's yours, Nora." He stood, squaring off in front of her.

She shoved a box at his chest. "I'm not asking you for a handout, Kieran. This is my place, and I can handle running it without charity, thank you very much."

The box warmed his fingers. "What about from Seth, then? He's not hurting for coin either."

Nora opened the last box. "Seth shouldn't have to bail me out. Then what will he have to show for all those years of work when he decides to settle down and start a family?"

"How do you know he even wants kids?" He sat back down and rested the box in his lap.

"I have eyes, that's how. Haven't you ever watched him when there's a kid around? He always lights up and can't resist playing with them."

"He is a big kid at heart, I'll give you that." Come to think of it, Seth never shied away from courting ladies who were single mothers. Maybe he really did long to be a father one day... He bit into his burrito with a groan. "This is good. *Really* good."

Nora waved off his praise. "I refuse to stand in the way of Seth having the life he deserves. It's bad enough Ma roped him into working for me for free." She sank onto the bench beside him.

"Maybe Moira thinks you deserve a good life, too."

Nora sighed, placing her barely touched burrito back in the box. "I wish she'd worry about herself first."

Her defeated tone made Kieran's stomach sink. "Is something wrong with—"

"I have grapes that need mashing. Are you ready to start with the sanding?"

Kieran stood. "Sure."

"I'll leave you to it, then."

Guess Nora had reached her limit on talk for the morning. It was better that way. Less chance he'd get sucked into her life so deep he couldn't dig his way out. *Why do I feel like I'm already six feet under?*

They worked separately all morning. Kieran took solace in the rhythmic scratch of sandpaper on wood while trying his best not to spend the entire day staring at Nora.

It was a hard task to accomplish. Especially since she was working on the other side of the backyard, destemming each grape methodically before dropping it into an enormous bucket. His gaze kept lingering on her delicate fingers. She moved so effortlessly, absorbed in the task yet relaxed. He couldn't help wondering what it would feel like to have all her attention focused on him. *If only I could be so lucky...*

But the calm moment couldn't last forever. By late morning, he'd finished sanding. Clearing his throat, he stood. "I'm done, for now. What else do you need help with?"

Nora blinked. "Hm?"

He strolled across the yard, enjoying how the fresh aroma of her fruit chased away the lingering scent of sawdust. "The sanding's done. Want some help with your grapes?"

"I'm about through, actually. Unless you want to hop in and press them?"

"Me? Hop in?"

"I know a lot of the bigger vineyards use magic to release the juice, but I can't afford to hire out right now. Besides, this batch is small enough to do it the way my mother taught me."

"Think I'll pass." He'd hung around their place enough to have seen Moira ankle-deep in a barrel of grapes on more than one occasion. "Having a bunch of slimy grapes squishing between my toes doesn't sound like a fun way to cap off my day."

"Suit yourself." Nora hiked up her skirt and placed a booted foot on the picnic bench, then slowly began unlacing herself from the leather. "You don't need to stick around. Seth said he wouldn't be back to hang the shelves until tomorrow. Guess I'll see you then?"

He was too busy watching her boot hit the ground to answer. The action felt altogether too intimate. Yeah, they were in Nora's backyard, in broad daylight, and she was only undressing up to her ankles, but his brain wouldn't stop screaming, *Yes, more.*

"Kieran?"

"Huh?" He tore his gaze off her creamy skin and caught her bemused smile.

"See you tomorrow."

He plunked onto the bench beside her. "I better stick around. Those grapes look slippery. Seth would kill me if I left when I could've prevented your senseless demise."

She rolled her eyes as the next boot thunked on the grass. "I suppose my luck is terrible enough that I might be in danger of succumbing to death by grapes."

"Don't fret. I'll be here to catch you before you take a tumble."

She grabbed a washbasin off the table, then dragged a sudsy cloth over her skin. Kieran gulped, more mesmerized by the sight than he ought to be.

"Seriously, Kieran. You don't have to stick around."

He leaned in, plucking a fact Moira had shared with him long ago out of his head so Nora stopped trying to chase him away. "I thought the fermentation process got rid of all the impurities. If that's the case, why are you scrubbing so hard?"

"I could hardly sell the stuff with a clear conscience if I knew I stirred it with dirty feet." She giggled. "What should I sell next? My spit in a jar?"

"If you want. I bet there are shops in the capital where that would sell for twice what your wine does, so long as you popped your picture on the front of the bottle." He wasn't kidding, either. The city had all manner of shops and plenty of people who were into stranger things than that.

Her nose wrinkled. "Gross. I'm not that desperate." She grabbed a pitcher of clean water and rinsed off her feet, leaving her wet skin to sparkle in the sun. Then her brow wrinkled. "I forgot to drag that bucket closer. You mind?"

"Sure." With a grunt, he tugged the heavy container across the grass.

"Thanks." Nora placed her feet in the bucket of grapes and deftly stood. "See? What did I tell you? Nothing to it."

But as she lifted one foot, her other leg wobbled at the knee. Kieran lurched forward, catching her waist as she careened forward. "Spoke too soon." He chuckled. "You're lucky I was on watch duty."

A breathless laugh escaped her, her face pressed to his chest as she struggled to right herself. Every inch of his skin came alive as the warmth of her breath bled through his tunic. Her scent enveloped him, a captivating perfume filled with subtle spices and sweet notes that made his mouth water much more than the grapes. His fingers—the ones he still had, and those he only thought he could still feel—twitched with need.

Nora's in my arms. I never thought I'd feel this again... But after only a second, he shoved the blissful realization aside.

Nora wasn't his to hold.

As he pulled back slowly, ensuring she remained perfectly balanced, those golden-brown eyes zeroed in on his. Her breath hitched, and she breathed, "My hero."

He sensed she only said it in jest, but with her gorgeous eyes locked on his and her lips a mere inch away, he wanted so badly for it to be true. If things were different, he'd be everything she needed and more.

Hero. Conqueror. Lover. The panting dog at her feet. Goddess, what he wouldn't give for just—

"Hello!" A cheery feminine voice intruded on the moment.

"You expecting someone?" he asked, putting more distance between them.

Nora frowned, lifting her hands off his shoulders and thrusting them out for balance. "Nope."

Probably someone looking for a neighbor...

That assumption was dashed a heartbeat later when a blonde head poked through the back gate. "I hope you don't mind that I stopped by. Your mother told me where to find you, Kieran."

Fantastic... Plastering a benign smile on his face, he called, "She did, did she?"

He flipped to fully face the woman currently sweeping into Nora's backyard like she owned the place without waiting to be invited in. *Entitled? Check.*

He'd give her one thing. She was a looker. Slim, tall, and curvaceous, with flawless porcelain skin and a face that would bring most men to their knees. Ocean-blue eyes sparkled above a delicately sloped nose, her heart-shaped lips painted to match a stunning pink dress that stopped just before brushing the ground. *Effortlessly beautiful? Double check.*

"Let me guess... you must be the elf Mother's been insisting I meet."

She stopped in front of him and thrust out a manicured hand. "Tamora. It's lovely to make your acquaintance."

He shook her hand perfunctorily, though his heart wasn't in it. Even more so as a blast of cloying floral perfume struck him, washing away Nora's more delicate fragrance. Still, he couldn't be rude. "Nice to meet you, Tamora. I'm sorry to be the bearer of bad news, but my mother shouldn't have sent you here on a social call. I'm much too busy today, I'm afraid."

Tamora pouted. Honest to the goddess, she full-on pouted, like that would actually make him change his mind. In reality, all it did was make him even more certain he wanted nothing to do with this girl.

As he scanned her more closely, he realized *girl* wasn't that far off. Tamora's face was unlined, and he suspected if he asked her age, she wouldn't be anywhere close to his thirty-five years. Truthfully, he wasn't planning to ask. All he wanted was for her to leave so he could spend more time with the woman she'd so blatantly ignored.

It seemed said woman wasn't in the mood to ignore Tamora. After clearing her throat—an action that *still* didn't get Tamora to acknowledge her existence—Nora spoke in a voice so achingly sweet his mouth nearly puckered. "Don't be silly, Kieran. You're free to socialize all you'd like."

He turned, eyes narrowing dangerously. "No, no. I couldn't go now... not with the danger."

Nora lifted her feet one at a time, her jaw tight as she stomped, seeming to relish how the grapes squashed beneath her feet. "No danger here. Go. Have fun getting acquainted."

Wonder if she's picturing those as Tamora's head... or mine?

Tamora slung her bony arm through his elbow. "Wonderful! You can walk me back to Westpass. One can't be too careful these days. Who knows, I might even run into some danger on the streets. You'll protect me, won't you?" Her inky-black eyelashes batted at him, and Kieran's stomach dropped.

No way out of this without looking like a complete ass. None that he could see, at least. With a sigh, he shot the girl his most flirtatious smile—the one he usually reserved for ladies he intended to bed. Not that he'd changed his mind. He had zero interest in getting to know Tamora intimately. But as long as Nora was content to make his life miserable, he might as well return the favor.

Then again, he had no way of knowing if his strike would fall flat. Nora might delight in having him off her hands.

Wouldn't that be a pity?

But if she got jealous, even slightly, that would be... enlightening. Not that he intended to do anything to remedy it, but it would be nice to discover whether this insane attraction he'd been cursed with was returned or unrequited.

So, he dialed up the charm to one hundred. "As you wish, my lady. I must say, that frock is the perfect match for your lips. Quite... striking."

Tamora tittered and slapped his shoulder lightly. "Oh, stop. You're far too kind."

He spun her unexpectedly, making the dress twirl, and Tamora clasped her chest as if breathless. But Kieran's eyes were still locked on Nora. "What do you think, Nora? Isn't it just stunning?"

She stomped down so hard a dollop of juice splattered her knee. "Yes, you're right. The fabric looks so... expensive. You two better take off. It's far too dirty around here."

Kieran's gut clenched. Getting dirty with Nora sounded so much better than escaping with anyone else. But she'd backed him into a corner with her *helpful* decree.

So, when Tamora dragged him away, muttering, "How true. I would hate to ruin this frock. My mother had it made custom for my graduation," he groaned internally, but followed.

"Your graduation was recent, then?" he asked as they exited the backyard.

"Oh, not at all. It's been at least"—she paused with her gaze lifted to the sky, like the math was far too difficult to calculate—"oh, several months now."

Months... fantastic. Why does Mother want to saddle me with a child?

"Congratulations." If she was willing to play dumb, then he might as well, too. "Oh, is that why Mother wanted us to meet? Are you in need of a mentor now that you're striking out in the world?" He puffed out his chest proudly as their boot steps rang out on Main. "Well, look no further. I've done the same for many young boys and girls just like you."

Her lips puckered like she'd sucked on something sour. "No. That's not it at all. Your mother—"

"Please, don't be modest. I can tell you're an intelligent young lady. If you'd like me to connect you with my contacts at the capital, I'd be more than willing," he barreled on, not giving her a moment to cut in. "I'm even on good terms with the prince. I hear he's on the lookout for a new bride."

A calculated gleam shone in her eyes. *No trouble adding up those numbers, I see.*

"The prince? Truly?"

"Yes. He's quite handsome. And rich too." He grinned as Tamora's eyes widened. "Would you like a letter of introduction? I don't think it's too late to join the next ball, if you make travel plans soon."

"Well, I do love dancing. There's so little revelry in Everpass these days, don't you think?"

He patted her arm. "So true. Don't worry, Tamora. You'll be dancing through the streets of Fairvale in no time. You can even stay at my villa while you're there. It's sitting idle, since I'm here for a visit."

By the time they made it to Tamora's home, he'd fed her enough stories about the capital and its rich prince that she was practically frothing at the mouth. "I'll drop the letter off with your steward first thing. Travel safe now."

"I can't thank you enough, Kieran. I'm so pleased we met." Tamora clasped his hand, her demeanor completely changed from the coy front she'd first put on, and more like who he suspected she really was down deep. An excited young girl desperate for love and adventure.

She'd have a much better time finding that where he was sending her. Not married to an old washed-up spy like him.

He strolled away, whistling. What was his mother thinking? Tamora didn't suit him. Not in the slightest.

And what was Nora thinking? Is that who she thought he wanted? Some fresh-faced beauty who'd barely escaped the schoolroom?

That couldn't be further from the truth. He'd always valued a woman's personality over beauty, even more so as he aged. And he couldn't fathom a life spent shackled to a girl who only thought of him as a prize to be won. It was clear that was what Tamora was searching for. He was only happy he had the means to send her off on a mission for a more valuable catch.

If he ever decided to settle down—which he wasn't sure he was ready for—what he'd really need was a partner. Someone who would stand by him through all the ups and downs of life. Something told him that if he ever found that, it would be the greatest prize of all.

As he reached the turnoff to his road, a familiar lad on the street caught his eye. While staring much too hard at a set of ankles for the second time that day, a brilliant idea stole over him.

Jogging to catch up, he called out, "Oliver! Hello."

The teen slowed, dragging a hand through his curly brown hair. "Do I know you, sir?"

"We met this morning at Stellar Spirits. Or, rather, I was there when you stopped by."

Oliver gulped. "Oh. Hello. Can I help you with something?"

He grinned, slinging his good arm around Oliver's shoulder. It wasn't hard to do since they were about the same height. "I'm glad you asked. There is something I desperately need help with. Are you free right now, by chance?"

MASQUERADE

Nora

T he bar door scraped against the floor, and Nora flashed a tired smile. "Ali. Not up to cooking again?"

Ali curled a strand of short black hair behind her ear, scanning the tables. A group of travelers huddled together in the back, talking among themselves as they sipped their mead, but the place was relatively quiet. She frowned. "I thought I was late. Didn't anyone else show?"

Nora finally noticed the paperback clutched in Ali's arm. "Book club was tonight? Shit, I forgot."

"Looks like everyone else did, too." Ali sank onto the stool next to Maalik's and tossed her cloak on the stool beside her before smoothing a hand down her black trousers. "I can't believe they didn't come."

When she'd opened Stellar Spirits, one of the first things she'd attempted to draw in customers was a book club—much to Ali's delight. She was a huge bookworm and had even begged the owner of the Golden Lark to host a meeting there a few years back, but of course, he'd declined.

Since Nora had been known to cuddle up in bed with a book from time to time, she decided it might be fun. And it had been. They'd attracted a group of four women to start, but lately their eagerness for the written word had fizzled.

"Can't say I'm surprised. Denna just gave birth to twins. And Andra's out of town." Nora pulled out a mug and filled it with Ali's usual—apple cider. She never drank anything stronger when she had to head home and take care of her daughter.

"Guess we need to find some new members." Ali sighed. Then her gaze turned calculating, and she swiveled in her seat. "Are you a reader, Maalik?"

He tugged at the collar of his checkered button-down. "Depends. What's the story?"

"Here. Have a look." She slid the paperback across the bar. "This was last month's. We'll pick a new one at our next meeting."

Maalik squinted at the back cover. "This looks too... lovey-dovey. You got anything with murder and mayhem?"

"Lovey-dovey?" Ali snagged the paperback, eyebrows waggling. "You wouldn't think so if you'd read it."

"What are you talking about?" Maalik asked.

Nora chuckled. "Ali has a very specific taste in books." The first month she'd chosen the featured read, two of their original four stopped coming. "The characters spend a lot of time together... in bed."

"Or in the shower," Ali added. "Pressed up against the wall. It wouldn't be entertaining if the author didn't switch things up every so often."

Maalik's cheeks reddened. "Oh…"

"Us unmarried folk need to get our jollies where we can, am I right?" Ali grinned. "So… you in?"

His upper lip curled. "If you pick one with mayhem… maybe."

"Challenge accepted. I'll find one with my type of action and yours." Ali tapped the front of her book. "What did you think of this one, Nor?"

Nora winced. "Sorry… I kind of forgot about it. Can I take a rain check on the discussion?" Honestly, she'd been too depressed to finish. It was hard to stay invested in fictional characters' happily ever after while her life was imploding.

Ali loosed an aggravated sigh. "Figures. You have enough action happening in your real life that you don't need it in your fiction."

She scoffed. "Guess again."

"Don't tell me you didn't make a move on that fine specimen of a man while you were all alone today?"

"Ali…" she hissed under her breath. "Shh. Someone might hear you."

She waved at the table in the back. "C'mon. They're too busy chatting each other up to pay attention."

Nora pointedly stared at Maalik.

"What? You want me to pretend not to hear you in the bathroom again?" Maalik pressed his palms to the bar.

"No. Stay." Nora grabbed her trusty rag and started scrubbing, though the bar hardly needed it. She wasn't sure how she ended up with a grumpy half-troll as one of her main confidants, but she might as well roll with it. "You can help me convince Ali to stop her ridiculous matchmaking attempts."

Ali blinked innocently. "I don't see why I should. You two would be so cute together."

"In what world?" She barely resisted the urge to roll her eyes. "Did you forget that we come from two very different sides of town?"

Maalik's mug thumped on the marble. "Kieran has never struck me as the type to be bothered by that. Hell, he's been running with your brother since they were kids."

Great. He's supposed to be on my side. "Sure, Kieran doesn't care, but his family sure does. You should've seen the ditzy elf his mother sent sniffing after him in my backyard this morning."

"No!" Ali's eyes widened. "What happened?"

Her gut roiled at the reminder. Tamora hadn't said hi or even looked in her direction while she pouted and primped for Kieran. Yeah, she was beautiful, but she was still a complete bitch.

And he'd left with her.

Honestly, though, why wouldn't he? Tamora was young and gorgeous, no doubt breezing through life without a single complication. The perfect piece of arm candy for a distinguished retired spy.

"Some pretty young thing came looking for him... and they left together." Nora shrugged nonchalantly, ignoring the dull ache in her chest. "Don't you see? He's *not* interested in me."

Ali's eyes narrowed. "Really? Tell me what happened. Word for word."

"She's right." Maalik shoved his empty forward. "I bet there's more to it than you're letting on."

"I don't see how that matters." Nora snagged the mug. "But fine. She showed up. Claimed his mother sent her. Kieran told her he was busy, but I said it was okay if he left. So... they did. End of story." Sure, she was leaving out a few details, but that was the basic gist.

"So, he didn't leave until you gave him the okay?" Ali lifted a brow. "Sounds like you shot yourself in the foot with that one."

"Agreed." Maalik folded his arms across his chest.

She set the refilled mug on the bar. "It's none of my business who he takes for a stroll."

"But you want it to be..." Ali smirked.

"No. I don't." Only the heat creeping through her cheeks betrayed her thoughts, and Ali wasn't one to miss it.

"Yes, you do! Stop lying to yourself, Nor." She lowered her voice. "He was your first crush. Quit pushing him away and make a move."

Nora hung her head. "I can't."

"Why not?" Ali clicked her tongue. "Wait until you're alone and kiss him. You won't know if you never try."

"That's just it. I did try." Her chest tightened.

"What? When?" Ali asked excitedly. "Goddess's sake, you should have led with that instead of telling us about the stupid elf girl."

She lifted her head and stared blankly at the wall. *I can't believe I'm about to tell her this...*

Until now, she'd never shared the pitiful tale with anyone. But she knew her friend. If she didn't give her a reason to quit, Ali would keep urging her to go after Kieran until her lips turned blue.

"It wasn't today." She heaved a deep sigh. "Kieran and I kissed once, a long time ago."

Ali's mouth fell open. "Back when you had that crush? But I thought he was way too old for you."

"No, not then." Sure, she'd wanted him to kiss her when she was twelve and he was seventeen, but in retrospect, that was never going to happen. "I visited Seth in the capital the year I turned twenty. There was this masquerade ball I was dying to attend. So for my nameday, Seth mailed me the tickets and told me to meet him there."

"A ball. That sounds amazing." Ali placed her bent elbow on the bar top and rested her tilted head on the back of her fist.

"It was." Her eyes closed as she pictured it in her mind's eye. Merry music rang out from a ten-piece band. Rich fabric in every color of the rainbow swung around the ladies' hips. Men in dark suits, their faces hidden behind sparkling masks, prowled through the crowds, twirling women on the dance floor or dragging them into shadowed alcoves.

"Did you say it was a masquerade?" Maalik shook his head. "I'm surprised Seth would invite you to that. Sounds like a perfect excuse for debauchery."

"I'd begged him to take me for years. I suppose I wore him down in the end."

"What did you wear?" Ali asked.

A nostalgic smile crossed her lips. "The most beautiful dress I'd ever seen. I saved for ages and paid a dressmaker to make it custom. It was the same golden-brown as my eyes and fit like a glove. The mask was lace and covered the top half of my face, topped with stunning golden feathers."

"I wish I could've seen it. I bet you looked like a completely different person," Ali mused.

She sighed. "Yeah. That was the problem."

"What do you mean?" Maalik asked.

"When I arrived at the ball, I couldn't find Seth. And I was getting a lot of unwanted attention from men who were clearly looking for more than a dance."

"No kidding." Ali giggled.

"I spotted Kieran first. I hurried over, wanting to escape from the creeps... only he didn't recognize me."

"Stop…" A slow grin overtook Ali's face. "You didn't tell him who you were?"

Her cheeks warmed. "Well… no. He'd always seen me as just Seth's little sister." But he hadn't then. Kieran hadn't been able to tear his eyes off her in that dress… and she'd soaked up his adoration with glee. "I know I should've said something right away, but then he asked me to dance."

She closed her eyes, letting the memory wash over her. She could picture it like it was yesterday…

Ten years ago…

Gold silk swirled around her legs on the dance floor, her heart thrashing against her chest like grapes in a barrel. *Goddess… this is like a dream.*

Kieran's warm fingers wrapped around hers, one palm resting lightly against her hip, making her skin tingle. He wore a black half-mask, but she'd recognized him instantly. She'd never mistake him for anyone else, even though they'd been apart for ages.

He'd grown even more handsome while living in the capital. She marveled at his taut, sinewy forearms and the confident air he exuded. While other men strutted around the dance floor, Kieran glided, leading her through the unfamiliar moves effortlessly, all while keeping those gorgeous blues locked on hers. It was enough to make a girl swoon.

He bent his head and asked, "Are you sure we haven't danced before? You seem so... familiar."

Her stomach twinged. This would be the perfect chance to come clean. But more than anything, she didn't want the moment to end. "I'm here visiting. This is my first ball, in fact. And no, we haven't danced." All of that was very true, but nonetheless misleading. Still, she couldn't dredge up the will to recant. Not while every second in his arms made her feel like she was floating.

"Hm. Well, I'm pleased I was here to share your first taste of the madness." His grip tightened around her waist as a couple, dancing so closely it was indecent, narrowly missed ramming them into another pair with their lips locked.

"Is it always this mad?" she asked, breathless. She wasn't sure she could blame the tightness in her chest on dancing. Not while Kieran kept staring at her dress like he wanted to tear it off.

"Not always. Stick with me and I'll make sure you don't miss the fun."

She lifted a brow before remembering he couldn't see it with her mask in place. "Fun, huh? What would that entail, exactly?"

"I could show you, if you'd like. But it would require a change of scenery." He smirked, spinning her closer to the dance floor's edge.

"You'd really tear me away from my first ball? What fun is that?"

The sexy chuckle that rumbled out of him plucked a string within her, somewhere so deep that she dared not consider, not unless she wanted a crimson stain to ruin the light-pink rouge she'd brushed across her cheeks.

"Later, then. As long as you don't dance until you drop."

"Drat. That was my plan, I'm afraid. Sounds like I'll miss out. What a pity."

He bent further, and his hot breath ghosted over her ear. "We can have plenty of fun off our feet, if you'd prefer it."

Dizziness washed over her, and she was lucky he held her so closely. If she'd been standing unsupported, she'd have surely wobbled at the knees.

She'd never known Kieran would be so... brazen. Truth be told, she loved every second. Excitement coursed through her, and an undeniable sense of *satisfaction*. She'd spent so many years pining for him. It was nice to be desired for a change.

But she couldn't keep up the ruse forever. Eventually, Seth would arrive, scoop her into a hug, and ruin the illusion. So as he lifted his head, she swallowed thickly, prepared to confess.

Only Kieran didn't just look up and simply meet her eyes. He swung them in a grand twirl, one that landed them behind a vine-covered archway that appeared to be the entrance to a hedge maze.

"Where are—" Before her question fully formed, his lips descended and pressed into hers. Nora gasped, her hands rising instinctively to his shoulders. Her mind swam, warring thoughts screaming at her to push him away. Or better yet, drag him closer.

He wouldn't be kissing her if he knew who she was. But goddess, he felt so *good*. His lips were achingly soft, a delicious contrast to the hard muscles beneath her palms. Before she knew it, she was kissing him back. Soft moans filled her ears, hers—and Kieran's too.

She reveled in every caress, loving the way he held her so softly, while his talented mouth took her to new heights. Then he deepened the kiss, and as his tongue slid against hers, her toes curled within her new slippers. His hand glided to the nape of her neck, and he dragged her closer.

A voice rang out loudly. "Sis? Where are you? Take off your mask so I can find you."

Seth.

She stiffened, and Kieran clearly took notice. He pulled back, scanning her with lust-drunk eyes. "Something wrong?"

"That's my brother. I promised to meet him." She stepped aside, out from the shadows of the archway.

"Your brother? Well, I'd like to meet him if you're—"

"Nora, there you are!" Seth gamboled over, a huge grin on his face and a green half-mask decorating his eyes. "Sorry I'm late. I hope no one bothered you." He spotted Kieran and halted mid-step. "What—"

"Don't worry. I found Kieran. He made sure no one bothered me."

Kieran split a look between them. One she couldn't help realizing was much different from the sultry gaze he'd gifted her before. His stare was full of shock... and disappointment.

I knew it. I shouldn't have let it go so far... Every second that he stood there, unblinking and quivering with repressed emotion, her heart crumbled a bit more until it was nothing but dust.

Thankfully, Seth didn't seem to notice the tension thickening. "Thanks, man. I'm glad you were here to protect her from those idiots." He slung a beefy arm around Kieran's shoulder. "Come on out of the shadows. All the fun's happening on the dance floor."

Kieran ducked out from under his arm, his tone falling flat. "I ought to let you two catch up. Think I've had about all the fun I can stand for one night."

"Aww, really?" Seth threw up his hands as Kieran strolled off without a backward glance. "Sorry, Nor. Kieran usually loves these things. I'm not sure what's come over him."

Nora forced a smile while her soul wrenched. "It's all right. We'll still have a good time without him." Even as the words slipped off her tongue, she knew them for what they were—a lie. She'd never have a better time at a ball than those few minutes when Kieran thought she was someone else.

Nora blinked, forcing the humiliating memory aside. "Long story short, we danced. Then... we kissed. Then Seth showed up, and Kieran left after he realized it was me he'd been kissing."

"Wow." Ali blinked. "I can't believe you didn't tell me this before! What was the kiss like?"

"Honestly, it was... magical." She still thought about that night more often than she cared to admit. Eventually, she'd moved on, telling herself it was foolish to hang on to hope after such an obvious rejection. She'd been chasing the feelings he'd wrung from her in that stolen moment ever since, but no other man's kiss had ever come close. "And... it was a mistake."

"Really? What if he was just... overwhelmed?" Ali asked.

She shook her head. "No. You weren't there. He tore off like I was diseased the moment he realized who I was. And he never came looking for me afterward. We still haven't spoken about it. I wouldn't be surprised if he doesn't remember it at all. I'm sure he's kissed plenty of girls at masquerades."

"Sorry, las." Maalik reached across the bar, squeezing her hand lightly. "Want me to throttle him for you?"

A startled chuckle escaped her. "No. It's ancient history. I'm over it. Truly."

At least, she'd thought she was. With Kieran here, all those old emotions kept popping back to the surface. Maybe if she kept reminding herself what was waiting if she put her heart on the line, she'd finally stop longing for him.

"I'm sorry too." Ali smiled sadly. "Ooo, I might even have something to cheer you up."

Nora bit back a groan. "I'm afraid to ask."

"Remember that new professor from the magic school I hired?"

As a glassblower, Ali had to work with witches to be successful. Charmed lamps that turned on and off with a touch were all the rage these days. Ali was always complaining about how dull the work was, but supplying the town with enough lamps to keep their homes magically lit brought in a steady income that allowed her to spend a little extra on more artistic pieces she enjoyed creating.

Still, she had no clue why Ali thought a professor of magic would cheer her up. "Sure. I remember."

"He arrived late afternoon and only imbued half of my lamps with light magic. He's staying at the inn overnight so he can finish in the morning. But guess what he asked me before he left?"

Maalik spoke up before she had the chance. "What?"

"He asked if there was anyone in town skilled with alchemy. I may have mentioned you."

Nora gaped. "Alchemy? Are you cracked in the head? I've never practiced alchemy in my life."

Ali pursed her lips. "Please. You've helped your mother with her potions."

"You know half of those don't even work." And *help* was a stretch, even if they had. She'd never done more than fetch her mother something from the garden if she'd asked.

Ali barreled on, unperturbed. "And what do you call what you're doing here? Brewing all that deliciousness. That's pretty damn close to alchemy, if you ask me."

Nora groaned, eyeing the bar top. *If I slam my head into it, will she get the message?* "I wish you hadn't told him that, Ali. What were you thinking?"

She grinned smugly. "Wait until you see him, Nor. Let me tell you, if all witches look like that, you can sign me up to be spellbound."

Maalik snorted. "Sounds like you should've recommended yourself instead."

Ali ignored the jab. "I assumed if I sent him here, your handy helper would be driven mad with jealousy, but now I'm thinking you should just have a little fun with him before he leaves." She lifted her brows. "Nothing better to take your mind off an old flame than finding a new one."

Nora rubbed her temples. "The last thing I need right now is another man complicating my life. Do me a favor and tell him you were mistaken. Please?"

"Seriously? You don't even want to meet him?"

"Honestly... no."

Ali hopped off her stool. "Fine. Guess I'll leave you here to wallow." She snagged her book off the bar and wagged it at Maalik. "Don't think you're off the hook, my friend. I will find the perfect book for next month's meeting. Let's meet here in two nights to vote on which one."

He snagged his mug. "Where else am I gonna be?"

"That's the spirit." Ali took off with a parting wave.

Nora's shoulders slumped. That was one less thing to worry about tomorrow. Too bad her worries were stacked so high they might collapse and crush her at any moment...

A Fleeting Taste

Kieran

Kieran strolled into town the next morning, the autumn chill biting at his cheeks. "Today I'll do better," he muttered to himself, the soft lilt of his words muffled by his steps clunking against the cobblestones. He needed to keep things casual—like he should've yesterday. Not that he had much choice. Seth would be watching his every move. It wouldn't be so easy to sneak peeks at Nora. "I shouldn't be watching her at all." Seth deserved better.

He'd leaned on his best friend so much growing up. It had been his only escape from the pressures that came with living under his father's roof. Tanyth had never been satisfied unless Kieran was the best at everything he tried. For a half-human being judged against full-blooded elves, that was easier said than done. He was always coming up short in his father's eyes, an unending disappointment that left him in a near constant state of anxiety.

All that melted away when he spent time with Seth. They'd whiled away lazy afternoons, talking about everything. Seth never complained, even if he said something incredibly stupid. Their friendship existed in a judgment-free zone—something they both craved while living with the disgrace of being a halfling. He'd quickly grown to treasure their closeness. It was something he'd never felt with either of his parents.

When he'd been invited to take part in the Crown's exclusive spy training after completing his schooling in Everpass, Seth had been the only friend he'd dream of inviting along. He'd been his rock back then. In so many ways, he still was.

Once he'd told his parents about the opportunity, his father had gifted him a villa in the capital, then tightened his purse strings. "You're a man now, Son. Can't keep relying on handouts," he'd insisted, before setting him loose with little more than the clothes on his back.

Seth had taken a job as a laborer, freeing Kieran to study and undergo the grueling training that only a third of the program's recruits passed. He'd have failed without Seth's support—there was no denying it.

They'd barely scraped by for the first few years, surviving on plain noodles and whatever they scrounged out of the grocer's bargain bin. Seth had stuck by his side through it all, hardly asking for a thing in return. Until now...

"Goddess's sake." *Why do I have to be obsessed with her?* For the second night in a row, thoughts of Nora had plagued him. He couldn't stop remembering how perfect she'd felt in his arms. Or the barest tremble in her lip after he'd caught her, as she drank him in with her whiskey-colored eyes. "Stop. Just... stop."

"Hey, man. You doing all right?"

Kieran flinched. "Seth. Hey, I'm good. How about you?" He met him on the road outside Stellar Spirits and flashed a crooked grin.

How long had Seth watched him wander down the road, lost in his thoughts and muttering to himself like a madman? Probably for a while, judging by the befuddled look of concern his friend was currently sporting.

Seth was dressed for a long day's work, a tool belt slung around his trousers and his long-sleeved tunic rolled up to the elbows. And then there was him... arms hidden in his jacket pockets and gaze darting around uneasily as he gave himself the realm's oddest lecture. They made quite the pair...

"You sure you're doing okay?"

"Yeah. Fine," he said tightly.

"I bet I can ask Nora to help hang the shelves if you need the day off."

"No need. I'm good, I swear." A thread of unease wound around his heart. Normally, if something was bothering him, Seth would be the first person he'd tell. Only now... he couldn't. No wonder the big guy was still staring at him, scratching his head.

Kieran straightened his shoulders and forced some levity into his tone. "Don't worry about me. I'm just sore about my mother's meddling yesterday."

"Ah." Seth ducked inside the bar, holding the door open for Kieran to follow. "What did she do this time?"

"Matchmaking, of course. And your sister was no help at all chasing the girl off." He raised his voice, making sure she wouldn't miss the accusation in his tone.

Nora glanced up from the books she'd spread out on the bar. "You're a big boy, Kieran. Surely you can handle rejecting ladies on your own."

Was that a hint of bitterness, or was he imagining things?

Seth chuckled. "Oh, this sounds good. Tell me more. I could use a good laugh."

"There's not much to tell." He prowled closer to Nora, unable to stop himself from taking a long look at her.

She sat on a stool, the skirt of her navy-blue dress brushing her shins as she swiveled a few inches before spinning in the opposite direction. A pencil rested behind her ear, her gaze darting across what he suspected was a ledger.

He forced his gaze back to Seth's. "Tamora came to find me at my mother's behest, but I eventually talked her into heading to the city to meet the prince. She's probably on her way to the mountain pass as we speak."

Seth barked out another laugh. "You did? How'd you manage that?"

Kieran winced. "Speaking of... I may have invited her to use the villa. You don't mind, do you?"

"Why would I mind? It's your place, Kieran. You can do what you want with it."

"I know, but you still have most of your stuff there." He clapped Seth's shoulder. "Honestly, I wasn't really thinking when I offered. I saw a chance to change her target, and I took it."

"It's fine. I'm sure she won't bother with a bunch of clothes far too large to fit her."

Kieran sighed. "You're probably right. Still, if there are any damages, I'll take care of them."

Nora snapped one book closed and opened another.

"What's eating you, Sis?" Seth asked.

"Nothing. Just surprised Kieran and Tamora didn't hit it off." She glanced up again and offered a halfhearted shrug. "After you went on and on about her dress, I assumed you fancied her."

It was Kieran's turn to laugh. "You would be wrong. I'm not planning to court a girl I need to finish raising."

"Oh, wow. She was that young?" Seth lifted a brow.

"Just graduated—months ago." He shook his head. "What was my mother thinking?"

Nora drawled, "Probably that you're the type of guy to sweep a young girl off her feet. Isn't Tamora the exact kind of girl you'd meet at all those fun balls in the capital?"

Kieran's stomach wobbled. He'd been trying so hard to forget that night. So far, Nora hadn't brought it up, but that comment made him wonder… "Balls aren't my scene. Haven't been to one in ages."

"That's true." Seth slid behind the bar and helped himself to Nora's water pitcher. "I keep inviting him to tag along, but he's developed a vexing habit of turning me down."

Nora bit her lip and lowered her head, like whatever was in her book was absolutely thrilling.

"Well, we better get started." Seth sipped from his cup as he peeked at Nora's writing. "Will the hammering bother you while you're working on your books?"

"I'll manage. Better you do it now before I open. You two chased away most of my customers with your sawing."

Seth scoffed. "Really? I thought we were attracting you new clients. I bet Tamora didn't know your place existed until Courtney sent her looking for Kieran."

Nora scribbled on the page. "Trust me. She still doesn't know it exists."

"Ouch." Seth tilted his head. "She was one of those girls, huh?"

"What's that supposed to mean?" Kieran asked.

Seth let out a loud guffaw. "You're a shrew magnet, that's what. No wonder you never keep them around longer than a fortnight."

No. I just had a fleeting taste of bliss that I crave more than my next breath but can never relive. Only I can't exactly admit to that, now can I? Kieran shuffled to the back door. "The shelves still out back?"

Nora met his gaze and nodded curtly. "Right where you left them."

He propped open the door, and then he and Seth carried the shelves inside. He'd have managed it quicker if he still had two hands to work with, but no one complained about the extra time he took to get his balance right. And they didn't offer to help either.

Frankly, he was sick of that more than anything else. He'd lost count of the times his mother had rushed to *help* him since he arrived home. Maybe if she'd shown an ounce of that devotion while he was a child, he'd be more willing to accept it now.

After stacking the last shelf on the floor, Kieran pressed his knuckles into his lower back and stretched while Seth kicked the door closed.

"Don't tell me you're tired already." Seth crossed his arms.

"I'm not. Just missing my bed in the villa. I never noticed till now how soft my old bed is."

Seth chuckled dryly. "Nothing like returning home after a long absence to put things in perspective."

"What? Your old bed not cutting it either?" Kieran straightened, eyeing Seth closely.

"Nothing wrong with where I'm sleeping. But Ma..." He sighed. "I'm worried about her."

He confirmed Nora was still engrossed in her books before asking, "Really? Why?"

"You know she's always been a little eccentric, what with her tonics and potions and all."

"Sure." Moira had been obsessed with her concoctions for as long as he could remember. Honestly, it would've been more surprising if Seth told him she'd given them up.

"Last time I stayed with her, she was so wrapped up in her garden. But lately, it's like she's taking the whole wannabe-witch stuff to the extreme."

"You sure that's not a timing thing? Not much to be done with the garden till spring, is there?"

"True, but..." Seth lowered his voice. "I caught her outside last night, chanting at the moon. That's a little out there, even for her."

"I'm sure it's nothing."

"You know I've never liked her pretending to be a witch. Why she'd want to be associated with people who are so distrusted by near everyone, I'll never understand." Seth wrinkled his nose. "Only, it's not just the witch stuff bothering me. Her memory is getting worse. When I found her out back, I was honestly afraid she'd wandered out without knowing where she was headed."

Kieran's stomach sank. It was pretty common for memories to dull as folk aged, but Moira wasn't a gray-haired elder yet. She ought to have a few decades before that became an issue. He nodded across the bar. "Have you talked to Nora about this?"

Seth's auburn bangs bobbed across his forehead as he shook his head. "I don't want to worry her. Besides, she's taken care of Ma this long. It's about time I take a turn. Especially now that she's running this place."

"I'd expect nothing less." A pang of regret struck him square in the chest. He'd dragged Seth to the capital. What if his selfish decision to have his friend tag along caused Seth to miss out on the best years of his mother's life? "Can I help? Anything you need, just ask."

"I was hoping you'd make that offer." Seth leaned in. "You mind taking the reins with the renovations here? Then I can tell Nora I plan to fix more than that old roof at Ma's place. I'll be able to really keep an eye on Ma, see if I'm worrying over nothing."

That meant he'd be spending a lot more time with Nora—alone. He wasn't sure if he should rejoice or gird his loins. "Of course. I'm in."

"Great." Seth grinned, then raised his voice. "Hey, Nor?"

She swiveled on the stool to face them. "Yeah?"

Seth crossed the room, and Kieran followed suit. "I was just telling Kieran Ma's place needs a bit more work than I originally expected. After we hang these shelves, I'm gonna head back there, if that's all right with you."

"Sure. I don't have a problem with that." Nora frowned. "Do you need any help? I can always close for the afternoon—"

"No need for that. It's nothing major. Just little things I can handle on my own." He patted Kieran's shoulder. "Besides, Kieran can help you with whatever needs doing here."

Nora swiveled back to her books. "Why don't you both go? I can—"

Seth leaned against the bar. "Nope. You're not getting rid of us that easily. There's still a lot to do here. Someone needs to paint those shelves, and repaint the wall too. Or were you planning to keep it that way?" He waved at the wall, which was currently splattered with stains that hadn't budged despite Nora's intensive scrubbing. "You ask me, it clashes with the rest of the place, but what do I know about interior design?"

"Of course I'm repainting."

"So you do need help. Or are you planning to do it all while you're serving your customers?"

Nora rubbed a hand down her face. "Fine. He can stay."

"Good. Now that we've settled that, let's get to work." Seth was all smiles as he ambled back to the pile of shelves.

At least one of us is happy. Something told Kieran that Nora wouldn't be quite as easy to please.

The Perfect Drink

Nora

"Well, what do you think?" Seth stood with his head tilted as he scanned his handiwork.

"Honestly?" Nora beamed. "I love them! Thank you so much."

It had taken Seth and Kieran the entire morning to hang the replacement shelves, but she had to admit, they'd done a fantastic job. She lifted a thumb to the center row, which hung perfectly level at chest height and spanned the length of her bar. "Look at that. They're as thick as my thumb."

"They're in there good and solid too. Your customers could dangle off them like kids on a rope swing and they wouldn't budge." To punctuate his point, Seth thumped his fist on the same shelf she'd been measuring.

A vibration tickled Nora's skin, but the wood barely wobbled. "These are incredible, Seth."

"Happy to help, Sis." He nodded to the bathroom as the door creaked and Kieran strode out. "She loves 'em, man."

Nora flashed a tight smile. "Thank you, Kieran. You did great work."

"Told you I knew how to handle my wood." He smirked.

Her smile vanished. "How could I forget?"

Seth chuckled. "I'm gonna take off for Ma's. You sure you don't mind, Nor?"

"Not at all. Give Ma a kiss for me."

"You bet. Later." Seth patted Kieran on the back on his way to the door. "Make sure she stays out of trouble while I'm gone?"

Nora choked down a scoff. *Don't you see? He is the trouble.*

Kieran leaned back on his heels. "Sure thing. See you soon."

The door swung closed with an ominous bang that set off a reverberating thud in Nora's chest. Fate had a funny way of sticking them together, when all she wanted was to forget the humiliating memories she'd recalled in such detail last night. What was she supposed to do now? Chat with him like everything was normal while she couldn't erase that kiss from her mind?

"Do you need to open soon?"

She nodded and crossed the bar. "It's a good thing you two finished when you did." She flipped the window sign to Open and unlocked the deadbolt. "It rarely picks up until later, though. Too many folks still working."

Kieran's brow furrowed. "Do you think the paint fumes will scare them off?"

"I'll open all the windows. We're lucky it warmed up today." The chilly morning had given way to a bright, sunshiny afternoon. So long as they worked fast, they could get the first coat of paint up before night fell and the air grew chill again.

"I'll help."

They opened the front windows swiftly. But as Nora attempted to heave up the first window overlooking the backyard, she frowned. She double-checked that she'd flipped the lock. Then she tried again with a grunt. "Goddess…"

"Problem?"

The smooth glide of the window lifting beside her made Nora's frown deepen. "This one's stuck."

"Let me take a look."

"It's fine. Just need to wiggle it, I bet." She pressed her palms flat to the plane of glass and tried shifting the window from side to side. It meant leaving smudges, but that seemed better than admitting defeat and asking Kieran to play white knight.

She spotted him closing in without having to turn, his blurry reflection captured in the glass. Was he… checking her out? No. Probably just scrutinizing the stupid window so he could waltz in and fix the damn thing—one-handed, no less.

"I think I almost have it." She wriggled it harder, getting her hips in on the action. There was probably a bit of something wedged in there, keeping the window from budging. If she could just work it loose…

"Nora." His voice was all velvet and smoke, unleashing a torrent of tingles across her back.

She sought out his reflection again, only to find it locked on her swaying rear. Nora froze.

He cleared his throat. "Scoot. Let me try."

"Fine." She sidestepped out of the way, hurrying to the next window.

Goddess... What was that? The sultry way he'd uttered her name echoed in her ears until another sound replaced it—the swoosh of the stubborn glass finally releasing under his hand. Heat burned her chest, and she shoved the next window a bit more forcefully than she'd intended.

"Easy. They'll break if you keep slamming them around like that."

She spun around with a scowl. "Good thing I'm best friends with the town glassblower."

Kieran pushed open the last window, his grin fading as he spotted her expression. "Did I do something wrong?"

Nora sucked in a deep breath, fighting to keep it together. What was she even doing? Kieran had done nothing. Not now, at least. Sure, he'd cracked a few stupid jokes, but that was to be expected between friends.

Maybe the problem was she didn't see him as a friend any longer. Not after that incredible kiss—and his subsequent rejection. But did she really want to bring up the past right now? Would she even like his answers if she asked about that night?

She sighed. "No. You didn't. I'm just in a foul mood today."

"Ah... Well, if you need to talk about it—"

She held up a hand. "It's fine. Come on. You can help me haul up the paint." The stairs creaked as she led the way down into the cellar.

"Sure we're just hauling up paint?" he asked, following closely at her heels.

"Of course. What else would we be doing?" Her boots thumped on the last step, and she reached up, turning on a lamp.

Kieran's breath escaped in an audible whoosh. "That's better. This place gave me the creeps without the light."

Sure, the cellar was a little dreary. She hadn't bothered to renovate it, seeing as she only used it for storage. Even so, it wasn't like she'd led him into a graveyard. "Seriously? You've faced off against traitors to the Crown, and a dark basement scares you?"

He shrugged. "I can't help it. Fears aren't exactly rational."

"I suppose that's true." She stopped beside a set of bins neatly lined up beneath a row of shelves on the back wall. "Plenty of folk are afraid of silly things."

"How about you?" He stopped beside her, watching as she rummaged through a bin for the painting supplies. "What silly thing scares you?"

Besides asking you about that night?

"Rats." An involuntary shudder made her shoulders tense. "They always loved to sneak into Ma's kitchen this time of year, when the weather started to turn. Just the thought of their sharp little claws and those dark beady eyes makes me want to scream."

"I seem to recall you always begging us to throw back the fish we caught when we were kids. I never would've suspected you weren't the realm's biggest animal lover."

"Most animals, sure." She'd always loved pets. Dogs, cats, horses, and yes, even fish. "I don't know what it is about rats. I can't stand them. Seth must've carted dozens out of the house over the years when we'd trap one. I couldn't do it."

"Hm. Not so different from my dislike of dark underground spaces."

She dug out a paint tray and a variety of brushes, then straightened. When Kieran stepped closer, she jerked her head at the shelf. "I've got this. Can you carry up the paint?"

He took another step, boxing her in. Her breath caught. Their gazes locked as he reached out, leaning so close she had to crane her neck to keep from breaking eye contact.

"This the one?"

The scrape of metal on wood clattered behind her ear. She gulped as Kieran dragged the can into her line of sight.

"Yep. That's it." He backed away, and her speeding heart slowed. "You head up first. I'll turn out the light."

"Sure."

When he made no attempt to talk her out of her plan, a tiny smile crossed her lips. "Don't race up there so fast you fall down the stairs and crush me." Her brows lifted when he didn't even bother with a snarky reply.

"You should have a light for the stairs, too. Weren't you just boasting about being best friends with the town glassblower?" He mounted the first step.

"I'm managing with what I've got." Enough light seeped down from upstairs that it wasn't completely black in the cellar once the light shut off. "Besides, I already owe Ali too much to be begging for more favors."

"How much do you owe her?"

"At this point? A small fortune. Luckily, she's not opposed to supplying me in advance or I'd never be able to replace all the bottles that were shattered when my old shelves fell."

"Sounds like a pretty good friend. Why haven't I met her yet?"

A twinge of discomfort struck her. Ali's beauty would no doubt impress Kieran once they met. And she clearly thought he was attractive as well.

Nora shook off the jealous thoughts. She didn't have any reason for them. Kieran wasn't hers, and Ali could court whoever she wanted. "I'm sure you will soon. She's stopped in the last couple of nights, after you left."

"I look forward to it."

She probably should've let Kieran get a good head start, considering the fear he'd confessed to. Hell, if she really wanted to be nice, she'd have let him reach the top. But she couldn't resist shutting off the light after he'd only climbed half the distance.

His steps quickened, and she stifled a giggle. Not lying, then.

What am I doing? Testing his honesty? What reason would he have for lying? She shoved the questions to the recesses of her mind as she emerged upstairs.

Kieran clunked the paint can atop the bar.

"Careful with that." She hurried forward. "I don't need the counter stained."

"Good point." He tapped his chin as he scanned the floor behind the bar. "You have something we can use to protect the tiles?"

"I do. I'll grab it." She dropped the brushes beside the paint and crossed the bar while fishing a key out of her dress pocket.

After climbing the stairs to the second floor, she dropped to her knees in front of her apartment's only closet. She dragged out a few boxes and had just opened the trapdoor to the storage compartment when a clatter lifted the hair on the back of her neck.

"Is this where you live?" Kieran asked.

Nora bit back a groan as she peeked over her shoulder. "This is the second time in less than a week you've creeped up on me while I was down on my knees."

"Sorry." He chuckled. "Can't complain about the view, at least."

She grabbed an old set of sheets out of the crawlspace and whipped around, glaring fiercely. "What view?"

He waved at the window. "Great view of Main from up here."

"Oh." She set the sheets down and began shuffling everything back in place.

"Quite small, though."

"Feel free to head back down if you're too cramped." Not that she'd invited him up to begin with.

"Thought you might need help."

"I'm fine." She stood, then brushed off her knees.

"I like it up here." His gaze roamed over her things appreciatively.

She clutched the folded sheets to her chest. "Thought it was too small?"

He wasn't wrong. The room barely had enough space for her double bed, a couple of dressers, and a single rocking chair she kept beside the large octagon window that housed a few herb plants. That was pretty much everything, except for the tiny closet and a cramped bathroom. She'd hung tall shelves, using the vertical space to house her books and some odds and ends, but honestly, she'd be lying if she didn't admit to feeling a tad stifled from time to time.

"It is, but it's cozy, too," Kieran drawled, his fingers trailing lightly over her deep-purple knitted bedspread. "Can't say I like you living above a bar. Especially one without a second exit. Aren't you worried someone might break in? And what if a fire breaks out while you're up here?"

Nora chewed on her lower lip, ignoring how her body flashed with heat at the sight of Kieran so close to her bed. "I can't afford to be worried. But if it makes you feel better, I don't plan to stay here forever. Once I'm in a better spot financially, I'll buy a house in town. Then I can rent this room out and gain another revenue stream. Though you make a good point about the whole exit business..." She frowned, adding another item to the unending list of renovations she needed to complete.

He stepped closer, and she couldn't help noticing how tall he was. The low ceiling almost brushed the top of his sandy hair. "You want me to carry that downstairs?"

She shook her head, gripping the folded cloth tightly. "I've got it."

Another footstep rang out, competing for dominance with the pounding thuds in her chest. "You sure? I came all the way up here. Might as well put me to use."

Don't look at the bed... The phrase repeated in her mind—fine advice after he floated that tempting offer. Apparently her traitorous body wasn't inclined to listen. Like they had devious plans of their own, her eyes shot from Kieran to the bed and back again. "I-I..."

The sexiest smirk she'd ever seen flashed across his lips. "You what?" He closed the distance until the only thing that remained between them was a few layers of bunched-up sheet—a poor shield, but that didn't stop her from wedging it against her bodice.

"I-I," she croaked, her voice failing her at the same time her skin erupted with prickles. *Goddess, why is my mouth so dry?* She licked her lips, but when Kieran's gaze locked on the movement and his head dipped, she nearly lost it. *Is he going to kiss me? I can't believe this is about to happen ag—*

"Hello?" the masculine voice of a stranger called up the stairs. "I'm looking for the owner. Are you up there?"

Kieran backed away, his gaze falling to the floor.

"Be right down." The staccato beat of her heels on the steps sang a cowardly tune. But she couldn't stay up there a second longer. Not while she was sure whoever interrupted them had saved her from making a terrible mistake.

What was she thinking? It would've been madness to kiss Kieran again. Forget for a moment that he'd crushed her heart under his boot in the past. It was the middle of the day, and her bar was open. She couldn't entertain male guests in her room while customers lingered downstairs, waiting to be served. Kieran was altogether too distracting, causing her to act more unprofessional than she had in her entire life.

Speaking of distracting… She halted at the bottom of the stairs and did a double take. She'd been right that the man in her bar was a stranger—but good goddess, he was stunning. Inky-black locks framed his chiseled face, his dark-brown eyes staring out of spectacles that didn't hamper his appeal in the slightest.

The soft rasp of his fingers brushing across his stubbled chin tickled her ears as he graced her with a striking smile. "Nora Rowen, I presume?"

She blinked. How did he know her name?

He thrust out a hand, and the sleeve of his long black cloak inched up, flashing a glimpse of black ink on his brown skin. Was that… a rune?

Damn it, Ali… I'm not prepared to deal with this right now. "I am. You aren't a professor of magic, by chance?" She took his hand tentatively and shook.

The stairs pounded behind her. Kieran popped out of the stairwell, frowning as the stranger pumped her hand slowly.

"Ah. So you've been expecting me."

"Who are you?" Kieran's gaze raked across the man's fine black suit and white button-down before ending on their linked hands.

Frankly, being around them both had Nora a little light-headed. She couldn't remember the last time she'd been in such close proximity to two beautiful men. Thankfully, the cool breeze was whipping through the bar, or she'd likely have to resort to fanning herself.

She retracted her hand. "Yes. I'd like to know that as well."

"Professor Doran Wilder. I teach alchemy at Maudwin University of the Arcane." His smile didn't slip, even when he stuck out a hand to Kieran, only to have it ignored. "Pleased to meet you. Do you work here as well?"

Nora cleared her throat. "I'm sorry. I thought Ali was planning to tell you about her mistake. You see—" Her explanation cut off on a gasp as a white owl landed on the windowsill behind the professor.

Doran's hand fell to his side. "Don't mind Pearl. She's with me."

"You have a pet owl?" Nora gaped at the gorgeous creature, wondering if her eyes were currently as saucer-like as the black-and-gold set staring back at her.

"Pearl is my familiar." He chuckled softly. "I spend so much time at the university these days that I often forget they aren't a common sight in villages like Everpass."

Of course. She'd heard that witches often traveled with companion animals they dubbed familiars, though she wasn't too knowledgeable about them. "Yes, well, as I was saying—"

"Perhaps we can talk over a drink?" He nodded to the bar. "I've worked up quite a thirst after the morning's work."

She thrust the sheet out to Kieran and hurried behind the bar. "Of course. Grab a seat and let me know what you'd like. Though I'm a bit low on stock at the moment, I'm afraid."

"Yes, Alsira told me about your unfortunate turn of bad luck." Doran's eyes narrowed on the new barren shelves as he sank onto a stool. "It's one reason I popped in. Besides needing to parch my thirst."

"What can I get you?" Nora asked with a smile. She glimpsed Kieran's stony expression as he joined her behind the bar, but chose to ignore it. Customers took precedence.

"Well, as much as I enjoy a good tipple, I need to begin my return journey to Maudwin today, so I'll pass on the spirits. Keeping that in mind, I'm up for anything."

She leaned in. "Are you asking me to surprise you, Professor?"

He chuckled, resting his elbows on the bar. "If you would be so kind, Ms. Rowen."

Nora scrutinized Doran closely. This wasn't the first time a patron had put their taste buds' fate in her hands. In fact, she'd built a reputation in Everpass for giving the best recommendations. She'd discovered she had a knack for guessing people's favorites when she first started as a barmaid at the Golden Lark. Every time she'd watched a patron's eyes close with bliss as their taste buds rejoiced, it confirmed she'd made the right choice saving up to follow her dreams and open her own place.

Doran would be no different. As she continued to study him silently, she pondered her options. Should she serve him a tart and tangy juice? Or a delicate floral tea? No... he might like them well enough, but those weren't the perfect fit for him. She ended her perusal by staring deep into his chocolate-brown eyes. Ah... that was it!

Before she could announce that she knew just what to make, something jostled her from behind.

"Sorry." Kieran backed away, shaking out the sheet with a flourish. "Didn't mean to wreck your concentration. Or whatever that was."

"I was deciding what to make the professor." She grinned at Doran. "I know just the thing. Give me a moment. I have to grab something from upstairs." She flashed a warning glare at Kieran and hissed, "Alone," as she passed him.

Glee bubbled in her belly as she hurried upstairs. She wasn't sure why, but discovering the perfect drink always made her day brighter. Once she returned with the right ingredients, she'd make Doran's. She just knew it.

Extraordinary

Kieran

The old sheets stretched, pulling as taut as Kieran's battered nerves. What the hell did a professor of magic want with Nora?

He'd tried to ignore their conversation and start setting up the space to paint. Then, when Doran announced he'd be leaving that day, a massive weight had lifted from his shoulders. But hardly a moment passed before Nora started staring at the prof like she was drowning in his eyes.

Was it petty to knock her out of the trance the damn witch had ensnared her in? Sure. But he wasn't about to apologize for it.

A loud hoot made Kieran's skin prickle. He eyed Doran, wishing he could say what he was really feeling. *Go home and take your stupid owl with you.* But Nora would be horrified if he chased her customers away.

"You don't need to look so worried. I promise I won't put a hex on you." Doran smiled, his tone good-natured enough that Kieran would've likely been drawn to him if they'd met in any other setting.

"I'm not worried," Kieran stated.

Doran lifted a single brow. But he was either too polite or too cowardly to call out Kieran's reply for the bullshit it clearly was. "I know my kind doesn't have the best reputation in small towns like this one, but I swear I'm only here with good intentions."

"Whatever you say." Kieran focused on lining up the sheets perfectly. If he kept looking at Doran, he might take a swing at his stupidly handsome face. *Does Nora think he's handsome?* The thought bounced around in his brain incessantly as the door to her cramped apartment banged open and shut.

"Got it." Nora grinned, a handful of something green peeking between her fingers. "I'll have that drink ready for you in no time."

"Perfect." Doran smiled back, making Kieran choke down the urge to knock loose a few of those pearly whites. "While you're working, I have an offer I'd like to discuss."

Nora slid into the kitchenette and turned on the kettle. "Is this about alchemy? You should know, Ali was exaggerating when she told you I practiced it."

"Yes, she said as much this morning." Doran shifted on his stool. "But she also told me about the unique skills you've honed over the years. I imagine it wouldn't be hard for someone so familiar with brewing to learn the ins and outs of what I do."

She bit her lip. "Don't you have students who can help you?"

"Of course. But so few of them are in complete control of their power. It's one reason the work we do at Maudwin is so important.

What I really need is an assistant who doesn't need to worry about their innate magic wreaking havoc on my supplies."

Nora grabbed a jar, scooped a spoonful of something out of it, and dropped it into a large mug. "And you're offering me the job? But... you barely know me."

Doran tilted his head. "I am. Call it intuition if you must, but I'm certain you would excel at alchemy."

Intuition, my ass. He can't be serious...

The tea kettle whistled, and Nora flicked off the burner. "I'm flattered. Truly." She poured the steaming liquid into the mug. "But I already have a job. Running this business has been a dream of mine for a long time. I have no plans to give it up."

Kieran's heart lifted. Of course Nora was too smart to agree to work with a stranger she'd just met.

"I can certainly understand that." Doran adjusted his glasses. "What if you could do both?"

Nora carried the mug to the bar. "How would that even be possible?"

"The salary as my assistant is quite substantial. With the funds, you can hire someone to handle the day-to-day tasks here. And you'd have the summer free to oversee the business personally."

She slid the mug toward Doran, her lips pursed like she was actually considering it. Kieran's stomach churned as he snagged the paint can off the bar and carefully pried off the lid.

Nora wouldn't take the job... would she?

"My word." Doran smacked his lips together. "This is... extraordinary." He set down the mug, beaming from ear to ear.

Her cheeks flushed. "Thank you."

"I haven't had hot cocoa since I was a little lad. But this is so much more refined than what I remember. What did you add to give it that wonderful freshness?"

"Fresh mint leaves." Nora returned his smile with a delighted one of her own. "I'm glad you like it."

Doran rapped his knuckles on the bar. "This makes me even more certain you'd fit in perfectly at Maudwin."

Nora shuffled from one foot to the other. "Thank you for the offer, but—"

"Please. Take some time to consider it. My current assistant is retiring in a few months, so I don't need your answer yet." Doran lifted the mug and took a long pull. "I do hope you'll be interested, if only so I can trouble you for more drinks. It'll be a massive step up from the weak coffee my assistant is forever brewing."

Kieran turned so they wouldn't spot him rolling his eyes.

"I will think about your offer, as long as you promise not to stop searching for a replacement," Nora said.

Doran chuckled. "Fair enough." The stool scraped as he stood. Metal clanged on the bar top.

"Hold on. I'll grab your change."

"Keep it." Fabric rustled. Pearl hooted once, then lifted off. "It was lovely to make your acquaintance, Ms. Rowan."

"Please. Call me Nora."

"And you must call me Doran." He flashed another bright grin before strolling toward the door. "Farewell, Nora. Until we meet again."

"Goodbye, Doran," Nora called after him.

Well, wasn't that just adorable? Kieran's lips curved into a sneer as the front door creaked on its hinges.

Nora's soft humming filled the silence.

He grabbed a wooden paint stirrer from the pile of supplies. "You aren't seriously considering that job, are you?"

She emptied the mug, then placed it in the washbasin. "Why shouldn't I? It might be fun."

"More like dangerous. Don't you know what they study at that school? It's not all alchemy. I hear there's folk there studying necromancy. Sure you want to mess around with witches who are trying to bring back the dead?"

"I'm not as superstitious about witches as Seth is." She shrugged. "Besides, I'm sure Doran would keep me safe. After all, his old assistant is retiring. Seems he didn't have any trouble keeping them alive."

Kieran gritted his teeth as images bombarded him of Nora and Doran working closely together—alone. How long before the handsome professor was no longer satisfied with only her delicious drinks and attempted to sample more of what Nora had to offer?

"Relax. I'm not planning to take it. Why do you think I told him to keep looking?" She set the mug on the drying rack.

A bit of the tension in his bones melted away. "Probably for the best. I don't think your mother would be pleased to see you go."

Nora chuckled. "I don't know about that. She'd likely pop in every chance she got. You know how much she fancies magic."

She might be right on that count. Moira would be liable to worm her way into classes using Nora's connections. "What's stopping you, then?"

"Everpass is home. I know you couldn't wait to escape, but some of us actually enjoy living here." She polished the counter, her lips twisting.

"Hey, I like it here too."

She scoffed. "Really? Then why didn't you ever visit when Seth came home?"

He smirked. "How do you know I didn't? Keeping tabs on me, Nora?"

"You'd like that, wouldn't you?" She tossed down the rag and crossed her arms.

Yes... "Course not. I just find it curious that you're so well-versed with my travel plans."

Her cheeks flushed again, and he took pleasure in the fact that they were a good deal redder than when the professor complimented her. "I wasn't keeping tabs. But Seth always tells us what he's been up to—and that always includes a good deal about you."

"Ah..." His hand stilled, the paint swirling like all the sourness churning within his gut. "Well, my absences had little to do with Everpass."

"Just too much fun to be had in the capital?"

"More like less judgment from my folks."

Nora's face softened. "Oh."

He hurried to change the subject. "So, is running this place really your dream?"

"Yeah. Though I probably should've chosen something easier. I saw how much Ma struggled with her business, but I've always wanted a place of my own. Now I have it." She traced her hand lovingly across the bar.

"You're well-suited to it." Kieran had to admit, she'd surprised Doran flawlessly earlier. And everything she'd served him had been absolutely delicious. If she overcame this supply hurdle, he suspected she had a long, profitable future ahead of her.

"What about you? What are your plans, now that you're done working for the Crown?"

He poured paint into a tray. "Honestly? I'm not sure. I always dreamed about finding adventure. But I suppose my adventuring days are over. Doubt if I'll have much opportunity for it any longer."

"You won't with that attitude."

Glaring, he said, "Pardon?"

Nora leaned against the bar. "There're adventures all around you. If you can't find one that suits you to join, then make your own."

He snorted. "Right... I fail to see what adventures there are in Everpass."

She grabbed a paintbrush and dipped it in the tray. "Maybe you're not looking in the right places."

"Maybe you're full of shit."

"Excuse me?" She shot him a sideways glare as she started painting beside him.

"Give me one example, then."

Nora brushed the wood methodically. "You could sign on as a runner. Lots of travel opportunities there."

"No thanks." He'd worked with runners plenty in his former life. It could be a fun gig carrying letters and parcels from one village to another, if not for the terrible pay and grueling hours. Honestly, the pay wasn't a deal-breaker, but he'd begun enjoying the slower pace of life in Everpass. And there was one face in particular he was becoming quite fond of seeing every day. But he wasn't ready to admit that, so he said, "That job is meant for a younger fellow than me."

"What about the fire brigade? They're always looking to hire."

Score one for Nora. Only... "I doubt they'd be too keen to ask for help from me." He lifted his arm, showing off the missing piece that he'd once again practically forgotten about until this moment. Nora appeared to have that effect on him.

"I don't know about that. You've proven to be perfectly capable at every task I've given you so far. If you want to join the brigade, you should. You'll never know if you don't try."

"Capable, huh? That's what you're going with?" he teased.

"I could think of a few other descriptors, but we're trying to build you up, not tear you down."

Laughter spilled out of him, so light and carefree he hardly recognized it. Goddess, how long had it been since he'd laughed like that? Weeks, at the very least. "You know what? You're pretty amazing, Nora."

Her head dipped low, and the smooth, slow stroke of her brush faltered. A bead of paint dripped from her brush, and it was dangerously close to slipping off the beam and splattering her dress.

"Got it." He darted in, catching the paint with his brush. But as he turned to grace her with a smile, he realized how close he'd gotten.

Nora's breath hitched at the same moment her gaze lifted to his lips.

Not this again. He'd narrowly stopped himself from kissing her earlier, while they were alone in her bedroom. If that damned professor hadn't shown up, he'd have had her back pressed against the wall, their tongues tangling in fiery passion.

But no one was there at that moment to shove open the door. And Nora just kept staring at him, her face so close all it would take was one little inch...

He closed the space between them, pressing a soft kiss to her lips. *What am I thinking?* His mind screamed at him to pull away, but before he could, Nora leaned in, her mouth brushing against his and setting off a cascade of longing so intense nothing in the entire realm could convince him to move.

Nora's hand wrapped around his neck, and he groaned, sinking into the sensation. Her captivating perfume enveloped him, tinged with the sharp bite of paint. His lips tingled, his skin breaking out in goose bumps under her touch.

Memories flashed of the last time they'd kissed. One kiss was all it took to have him obsessed with the masked beauty. At the time, there'd been no doubt in his mind that he would do anything for a shot with her. But then it all fell apart when Seth arrived.

He thought he'd lost his chance for good then. After he forced himself to walk away, even though he sensed the devastation in her eyes. And yet, somehow, here he was, just as addicted as before.

Goddess... Seth. He'd promised. He couldn't betray his best friend. No matter how incredible Nora's kiss made him feel...

He pulled back, his chest heaving. "Nora... We can't. I'm sorry."

"You're *sorry*?" She tore her hands off him and stepped back, shaking her head. "I thought you'd grown up, Kieran, but I guess dark basements aren't the only thing you're still afraid of."

"Nor—"

The door picked the worst possible moment to swing open. A group of imps hurried in, and Nora rushed to serve them, ignoring him completely.

Kieran turned back to the paint with a sigh. *Why did I do that?* He just couldn't leave well enough alone.

He'd be lucky if Nora didn't throw him out, and he lost his only chance at a cure. Now he needed to figure out some way to help Nora without giving in to his desires again.

Something told him that would be easier said than done...

Smitten

Nora

She rubbed her shoulders, shaking off the urge to close up early and sleep for about a hundred years. Stellar Spirits had been swamped all afternoon and well into the evening, which she was enormously thankful for. She needed every sale if she wanted to stay afloat and build back her stock. Still, staying busy didn't come without its own set of problems—chief among them being an exhaustion so heavy she struggled to keep her eyes open.

At least the end was in sight. As closing time drew near, the crowd of customers thinned. Now she was elbow-deep in the washbasin, finally making a dent in the dirty dishes that had amassed.

"Thank you, Nora. Everything was delicious." A plump older woman, her short white hair styled in a halo of curls, stopped at the bar, a stack of dishes in her hands.

"That's high praise from you, Chef." Nora frowned. "You shouldn't trouble yourself with the dishes. I would've cleared those." Even as the words left her mouth, she knew they were wasted. Vilotta, who insisted everyone call her Chef, came in weekly with her husband, and each time she insisted on clearing their plates from the intimate table for two they always claimed.

"Don't be silly. I know exactly what it's like serving folk all day long. It's the least I can do."

Her husband, Edgar, held out a threadbare cloak. "All set, dear?"

The pair had been married for decades but still shared a meal together on their day off. And it was blatantly clear from how they doted on each other, holding hands and giggling like teenagers, they were still very smitten. It was rare proof that long-lasting love could flourish.

Normally, she enjoyed nothing more than basking in their joy. But after today, she wasn't so keen to. Not when she was more certain than ever that she would never experience a love like theirs.

"Thank you, sweetheart." Vilotta smiled sweetly as Edgar wrapped her coat around her. Then the pair set off together, arm in arm. "See you next week, Nora."

"You bet. Have a great night." Her shoulders slumped as she grabbed the dishes. A flash of black sky winked in the doorway before the door swung shut. Not much longer now, and she could close. Get that rest she desperately craved.

Too bad that wasn't the only thing she couldn't stop craving...

The door banged open as she rinsed the first plate. Maalik trudged in, looking almost as exhausted as she was, his striped button-down and khaki trousers rumpled beneath his dark-brown cloak.

"You're stopping in late. Having your usual?"

"Please." He thunked atop his preferred stool and heaved a weary sigh.

"Long day?" She abandoned the sink and dried her hands before grabbing a clean mug.

"That's putting it mildly. My boss found a discrepancy in the books. Made us stay late and weed through the last six months' worth of figures—twice."

She slid a frothing mug across the bar. "That sounds... tedious."

"Tell me about it." He took a long pull from his mug. "I can't stand that place. Too bad I don't have the skills to do anything else."

Maalik worked at the bank, a career that evidently wasn't suited to him. Encouraging him to ditch the thing that was the most likely cause of his habitual desire to drown his sorrows would be bad for business, but she'd never been shy about supporting a friend.

"You shouldn't stay there if it's making you miserable. Surely there's something else you can do."

"If there is, I haven't found it yet."

"Well, I hope you do." She patted his hand before attacking the dishes again.

He slugged back another big gulp. "I almost forgot. I spotted something today that you might be very interested to know."

"Oh yeah? About what?"

Maalik leaned across the bar, lowering his voice. "It's about the company that's renting you this place."

"What about it?"

"Do you know who owns it?"

"No." Her fingers tightened around the dish in her hands. "Who?"

"The Dornelises." He drained his mug and inched it forward.

Nora's chest pinched as she grabbed his empty. "Are you sure?"

"Positive. I spotted it on a bunch of paperwork while wading through those numbers today."

"Maybe it's a coincidence..." Kieran might not even know. His father owned lots of real estate, but as far as she knew, Kieran wasn't interested in helping run his businesses. In fact, their relationship seemed more strained than friendly.

He lifted a shoulder in a lopsided shrug. "I just wanted you to know in case pretty boy has ulterior motives for helping you."

She slid the refilled mug across the bar, then reached for her necklace, smoothing her fingers over the crescent moon pendant. "I doubt that. He's been best friends with Seth forever. I can't imagine Kieran would do anything to spoil their relationship."

He cradled the mug. "You're probably right. Just... be careful. I would hate to see him hurt you again."

Little late for that. "Thanks, Maalik. I appreciate the heads up."

They fell silent, the soft slosh of water and ale the only sound in the nearly empty bar. Thankfully, Maalik didn't press her to chat. She was in no condition to keep up with small talk while her mind raced.

She'd barely spoken to Kieran that afternoon, after that disaster of a kiss and the repeat rejection. He'd painted her shelves, then cleaned up while she raced back and forth, cooking, making drinks, and waiting on customers. Then he'd packed up and left, disappearing during a particularly busy point when she didn't even notice his departure. At the time, she'd figured he didn't want to bother her with a goodbye while she was busy, but now she couldn't stop questioning everything.

Was Kieran helping her for nefarious reasons? Why didn't he tell her his family owned her bar? She gasped as she recalled a particular clause in her lease. One that gave the owners the right to rescind it early if the business was under duress. Was Kieran reporting back to his father, telling him all about the troubles she faced, or was he as clueless about who owned the place as she'd been?

No. Just because he didn't want to kiss her didn't make Kieran a villain. She needed to stop thinking the worst. First thing tomorrow, she'd ask him to explain. Surely there was a reasonable explanation...

The next morning, Kieran arrived as she finished handing out the last of her leftovers, looking ready to work in a gray long-sleeved tunic and black trousers. "What's for breakfast?" he asked cheerily as he dragged a hand through his windswept dark-blond hair.

Nora blinked, taken aback by his display of normalcy. *What a surprise... Guess he's gonna act like that kiss never happened.* "Nothing today. The kids cleaned me out." The back door creaked on its hinges as they stepped inside.

He huffed. "Figures. I should've guessed it when I saw how busy you were yesterday."

"Not a terrible problem to have. Think you can survive until lunch?"

"I don't know. Might need to trouble you for a mug of hot cocoa, since I know how *extraordinary* you make it."

"Funny." She ducked behind the bar and slipped off her shawl. "I need to balance my ledger. You mind hauling up the supplies without me?" She smoothed her brown dress, then reached for her books.

Truth was, the figures were fine. She just needed a plan to bring up his family's ties to her rental without it coming across as an accusation.

"Sure." Kieran shot her a grin as he headed for the cellar.

He wouldn't smile like that if he was secretly plotting against her, right? She was probably worried about nothing.

But when Kieran hollered up the stairs a moment later, her blood ran cold. "We have a problem. You better get down here."

"What problem?" She raced down the stairs, her heart in her throat. "Holy shit."

Paint was splattered everywhere, dotting the shelves and floor in half-dried puddles. All the expensive, color-coordinated shades she'd saved from the initial remodel were spilled out—wasted. And worse, some of it had leaked into the storage bins, destroying most of the supplies she'd scrounged up to start her next few batches of liquor.

"I don't know how this happened." Kieran scratched his head. "It was fine when I left last night, I swear."

"You... ruined it." Nora's chin wobbled almost as much as her voice. "I can't afford to replace all this."

Kieran stepped closer. "I didn't—"

"Did you do it on purpose?"

"What?" His jaw dropped. "Why would I?"

"Hmm... I don't know. Maybe you're sabotaging me for your father so he can lease this place out to someone else." She watched his face carefully, praying his shock would only grow. But when Kieran backed away, lowering his gaze, her head spun. "You knew." She jabbed a finger at his chest. "You knew he was my landlord all this time, didn't you?"

"Please, let me explain."

She shook her head. "No. I don't want to hear it. Get. Out."

"What? Nora—"

"This place might not be mine for much longer if your father gets his way, but it is now." She crossed her arms, glaring fiercely. "Go, Kieran. I don't need your *help* any longer."

Kieran scrubbed a hand down his face, his gaze darting from the spilled paint to Nora and back again. Then he loosed a deep sigh. "I'm going to fix this, Nora. I promise."

The door slammed on its hinges, and Nora sank to the floor, cradling her head in her hands. Another mess stared back at her, just as devastating as the last.

Her stomach churned, the cloying scent of paint doing little to ease the sickness in her belly. But she couldn't bring herself to move. Especially not when she replayed everything in her mind.

She'd been right to kick him out... hadn't she? She'd entrusted Kieran with the last of her paint. He'd been the only person in the cellar last night, and the first to come down this morning. No one else could've done this but him.

But even as the logic bolstered her, she couldn't help feeling like she was in the wrong.

She should've at least let him explain... Sure, it would've probably been bullshit, but at least she wouldn't be sitting there with the gnawing worry that she'd just made a terrible mistake.

"Hello?" a familiar voice yelled down the cellar steps. "You down there, Nor?"

"Yeah." Nora cleared her throat. "Yeah, I'm down here, Ali."

Footsteps pounded on the stairs, followed by a gasp. "What happened?"

She shoved to her feet, numbness spreading through her chest. "Oh, you know. Just me, having the worst luck in the realm, as always."

Ali's strong arms wrapped around her. "I'm so sorry. How can I help?"

Nora patted her friend's back weakly before breaking free. "You can't. Not unless you find someone who'll sell me replacements for my ruined ingredients—on a payment plan." She gritted her teeth, knowing what she'd asked for was impossible. No one in town sold goods without payment on delivery.

Ali nibbled her lower lip as she surveyed the mess. "How did you manage to dump paint over everything?"

"I didn't. It was Kieran."

"Really?" Ali's eyes popped wide.

"Yes..." Nora sighed. "Well... maybe."

"What do you mean, maybe?"

Her nose wrinkled. "I kind of threw him out while he was trying to explain."

Ali cocked her head and speared Nora with a shrewd glare. "Why would you do that?"

With a sigh, Nora laid out everything that'd happened since they'd spoken last, including Professor Doran's job proposal, Kieran's hot-and-cold act yesterday, and Maalik's warning. "And that's why I blew up at him when I saw this mess."

Ali frowned. "I suppose that explains why he'd be willing to help you for free, if he was planning to sabotage you all along." She rubbed her temples. "But then why all the flirting? And kissing you again. I don't know. Seems fishy to me."

"That's what I was worried about..." Nora ascended the stairs. Times like this definitely called for a drink. "You think I should've let him explain?"

"I hate to say it, but yeah." Ali sank into a stool. "My advice? Clear the air. Not just about today, but the past too. You'll never be able to move forward with the repairs if you can't trust the guy working for you."

"If he even comes back. I'm not so sure he will, after I kicked him out." She slid a mug of cider to Ali.

"Sounds like he was pretty determined to fix things when he left."
Ali sipped thoughtfully.

Could she count on Kieran returning? Did she even want him to?

If he did—which was a pretty big *if* at this stage—Ali was right.
Something had to change. She couldn't keep tiptoeing around their
past and ignoring how it was eating her up inside not knowing where
Kieran stood back then—hell, and where he stood *now*.

She didn't trust Kieran. Not like she should. And she couldn't keep
working with him if she was constantly worried he was one step away
from double-crossing her. The truth might hurt, but she'd rather he
admitted he wanted nothing to do with her romantically than be stuck
in their current limbo. Then they could finally move forward—as
friends.

Nora filled a mug with ale, letting a bit of the frothy foam spill over
her fingers before settling it on the bar. "Maybe I should write Doran.
You think he'll give me an advance on my salary if I accept his job
offer?"

"No." Ali slammed her mug down with more force than necessary.
"You can't take that job! I'd miss you too much."

Nora splayed a hand over her chest, blinking repeatedly. "Excuse
me? You were the one who invited him here in the first place."

"Yeah, so you could boink him. Not run off with him into the
sunset!" Ali crossed her arms, her brow creasing. "We're supposed to
make it here together, remember? How are we going to do that with
you traipsing off to Maudwin?"

Ali was right again. Back when they first met, while slaving away
under their respective bosses, they'd bonded over their shared dreams.
Now here they were, running their own businesses, just like they said
they would.

Nora's face crumpled. "I'm sorry, Ali. I really don't want to leave. You know that. But I'm running out of ideas. Maybe this could be the answer."

"Maybe..." Ali slugged back the rest of her cider. "Can you at least wait and see what fix Kieran shows up with before you uproot your life?"

"I suppose that would be wise..." Nora sighed, letting the bitter swig of ale wash away the urgency thrumming through her belly.

"Things will look up soon, Nor. I have a good feeling about this." Ali patted her shoulder as she stood. "Look, I gotta head out. Open the shop. But I'll see you soon, yeah?"

"Sure." Nora dumped out the dregs of the amber brew with a sigh as the front door slammed, wishing she could have another. Too bad she had far too much cleaning to do. Drowning her sorrows would have to wait.

Business Proposition

Kieran

His boots slapped the cobbles, the chill wind nipping his cheeks as he paced through Everpass. "Stupid paint," he muttered under his breath.

How could Nora think he'd spilled it deliberately? After everything he'd done to help...

This was all his fault. Not the paint. He'd stashed it safely in its place last night, the lids secured tightly. He'd even double-checked.

No, what he'd done was worse. If only he'd told her from the start, then she'd never have suspected him of sabotaging her. He'd known he was playing with fire by keeping his father's ownership of her bar a secret, and he'd done it anyway. He shouldn't be surprised that he'd gotten burned when she discovered the truth.

He had to make things right—and he would. But how?

"Stupid perfect kiss," he mumbled, scrubbing a hand down his face. He'd stopped himself from knocking on Moira's door a half-dozen times already. Seth would know what to do... But the thought of facing him while he couldn't wipe the memory of Nora's lips from his mind rankled within him, making him turn aside each time.

He couldn't count on his best friend's help. Not when Seth was bound to see the turmoil brewing inside him. They were too close. Seth would take one look at his guilt-ridden expression and realize he'd done more to his little sister than ruin a few of her supplies.

What he'd done was so much worse. He'd given into the undeniable attraction boiling in his veins and taken what he didn't deserve. Then he'd ruined Nora's peace of mind.

When she'd flown down those stairs and spotted the mess, he'd watched her entire body stiffen—the instant tension of a woman who was at her wit's end. And yeah, even though it *definitely* wasn't his fault that paint had spilled, he'd still been the one to witness all the hope drain out of her. Was it so wrong that he wanted to be the one to fix it for her, too?

If only he could figure out how...

As his aimless steps drew him toward a strip of shops, he stopped short, staring at a dazzling stained-glass sign in the shape of a golden hourglass hung prominently in the front window of a bright-blue two-story building.

"Maybe it's not *my* best friend I need..." With a grin, he shoved open the door, wincing at the loud bells that chimed in his ears.

"Welcome to Our Glass," a woman called loudly from somewhere within. "I'll be with you in just a moment."

He ambled through the shop, marveling at all the pretties. Most of the shelf space was reserved for practical things—vases, bottles, cups, and bowls by the dozen, some in color-coordinated sets, others unique statement pieces that would look at home in the grandest palace. Lamps in all shapes and sizes covered one wall, softly glowing with light magic. A glass case wrapped around the opposite wall was full of small treasures. Pipes, jewelry, animal figurines, and so much more. He could've wasted an entire afternoon staring at everything.

"Wow." Nora's bestie was crazy talented. His skin thrummed with nerves. Hopefully she was crazy nice too, because he was about to ask her for a hell of a favor...

"Sorry 'bout that." A door swung open, bringing with it a blast of heat and a dark-skinned woman sheathed in a long-sleeved button-down and black pants. "I was in the middle of—" Her hands stilled on the ties of her apron as her full upper lip curved into a sneer. "I'll have you know I have a firm 'you break it, you buy it' policy, Kieran Dornelis."

He winced. "Already double naming me? We haven't even been properly introduced."

"Name's Alsira Mikelli. My friends call me Ali, but it's Ms. Mikelli to you." She tossed the apron on the counter and popped a hip, then crossed her arms.

He grinned sheepishly. "I'm guessing you've spoken with Nora today?"

"Sure did." Her dark-brown eyes narrowed. "That's why I'm watching you like a hawk. If you've come here to continue your reign of destruction, I won't go as easy on you as Nora did."

He palmed the back of his neck. "I didn't come here to destroy anything. I came to ask for your help."

"With what?"

"Fixing that mess in Nora's basement."

Her brow arched. "So you did do it."

"I never said that."

She scoffed. "Sure you didn't."

"Ali—" At her glare, he blurted, "Ms. Mikelli, please. I swear it wasn't me who spilled that paint. Yeah, I knew my father owned Nora's bar, but I certainly wasn't in league with him to destroy her. That's the last thing I want. You have to believe me."

Her lips pursed, her dark stare pinning him in place as she scrutinized his expression. A bead of sweat rolled down his back.

She released a weary sigh and rounded the counter. "Say I believe you... What are your plans to make things right?"

"That's the problem. I-I don't know what to do... I already offered to give her a loan."

Ali tilted her head, making her black locks bob against her shoulder. "Nora wouldn't accept that. She's too determined to sink or swim on her own."

It would be so much easier if she'd just take his money. But he had to respect her for standing her ground. There was something to be said about earning your place without relying on handouts. He'd been mad at first when his father cut his purse strings, yet when he accepted his place in the guard after earning the position, it had been one of the proudest moments in his life.

"Then what will she accept?" Sure, he'd graduated on his own, but Seth had been there with him every step of the way. Nora had to learn that it was okay to lean on friends when times were tough. And he was determined to be there for her. "If you know how to fix this, please tell me. I can't stand by and watch her drown."

She peered at him again, staring so long and intensely he fought the urge to squirm. Finally, her face softened. "You really do want to help Nora, don't you?"

"I do."

A sneaky smile spread across her face. "Good. I have a plan, and you're coming with me." She strolled to the back wall and methodically touched every lamp, dimming their magical glow until the shop was washed in shadows. Then she marched to the front door and flipped the Open sign around. "Come on. Daylight's wasting."

Kieran followed, his heart pumping fast. "So what's the plan? Where are we going?"

"You'll see." She flipped the lock on her store, a wicked gleam in her eyes. "Trust me. You'll fit right in where we're headed."

"Oh good. That sounds promising." He followed her with a grin, though it faded fast when he registered the soft sound of her snickering under her breath.

Kieran huffed, his lungs burning from the breakneck pace Ali set as the first hour of hiking into the countryside ran into the next. "Are you ever going to share where we're going?"

"Come on, slowpoke. We're almost there." She blatantly ignored his question, like every other time he'd asked it.

"Goddess's sake. She's trying to kill me," he muttered, tasting metal in the back of his throat as he trudged behind Ali up a steep hillside.

They'd left Everpass's cobblestone streets ages ago, heading south on winding country roads through farmland and fallow fields alike. But Ali hadn't stopped at any of the charming farmhouses dotting the rolling hills. She kept barreling forward at a pace that the average human—or elf, for that matter—would struggle to keep up with, yet it didn't seem to bother her in the slightest.

He was beginning to suspect Ali had just dragged him out here to exhaust him. Then she'd leave him alone in the wilderness with no supplies and skip off on her merry way. But as they climbed atop the hill, Ali's arm snaked out, pointing to a farm resting in a valley next to a stunning lake. "That's it. Come on."

"What's the rush?" he wheezed, forcing his legs to move. "We're almost there."

"Can't slow down. I gotta get home before..." She trailed off, then shot Kieran a glare. "Forget it." Then she made a show of drawing a huge breath through her nose. "What did I tell you? Smell that? You fit right in."

As they closed in on the massive barn, an unmistakable scent hit his nostrils. "Are you implying I'm full of shit?"

She snickered. "You said it, not me."

"Funny." No wonder Ali and Nora were best friends. They both had no problem giving him hell. "So, what are we doing here?"

He jerked to a stop as a rooster pranced out of a henhouse, crowing once before his beady black eyes zeroed in on him—and it ran straight at him. "Whoa!" Kieran dodged, jumping back as the little guy pecked his boots.

"Bok Peckman, leave him be!" A young woman, her brown skirt swirling against her legs and twin plaits bouncing on her shoulders, raced toward them, shooing the crazed rooster away.

Bok tilted his head, aiming a final death glare Kieran's way before he raced back the way he'd come.

"Sorry about that. He takes his job protecting the girls very seriously. We really should give the coop a wide berth." She waved them toward the farmhouse while giving them a cool once-over. "I'm Paige Barclay. Nice to meet you." She thrust a hand out to Ali, who wasted no time shaking it and finishing the introductions.

Paige rubbed her palms down her skirt after Kieran took a turn shaking her hand. She was pretty in a wholesome, girl-next-door kind of way, with pale freckled cheeks, sun-kissed golden-brown hair, and a petite figure, topped with a serene smile that set him at ease. "So, what can I help you folks with?" she asked.

Kieran eyed Ali curiously. He'd been wondering the same thing. Why did she drag them both out to a county farm—to meet with a stranger?

"I have a business proposition for you," Ali began.

Paige lifted a hand. "If that's the case, give me a sec." She hollered over her shoulder. "Ma? You better get out here."

Silence reigned, punctuated by the chirp of crickets floating on the breeze. Then a woman yelled back, "Bring 'em inside. I'll put the kettle on."

Paige grinned. "Would you folks care for some tea?"

"Sure, that'd be great." Ali followed, with Kieran trailing behind more warily.

They entered a sunny kitchen, more cramped than he'd have expected, but tidy and organized. A basket of eggs sat on the table, and a woman who looked like an older version of Paige stood beside the stove. At her feet, a fat little brown-furred sausage-shaped dog hovered, its tail tucked between its legs and an alert gaze bouncing between them.

"Who are you?" The woman's tan skirt swished as she pulled a few pristine ceramic teacups down from a shelf to join the battered pair already perched on the kitchen table.

"I'm Ali, and this is Kieran."

The woman offered them a nod each, then cleared her throat. "I'm Opal. What brings you travelers by?" Her shrewd gaze bobbed across their faces. "If you're wanting moon tea, you've come to the wrong witches. We aren't healers."

Tingles prickled his shoulders, and his pulse sped. He spun to face Ali, shooting her a hard glare. Was she crazy? He'd never have agreed to hike all the way out here if he knew she was about to drag him into a coven. He took a steadying breath while trying to forget all the horror stories about hexes he'd heard over the years.

Once again, Ali ignored him completely, focusing on Opal like he wasn't there. "Trust me, *we* won't be needing any of that—ever."

"You said something about a business proposition." Paige settled into one of the kitchen chairs and gestured for them to do the same.

Ali sat across from her. "That's right. I asked around Everpass and heard that you've worked with payment plans in the past."

"We've been known to dabble… but not without collateral," Paige answered.

Ali turned to him with a pointed stare.

"Ah…" Now his true purpose here finally made sense. He pulled out the baubles Ali asked him to fetch from his room before they left Everpass. Truthfully, he wasn't even mad about it. Nora deserved a chance to overcome the bad luck that had befallen her. The few pieces of antique jewelry he rarely used were a small price to pay. "Will this do?"

Opal's eyes lit up, and she snatched his grandfather's pocket watch out of his hand, lifting it to her nose and examining it shrewdly. "Hm… Very nice." She nodded to Paige, then scooped the rest out of his palm.

"What do you need? And when can we expect your payment?" Paige asked.

"I have a list." Paper crinkled as Ali dug in her pocket. "We have a fallow field in Everpass that we'd like seeded. Within a few weeks, Nora will be ready to hand over the first portion—"

Paige held up a hand. "Let me stop you right there. Who's Nora?"

"The owner of Stellar Spirits," Ali explained. "We're here on her behalf."

"No." Opal thrust the jewelry back in his hand so swiftly Kieran had to juggle it in his fingers to avoid watching it clatter to the floor. "We don't deal with go-betweens. Too risky."

Paige pursed her lips before handing the list back. "She's right. We have the means to help, but we can't draft an agreement without speaking to whoever's responsible for repayment. In person."

He tugged at the neck of his tunic. That would be risky. Once Nora learned he'd put up collateral, she was liable to call off the deal.

He flashed his most winning smile. "Surely we can come to an arrangement without her direct involvement. Ms. Rowen is far too busy running her establishment to make the trip out here personally." He stepped forward, hand outstretched to pat Opal's arm reassuringly.

The little dog was clearly disinclined to allow it. Kieran snatched back his palm before it connected, grimacing as his ears were assaulted with a maddening chorus of howls and yips.

"Tibbie, relax. He was just leaving." Opal shut off the burner, cutting the heat to the kettle before it finished warming. Kieran's hopes cooled with it, settling in his stomach like ice. "If your friend can ever carve out time in her *demanding* schedule to grace us with her presence, then we can talk."

Ali speared him with a withering look as the old woman shooed them out of the kitchen and through a simply furnished sitting room, toward the front door.

Oh no... How could he fix this?

It was clear from Opal's icy tone she thought Nora was too stuck up to meet with her in person. He should've realized these humble farmers were frequently snubbed by the shop owners in Westpass.

Now they must think they were in for more of the same. Especially after he came in, throwing around gem-encrusted trinkets like they meant nothing.

How could he get her to see that Nora wasn't anything like that?

Try as he might, he couldn't come up with a solution. With each shuffling step he took toward the front door, his heart sank more, until it felt like he was trampling it—along with all of Nora's hopes and dreams.

But as Opal reached for the knob, Ali gasped.

He turned as she halted in front of a bookshelf, her eyes wide and excited.

"This collection... It's amazing." Ali trailed a hand along the well-worn spines.

Paige's cheeks pinked, and she shuffled from one foot to the other. "Oh. Thank you."

"It's yours?" Ali lifted a brow.

"We share them," Opal announced, a bit of warmth returning to her voice. "Are you a reader?"

"Yep. Always have been." Ali grinned, plucking a novel off the shelf. "In fact, so is Nora. She even started a book club. This was our selection two months ago."

Kieran spied a man on the cover staring out with a sultry expression, his bare chest on full display, before Ali handed the book to Paige.

"Really?" Paige's eyes lit up. "This one was so good, but Ma hasn't read it yet. I've been dying to talk to someone about it. What did you think of the ending?"

Ali pressed a hand to her chest. "That cliffhanger was brutal. I can't wait for the next—"

Opal burst in. "Hey, save the spoilers!"

"You two should join our book club! We were just talking about finding new members." Ali clapped her hands. "Next meeting is tomorrow evening at Stellar Spirits. We're voting on what our next read will be."

"You want us to join your… book club?" Opal's voice wavered, sounding more than a little dumbfounded. "In town?"

"Yes! Please say you will!" Ali waved at the shelf. "You clearly have fantastic taste."

Ali was a genius! What better way to convince them Nora deserved help than by introducing them in a casual setting? But would they agree?

Paige shrugged.

Opal blinked twice, then sighed. "All right. I suppose we can come."

Ali clapped again and let out a delighted squeal. "This is going to be great, you'll see." Her enthusiasm was so infectious Paige and Opal both grinned back at her.

"Well, I reckon we can bring that agreement with us when we visit. Save your friend the trip out here." Opal finally grabbed the knob and ushered them out. "See you tomorrow."

Paige followed them onto the raised wooden front porch. "I'm glad we got that sorted. I suppose you'll be wanting to hang on to your jewelry until we've reached a formal agreement."

"No. Take it now. I don't mind." He pulled out the items again.

"You sure?" Paige tilted her head. "What if your friend doesn't agree to our terms?"

"Then I'll walk back and get them." The metal clattered together as he deposited the jewelry into her hand. "But I really could use one more thing that wasn't on that list, if you have some to spare."

"He's joking." Ali jabbed his side with her elbow so hard he choked back a grunt.

Ignoring the daggers shooting from her eyes, he said, "Actually, I'm not."

Sure, Ali might be right to suspect he'd muck up the deal after he'd almost gotten them thrown out earlier, but this was important. There was another problem that'd been nagging at him, and he wouldn't sleep well until he fixed it. Since they'd likely arrive back in town after all the shops closed, he needed to procure the means to fix it elsewhere.

Paige pocketed the jewelry. "What do you need?"

"Nothing. Don't worry about him." Ali hissed out of the side of her mouth, "We're here for Nora, remember?"

"I know we are. This is for her, too." He aimed a soft smile at Paige. "Do you happen to have any extra rope?"

On the House

Nora

“Here you go.” Nora handed a paper container to a little boy wearing threadbare mittens. She'd repurposed last night's ham and veggie bake into omelets this morning.

He shot her a toothy grin. “Thanks, Ms. Nora.”

Before he raced through her gate, he tore open the lid and didn't even pause to shuck off the mittens before shoveling a mouthful into his face. She stifled a giggle.

The last season had been hard on many. After several summers filled with droughts, the farmers were dealing with an unprecedented shortfall. Of course, the Crown stepped in where it could, but many of the folk in Everpass were too proud to take handouts. If only these children's parents would set aside their feelings, perhaps there wouldn't be so many relying on her breakfasts...

A sigh spilled out of her lips. She wasn't too thick-headed to realize an abundance of pride might be her downfall as well.

Should she ask Seth for a loan? After so long in the capital, he must have something squirreled away. And they were family...

No. She wouldn't be the one to drain her brother dry. Not when she knew he longed to buy a farm of his own and start a family.

While she'd always loved days spent in town, her brother was the opposite. Growing up, he'd grumble on market days but enjoyed nothing more than spending a long afternoon down at the fishing hole. And he never once complained when Ma gave him chores in the garden.

She'd always known he'd return to a simpler life one day. That he'd willingly endure year after year living in a city far larger than Everpass said something about the power of his friendship with Kieran.

And here she was... mucking that up too.

Maybe Kieran was right. She had no business kissing him—ever. Not when Seth could get hurt because of it.

"Good morning." Curly brown hair flashed above the gate before it swung open.

"Oliver. Good morn—" She froze, her eyelashes the only thing moving, fluttering furiously. "What are you wearing?"

While grinning from ear to ear, the teen did a slow spin. "Looks great, doesn't it?" He stopped beside her, pride shining in his expression as he modeled the embroidered button-down shirt and tweed trousers. "You won't believe where I got this stuff."

Nora's chest twinged. "Oh... I think I might." Truth was, she recognized it already. You don't spend your preteen years crushing over a guy without committing his clothing to memory.

"That fellow helping with your repairs spotted me on my way back from cleaning the Jones's chimneys. He paid me to cart all his old clothes out of his closet, *and* he let me keep whatever I wanted. Isn't that wild?"

She forced a grin. "Sure is. Here. You better get going or you'll be late for class."

"Thanks." Oliver snagged the food and departed with a wave.

Had she misjudged Kieran? How could he be so sweet to Oliver, then turn around and sabotage her deliberately?

She rubbed her temples, then scooped up the last two boxes of leftovers. And yeah, she might have peeked over the fence a few times. But no matter how much she looked, Kieran's smiling face didn't appear in the distance.

Of course he's not coming back. Why would he after you threw him out?

The back door creaked as she slipped inside her bar—alone. The space felt different today. Almost... empty.

She dropped the boxes on the bar with a sigh. How had a few measly mornings spent with company caused her to feel its loss so acutely?

Absently, her fingers lifted to her neck to rub the crescent moon pendant on her necklace. Only... she couldn't.

"Oh goddess. No!" Her heart shattered. Her necklace was missing. The lone relic from her birth family was gone.

Sure, she'd never known them, but it didn't make the loss sting any less. And when compounded with everything else that had gone wrong in the last week, it was like adding insult to injury.

She wracked her brain, trying to recall the last time she remembered seeing it. Was it on her neck when she pulled on her favorite black dress that morning? Or when she washed last night? Truthfully, she couldn't recall. She'd been so occupied with thoughts of everything she needed to set to rights—and of Kieran—that she'd waded through those mundane tasks with only half her focus.

The urge to cry washed over her heavily. But she wasn't about to find anything if she sat down and wept. With a weary sigh, Nora collected herself and began the tedious process of retracing her steps.

Later that afternoon, Nora frowned as she stood over the washbasin. She'd wasted the entire morning hunting for her necklace. All for nothing.

She could've covered the shelves in another coat of paint—if any had survived the spill. Or whipped up a batch of liquor with the meager supplies she had left. Her time would've even been better spent hauling all the paint-covered plants out of the basement or cleaning the mess down there.

But had she done any of that? No. She'd spent the day on her hands and knees, yet again. Scouring every nook and cranny of her bar for the necklace she'd worn as long as she could remember.

No wonder the place felt off. It wasn't just that she was lacking company. She felt naked. Exposed in a way she'd never been before. Deep down, she knew that was foolish. It was only a necklace, after all. A simple bauble on a chain that could be replaced. Nevertheless, its loss ate at her. Without it, she felt hollow; an empty vessel brimming with darkness.

"Well, don't you look morose."

Nora startled, her gaze swinging up. "Maalik. I didn't notice you come in."

He snorted. "No kidding. What's wrong?"

She grabbed an empty mug, arching a brow. "You mean, today?"

"That bad, huh?" He settled on his favorite stool.

"I lost my necklace." The metal tap chilled her fingers as she poured him an ale.

"Sorry to hear that. You need a hand looking for it?"

"I've already searched everywhere. It's like it vanished into thin air."

"You really can't catch a break, can you?"

"Sure seems that way."

Maalik shrugged, making his checkered flannel pull taut across his chest. "At least you have me."

Nora's lips quirked up in a halfhearted grin. "True."

The door creaked as she slid the mug across the bar. She should be grateful she had any customers. It would be far worse if she'd been forced to spend the entire day alone with her thoughts.

"Ah... Chef. I wasn't expecting you again so soon." Nora tilted her head as the older woman shuffled in, wrapped in the same threadbare cloak she always wore and a plain navy-blue dress. "Are you here on your own?"

"No, dear. Edgar's just behind me. We'll take our usual table and drinks. And whatever special you have cooking." She lifted her nose, sniffing audibly. "Smells wonderful."

The praise sparked a little thrill in her chest. With all the time she'd dedicated to searching, she hadn't planned anything fancy—just baked ziti with meat sauce—but she had to admit, it did smell amazing. "Coming right up."

Vilotta marched across the bar, but before Nora grabbed fresh glasses to begin preparing their drinks, the door swung open once more, drawing her attention.

"Hello, Edgar. What have you got there?" She quirked a brow, staring at the mass of rope in his arms.

"Ah... Nora. This is for you." He deposited the armload on the bar in a heap, untangling a length of it that had wrapped around one of his cloak's buttons.

"What is it?" she asked cautiously.

"A rope ladder."

Her brow furrowed. "Oh... What's it for?"

Edgar grinned slyly. "Master Kieran asked me to bring it here for you. For the upstairs—just in case."

A myriad of thoughts hit her all at once. With it came a pleasant burst of surprise. It seemed Kieran cared so much about her safety that he'd felt compelled to send this after a single conversation in her room. She was struck with regret, yet again, for throwing him out so easily without even listening to his explanation. After all, didn't this prove he cared?

But as she met Edgar's eyes, embarrassment rose to overshadow all the rest. It was pretty clear from the twinkle in his eye he had formed an understandable assumption about what Kieran was doing in her bedroom.

Heat rose to her cheeks, and she grabbed the rope ladder hastily, stuffing it under the bar. "Thank you, Edgar," she muttered.

"Oh..." His face fell. "Should I not have brought that by? Kieran mentioned you might still be a little sore at him."

"Did he?" Nora replied sourly.

"Sure. We had a long chat last night when he showed up at my door, begging me to teach him how to tie those knots properly. He swore he wouldn't sleep soundly until he knew you were safe."

A pang lodged in her chest as she fingered the rope. "Kieran *made* this for me?"

"He did. Had a heck of a time with the knots, on account of his... you know." Edgar lifted his left hand and twiddled his fingers. "But when I offered to handle it for him, he insisted on doing it himself. I could've finished it in half the time, but he wouldn't hear of it. He even arranged for me and the missus to have an extra afternoon off as a thank you for teaching him."

Maalik huffed under his breath. "Appeasing his guilt, no doubt."

Edgar cocked his head and raised his voice. "What?"

"Nothing important," Maalik drawled, lifting his mug to his lips.

The older man might not have heard, but Nora sure had. Only... she wasn't so sure Maalik was right.

Was Kieran doing something nice to get back in her good graces? Or was this a genuine gesture of kindness? It was all so confusing. She should take Ali's advice and have a long conversation with him. Facing his inevitable rejection would be better than endlessly wondering what it all meant.

"I've been meaning to ask..." Edgar leaned in, lowering his voice. "Has your mother gotten any fresh supplies recently?"

Nora blinked, bewildered by the subject change. "Can't say that I know, I'm afraid. Why do you ask?" She busied herself with Vilotta's peach iced tea.

"Err... Just a little health matter I was hoping she could help me with." Edgar's gaze turned shifty. "I tried one of her tonics already, but it didn't quite do the trick."

She slid the iced tea on the bar top and grabbed an empty mug for Edgar's ale. If only all her worries could be solved with a simple tonic... Too bad her problems were far too complicated for a potion to cure.

For a moment, the weight of her issues nearly rose to swamp her. Tears pricked at the corners of her eyes, and her chest tightened. But as the ale drifted to the top of the glass, spilling over her fingers, she choked down the darkness by pure force of will.

"Whatever problems you're dealing with, Edgar, I hope they sort themselves out on their own." An odd tingle coursed through her as she handed him the mug.

"That's kind of you, Nora." A faint smile graced Edgar's face. "Sadly, I think this is one problem I might have to learn to live with."

"Can I help?" Nora asked, her voice thick with sincerity.

"No." Strangely, his cheeks reddened at her offer. "Nothing to worry yourself over. Thanks for the drinks." He scooped Vilotta's glass off the bar and hurried to their corner table.

Maalik nodded to the spot where the rope ladder hid. "What are you planning to do about that?"

"I don't know." Nora grabbed his empty mug and refilled it. She gathered from his serious stare he wasn't just inquiring about the ladder, but the man who'd crafted it. "Still haven't decided."

She ducked into the kitchen before Maalik peppered her with more questions. Prepping meals for Edgar and Vilotta kept her hands occupied, and she forced her mind to focus on the task, not allowing it to linger on Kieran for a full five minutes. That was a record for her these days...

She deposited the steaming plates on their table, ready to ask them if they'd like a drink refill, but while their glasses both sat empty, their chairs were abandoned as well. Probably just in the bathroom washing up. She strode behind the bar and began attacking the dishes again when the front door opened.

"I have good news!" Ali announced in lieu of a greeting. "I found two new members for book club."

"Really?" Nora grinned. "And here I thought you'd found all the readers in town already." Found was being generous. Dragged in kicking and screaming was probably a bit more accurate.

"They're not from town. I'm recruiting from the countryside now. So, I hope you two are ready to make a good impression tonight. I can't have you scaring away my newbies."

Maalik chuckled. "Hey, I'm a new—"

They all froze as an unmistakable noise filtered through the bar—moans of pleasure interspersed with a few deep grunts.

"Is that coming from your bathroom?" Ali covered her slack jaw with one hand. "Wow! I'll have what she's having."

Maalik shot a glance at the front door. "Who *is* that? Thought the only folk in here were—" His eyes widened before his head swiveled toward the empty table in the back. "Oh..."

Nora cringed as more amorous whimpers echoed in her ears. "Unless someone arrived while I was in the kitchen..." She turned to Maalik, her expression pleading. "Please tell me someone came while I was in the kitchen."

"Someone's about to come, if that makes you feel better," Ali deadpanned, before chuckling.

Nora and Maalik didn't join in. And when Maalik shook his head slowly, his face grave, Nora's stomach knotted.

"Wait... What am I missing?" Ali asked, her gaze glued to the bathroom door as it began to thump rhythmically. "Who's in there?"

She could hardly believe she had to say this... "You know that sweet older couple who work for the Dornelises?"

"Edgar and Vilotta?" Ali whisper-shouted. "Nooo... But they're both nearly seventy."

"'Fraid so." Maalik drained his mug and slid it to Nora. "I'm definitely gonna need another."

She grabbed it, grateful to have something to do other than stare in shock at her bathroom. "On the house."

"Um… I hate to bring this up, but school just let out," Ali said softly. "Shouldn't you do something about that?"

"Me?" It was difficult to spit that out without sounding shrill. "What am I supposed to do? Burst in there and tear them apart with a broom?"

Maalik choked on his ale.

"I don't know," Ali admitted. "But what if some kids wander in? You don't want to scar them for life."

"Why should *I* be the one scarred for life?"

Ali shrugged. "You signed up for this. It was bound to happen eventually with you serving up such a romantic ambiance."

Nora scoffed. "It's a damn bar, not a brothel."

Maalik had his mug lifted to his lips but seemed to think better of taking another sip while the chances of him choking were so high. His mug thumped to the bar just as the pounding in the bathroom intensified—along with the moans.

"Goddess…" Ali fanned her face. "Why aren't there more Edgars in the realm? You think he has a long-lost son hiding somewhere?"

Laughter spilled in the open windows out front, and Nora raced to shut them as a gaggle of kids ran down Main. It was rare that children stopped in, but not unheard of. She was renowned for her mocktails, after all. "You're right. I need to get them out of there."

Ali waved at the bathroom. "Bang on the door."

"How will they even hear me over all that racket?" Nora wrung her hands.

Maalik's stool scraped the tile as he stood. "I'll get them to leave."

"Really?" Ali plunked atop his chair. "This I've got to see."

Maalik halted beside the door, straightened to his full height, and spoke in a melodic voice that tickled Nora's insides strangely. "You have until the count of three to finish what you're doing and get out of there."

Nora dropped her head in her hands when the statement had the exact opposite effect she'd been hoping for. Instead of dimming the noise, Maalik's words seemed to spur them on. She'd be hearing those moans in her nightmares for weeks...

"One," Maalik said.

Thuds pounded against the wall like a jackhammer.

"Two."

Within the bathroom, both voices rose in an ominous chorus of impending conclusion.

"Three."

Nora plugged her ears, her cheeks burning more than when she visited Ali at work. Maalik spun slowly, a look of utter repugnance plastered on his face. Ali merely blinked, a hand splayed across her chest.

With the noises muffled by her fingers, Nora missed when they cut off. But only a few moments passed before the bathroom door opened.

All hope that someone else had snuck into her bathroom promptly evaporated as Vilotta stepped out. Her short white curls were mussed horribly, her cheeks flushed. "Terribly sorry about that," she muttered, though from the blissed-out expression she wore, it was pretty clear she wasn't speaking honestly.

Edgar followed behind her, hitching his trousers around his waist. "Nora. Ah, there you are."

Eyes bulging, she pointed to her chest. "Me?" Why in the realm did he want to speak to her after—*that*? She tensed, readying for whatever insanity came next. It seemed her day was stacking up with weirdness no matter which way she turned.

"Not sure what was in that drink you made me, but I'd like another." Edgar dug into his pocket, and then a handful of coins spilled on the bar. "Better yet, pour me a pitcher to go."

"We'll take some to-go boxes for our meals too, dear," Vilotta called.

"Sure. Coming right up." She ducked under the bar for the boxes.

Ali cleared her throat. "Say, Edgar, are there any single men in your family?"

RATS

Nora

As the day wore on, Nora's prediction unfortunately proved true. Her day turned stranger than any she'd experienced since opening. Countless items went missing, there one moment and gone the next. Her second batch of ziti burned before it had completed one third of its normal cook time.

And worst of all, a young woman in a delightful yellow sundress, who'd come in for tea, decided to hole up in the corner and sob into her cup. She was still at it now, a full hour later, and no matter what Nora said or did, she couldn't calm the poor girl.

A beefy traveler, with elongated pupils that made her suspect a few lizard-folk lurked far back in his lineage, sidled up to the bar. "Can't you throw her out? I've had about enough wailing to last me a lifetime." A disgusted sneer curved his thin lips as he stared at the forlorn woman in the back.

"I'm sorry." Frankly, with the attitude the stranger was serving, she wasn't feeling too inclined to apologize, but she couldn't help agreeing with the fellow. The crying was seriously grating on her nerves. But still... "She's obviously going through something. I'm sure she'll leave once she's pulled herself together."

She hadn't signed up to carry the burden of everyone's worries when she opened her bar, but that didn't stop folk from using her place to let off a little steam. And seeing the sadness seep out of this woman made Nora's protective side surface—even if her cries were slowly driving her insane.

Who knew what was going on in her life? She could've just lost her job or a loved one. She might live in some hellish situation that seemed impossible to break out of. If she needed a safe place to break down, Nora wasn't about to throw her out on the street.

"She a friend of yours or something?" the traveler asked.

Nora winced as a plaintive sob rose from the corner. "No. She's not from around here." Or if she was, she didn't recognize her. Long dark-brown curls hid much of her face, but she'd gotten a clear view of the girl's rosy cheeks and bright blue eyes when she'd first ordered her tea.

But that didn't change the facts. She was clearly going through something terrible, and Nora didn't have the heart to toss her out.

"Throw her out, then," the man insisted. "Buying one measly cup of tea doesn't give her the right to ruin my night out."

Nora abandoned the rag she'd been absentmindedly wiping the bar with and faced the traveler fully. "I don't recognize *you* either. What gives you the right to make the rules in my bar?"

The idiot didn't even have the sense to look chagrined. His arm flicked out, fingers pointing at his half-filled plate. "At least I bought a meal. I didn't sign up to eat it while listening to that bitch's caterwauling."

Goddess. She could stand a lot. In her line of business, constantly serving people whose lips had loosened after a drink or two, she'd heard it all. But while unwanted flirtations and crude stories that would make a more modest woman run screaming barely fazed her, this was one thing she refused to stand for.

"Get out."

The stranger reared back, mouth agape. "Excuse me?"

"I said, get out." She gestured wildly to the door. "Men who can't be bothered to speak about the women present with decorum are not welcome in Stellar Spirits."

He threw up his hands. "Hell, you act like you're running a damn church. It's a bar, you stupid—"

"Get out!" Nora shouted.

The stranger stalked across the room and snagged his plate off the table. "Not without my meal, I won't."

"Take it and go!" Anger pulsed through her veins, burning hotly. She didn't even care that he hadn't paid. Or that he'd taken her plate. He could keep it if it got him to leave faster.

He stalked off, plate in hand, toward the closest door, which happened to be the back, slamming it closed behind him.

Nora sighed, most of her anger disappearing with him. But not all. Because the woman crying into her teacup took that as an excuse to wail even louder. Nora's shoulders rose, tension pooling in her back and throbbing behind her temples. She inhaled deeply, fighting to keep calm.

"I-I'm sorry," the girl choked out between sobs. "I-I don't k-know what's wr-wrong with me."

Nora's heart softened. "It's all right. He was out of line. You can stay here as long as you—"

"Hey!" A shout from out back sent tingles pricking up her spine. "Aren't you forgetting something?"

She bit back a groan, swiftly crossing the floor and jerking open the back door. "What?"

The stranger stood in her back garden, shoving the last mouthful of ziti in his mouth. "I don't want your filthy trash." He tossed the plate onto the picnic table, where it spun like a top before finally settling down without breaking. Frankly, after the day she'd endured, the tiny spot of luck surprised her more than if it would've shattered into a thousand pieces. "Clean it up, why don't you?"

The coward chuckled cruelly as he backed away toward the gate. He held her gaze while reaching into his pocket. Then he stuffed a cigar in his mouth and lit a match, glaring at her all the while, like he was daring her to say something.

Nora's chest burned, her body trembling with barely restrained rage. She wanted to march across the garden and slap the stupid smirk off the stranger's face. But even though she'd likely never see him again, she knew better than to give in to her dark urges. Gossip traveled fast in small towns like Everpass. What would the townsfolk say if they learned she'd developed the habit of slapping her clientele?

So she settled for glaring at him from the back step, channeling all the animosity she could summon into her gaze.

The stranger continued to chuckle. Great enormous belly laughs that made Nora grind her teeth and curse the ass to an eternity roasting in hell.

The cruel thought filled her mind as he lifted the match to his cigar. The flame erupted, no doubt caught in some freak rush of mountain wind. "Ahh!" he shouted, dropping the cigar and flinging the match aside. "The hell did you do, you… you… damn witch!" Eyes widening like tea saucers, he sped out of the gate, running like he actually believed that nonsense he'd just spouted.

Shaking her head, Nora stepped into the garden. She was no witch. Never had the affinity for magic, though that would've elated her mother to no end. Most humans who had a natural talent for magic discovered during their teens and were forced to study to control it, though she'd heard it was different for other races.

As she plucked the plate off the table, the fire roared to life, setting a pile of dry kindling stacked near her shed ablaze.

"No!" She dropped the plate and raced for the back door. "Help! Fire!" she shouted at the top of her lungs, hoping someone would hear and race to her aid.

But she refused to sit back and let the flames blaze unchecked. The door flew open, banging against the wall. "Fire! Get to safety!" She half-expected the crying girl not to get up, even under the threat of being roasted to a crisp, but apparently Nora had discovered the one thing that could convince her to move.

"I'll get the fire brigade!" She leaped to her feet and disappeared through the front door.

Nora's pulse pumped furiously as she tugged an extinguisher off the wall. The fire brigade supplied all the businesses in Everpass with charmed tools. The oblong canisters were filled with water magic and could easily extinguish lesser fires before running out of steam.

But as she returned to the backyard, Nora's heart sank as her body flushed with heat. The small fire had grown into an enormous inferno in her absence. The entire shed was engulfed, the crackling fire over-taking it completely.

It didn't seem real. How had the flames spread so much in such a short time?

No way her lone extinguisher would smother that. But she had to do something...

Concentrating on the flames closest to the bar, she depressed the lever on the metal contraption. Water sprayed in a smooth arc, drenching the flames. Steam clouded the air, competing with the cloying smoke for dominance. Nora coughed, her eyes pinching half-shut to stave off the worst of the onslaught.

Please, please go out, she chanted in her mind. For a moment, it almost seemed like she was succeeding. The fire began to gutter out, especially the portion closest to the magical spray. But as she started to rejoice, the extinguisher sputtered. The water cut off, and the flames whooshed back to life.

Coughing, Nora backed away, her stomach sinking.

She was going to lose everything. If the flames spread, her bar would be next. The few meager possessions in her loft. Her hopes and dreams. Everything gone in a flash.

Frustration and despair crashed into her so strongly she nearly screamed.

Then the back door slammed open, and the girl popped out. "Here! Hurry, Lio!"

Nora gaped as a tan, dark-haired stranger wearing a homespun tunic and black trousers burst into the garden behind the girl. "I thought you were running to get the brigade?"

"She did." Lio strode forward, concentration etched on his brow. "Back up. Both of you. Go inside."

She opened her mouth, ready to yell at the fool as he marched toward the blazing inferno. Nora knew who was in the brigade, and this stranger certainly wasn't. Yet, before she squeaked out a word in protest, Lio lifted his hands and twin streams of water flew from his palms.

A hand tightened around her forearm. The girl dragged Nora inside the bar, and they watched from the safety of the back windows as he fought the flames. "He's a witch," Nora whispered.

"Not quite. Lio's a water nymph."

Nora blinked. "What?"

"My brother, Stelios. He can conjure water, nothing else. We moved to Everpass last week after they hired him on at the brigade."

"Oh." If he was new to the brigade, that explained the lack of uniform. Nora's gaze shifted between the ever-diminishing fire and the young woman. "I don't think I got your name."

"Sorry. That was probably my fault." She winced, rubbing her arm, gaze downcast. "I'm Katini, but everyone calls me Tini. Thank you for being so nice to me earlier."

The name certainly suited her. She was delicate and petite, a sharp contrast to her brother, who was so tall he'd likely need to duck through ninety percent of the doorways in Everpass, and stacked with all the muscle you'd expect from a member of the fire brigade.

"No, thank you, Tini. I don't know what I would've done if not for you and your brother." Nora truly meant it. Tini had been her savior. If that fire had blazed any longer, she had no doubt it wouldn't just be the shed that was destroyed.

The front door burst open. "Nora! Goddess, are you all right?"

"Ali." Nora's shoulders slumped. "I'm fine. But my shed sure isn't. Can you believe this?"

Ali hustled to the back of the bar and drew her into a tight hug. "You sure you didn't end up on the wrong side of a hex or something?"

"That would make more sense than all this bad luck hitting me out of nowhere."

Ali pulled back, seeming to notice Katini for the first time. "Hello. I'm Ali, Nora's best friend."

"Tini. Nice to meet you."

Nora cut in. "She was here when the shed caught. Then she brought her brother to put out the fire." She brightened, an interesting tidbit returning to the forefront of her mind. "He's a nymph too, like you."

Tini's face lit up. "So there are other nymphs here! I wasn't sure if we'd meet any."

But while she'd expected Ali to brighten as well, the opposite happened. Ali ducked her head, her normal welcoming expression never surfacing. "Yep. You found me."

Nora didn't have long to ponder what that meant. At that moment, Lio ducked inside, smoke clinging to him like cologne. "It's out. I doused it extra to be certain, but I wouldn't recommend sifting through the wreckage for a few days." The last word wavered as his gaze trailed to Ali.

Oh... This was *interesting*. Nora hung back, watching the pair as their gazes clashed. Maybe she was imagining things, what with her own suppressed lust so close to the surface in the wake of Kieran's return, but it was almost like the air sparked between them, heavy with attraction.

Bang.

The front door swung on its hinges far more than it had any right to with her favorite nine-year-old doing the shoving. "Mooommm. What's taking you so long? I'm hungry."

"Coming, sweetie," Ali replied, tearing herself away from the trance she'd been locked in with Lio and glancing at her daughter.

Lio's head swiveled from Ali to Echo in the doorway and back again. Then he stiffened, the sultry haze evaporating from his eyes, replaced with a hard stare that he directed Nora's way. "I'll bring a new extinguisher by later. Come on, Tini. Time to go."

"Thank you!" Nora called at his retreating back as he marched to the front door. He swept past Echo without saying a word.

Tini shot her a crooked smile as she dug into her pocket. "Sorry. He's not great at making friends. I'll see you later, Nora. Thanks for the tea. This oughta cover it." The coins clattered on the table as her footsteps echoed across the tile.

"Mooomm. My stomach is dying over here." Echo crossed her arms, pouting in a way that was simultaneously annoying and cute as hell. She was the spitting image of her mother, with the same dark skin and eyes, though she wore her black hair plaited into twin pigtails and favored brightly colored dresses, like the orange-and-white-striped frock she currently had on.

"I'm glad you're okay. I'll be back later for book club. Don't even think about canceling!" With a wave, Ali took off, leaving Nora alone in her empty, smoke-scented tavern.

Well... that could've been so much worse.

At least it was just the shed and not her bar. The old thing had needed to be replaced, anyway. Not that she'd planned to do it soon, what with her to-do list being so long already, but what was one more thing in the grand scheme? At least there was nothing important stored there. Only gardening supplies that could be easily replaced or borrowed from Ma.

She heaved out a weary sigh, ready to do something—any-thing—else, when a flash of white caught her eye. Her necklace! She twisted toward it and spotted the unmistakable sight of her opal crescent moon pendant disappearing into a crack in the wall, like some critter had found it and dragged it inside by the chain.

Shudders broke out all over her frame. *Goddess, why? Why did it have to be rats?*

There was no question in her mind that some ugly vermin had pilfered her necklace. Because what else would be the ultimate cherry on the shit sundae of a day that she'd been served? Of course, the one creature she feared more than any other *had* to make an appearance.

For a fleeting moment, she nearly broke down and wept.

Why can't just one thing go right on this cursed day?

No. She refused to give in to the urge. If her luck was determined to thwart her at every turn, then she'd have to make her own.

She was getting that necklace back. Rats be damned.

Please

Kieran

S tretching, Kieran's lashes fluttered as he slowly spun to face the window. For once, the harsh rays of the sun hadn't awakened him. Had someone snuck in and drawn the curtains?

He jolted up, staring blearily out of the glass as shadows seeped in. "I slept all day," he muttered as he shuffled out of bed and rushed through his morning routine. Although it seemed that late-afternoon routine would be a better descriptor today...

After staggering in during the wee hours, he'd collapsed in bed, exhausted. He'd only intended to rest for a few hours, counting on the sun to wake him as it always did. Yet, it appeared traipsing back and forth from the countryside, then staying up all night learning the ins and outs of knot tying were more draining than he'd expected.

Nora... Had Edgar brought her the ladder like he'd requested? He'd suspected she'd need some time before she was ready to hear him out. That was why he'd sent his gift in advance. But he'd hoped to show up just after lunch, after Edgar had dropped it off.

Yes, he hoped the ladder would soften her ire just a smidge, but it didn't change the fact that it was a needed addition to Nora's place. The thought of her trapped in that tiny room with no way out was nearly enough to set off a panic attack last night. If he hadn't kept busy looping and tightening dozens of knots with his hand and teeth, he'd have marched into Stellar Spirits and demanded she find somewhere safer to live.

Now, even if she refused to forgive him, at least he could rest easy knowing she had an escape route in case the worst happened. Sure, it wasn't perfect. He'd much rather her live in her own little cottage and not above a bar, but he couldn't exactly drag her out against her will.

Matters with Nora needed to be handled much more delicately. But he wouldn't let that stop him from setting things right. She deserved someone in her corner who would stand by her and give her the support to follow her dreams. And if that meant sneaking baubles to witches or tying knots by the hundreds, he was ready and willing to do it.

He only hoped he hadn't missed the start of her book club. According to Ali, they were meeting that evening to vote on their selection for the upcoming month. Kieran had hoped to sneak in a few hours with Nora before that so he could ease her into the idea of accepting help from the Barclays.

He stole another glance at the sky. Looked like he'd have to hurry now if he didn't want the witches showing up first and waving that contract in her face. So, after a few rushed adjustments to his gray tunic and black trousers, he grabbed his cloak.

Boots tapping loudly, he rushed down the grand staircase.

"Kieran."

With a gasp, he snagged the railing before tumbling down the last few steps. "Goddess, Father. Are you trying to make me lose a leg next?"

"Very funny." From Tanyth's dry tone, it was clear he meant the exact opposite. "I thought you were planning to tell me what's going on at that bar."

"Hm?" Instead of strolling past his father with a rushed hello, Kieran halted. "There's nothing to tell."

"Really? Then why did I learn about the fire from gossip instead of my own son?"

Kieran's heart stalled. "Fire?"

"Yes, a fire. It's all anyone can talk about. Honestly, you should've—"

He fisted his father's silky button-down, dragging him close. "What fire? Goddess's sake! Is Nora all right?"

Tanyth's icy gaze darted across his face. "Ah... You didn't know."

"Is. She. Alive?" he shouted, not caring one whit how his father's eyes bulged before darkening ominously.

"Yes. The girl—"

Kieran detangled his hand from his father's shirt and raced for the door, not bothering to stick around for the rest.

All he could see was her face. All he could hear was her voice yelling at him to get out. He could've lost her, and that would've been the last conversation they'd ever had.

He had to find her. Had to see that she was safe with his own eyes.

He raced through Everpass, the streets blurring around him until he stopped in front of Stellar Spirits. Then, like waking from a dream, he blinked back to reality.

Smoke lingered in the air, but the bar stood, seemingly still sound. A shaky breath wheezed out of his mouth, his legs wobbling with relief.

He shoved open the door and stepped inside. "Nora?"

The bar was empty. No customers. No one at all.

Had his father been wrong? Was Nora injured? Panicking, he turned back to the entrance, ready to bang on the door of every healer in town.

"Back here," she called.

Warmth pulsed through him, and his stomach unknotted. He marched through the bar, not stopping until he found her. She was crouched on the floor in the far corner, a crowbar in her hands, staring into a hole in the wall.

What was she doing? Had the stress of dealing with a deteriorating business driven her to tear the place apart? But why start there?

"Nora? I heard there was a fire. Are you all right?"

She lifted her gaze to meet his, and he nearly crumbled from the defeat in her eyes. "I'm okay."

"Are you?" He sank to the floor beside her. "You don't look it."

Her lower lip trembled, and he threw open his arms. She didn't move. Worry assailed him, sudden and sharp. Would she tell him to get out again? But then Nora sank into his embrace, and he wrapped his arms around her.

"I'm so sorry I wasn't here," he whispered into her hair. He breathed her in, inhaling her comforting sweetness laced with the stomach-churning stench of charred wood. "Tell me what happened."

"Just a day from hell. Be happy you missed it."

"I'm not." He pulled back and stared into her whiskey eyes, his heart breaking when he spotted them encircled with red. "I meant to come in after lunch, but I overslept. Maybe if I'd been here—"

"No. It's not your fault. And it's really not too bad. The shed out back is done for, and a rat stole my necklace, but no one was hurt. That's all that matters." Her words sounded weak, like she thought that by saying them out loud, she might actually turn them true.

"A rat, huh?" He eyed the hole. "Guess you're not going crazy and tearing this place apart for nothing." She tried to pull out of his hold, so he tightened his arms.

"You seriously don't believe that... do you?" she asked.

"No. But if you want to turn this place into rubble, I'll be your one-man demolition crew."

Her eyes widened, then narrowed. "I doubt your father would approve."

"He's never approved of me before. Might as well keep up the streak."

"Kieran." She shoved his chest, and this time he let her go. Nora backed away, but only enough to stare straight into his eyes. "I'm being serious."

"So am I, Nora." He held her gaze, making sure she wouldn't miss the sincerity shining there. "I'm not working for my father. Yes, I knew he was your landlord, but I swear, I couldn't care less about your rental agreement. Hell, if you'd let me, I'd buy the damn place and hand you the deed. But I know that's not what you want. You want to make this place a success all on your own. And I believe—no, I *know*—that you will."

Nora drew in a breath and flashed a wobbly smile. That was a good sign, wasn't it? Still, Kieran sat there, his pulse beating like mad while he waited for her to say something.

"I believe you."

He exhaled in a huge, relieved whoosh. But... Nora didn't look relieved. Not in the slightest. "What's wrong? How can I help?"

Her gaze dropped to her lap, watching her fingers as they tangled in her dark-brown skirt. "I don't know if you can..." Her voice softened, and he had to strain to make out what she said next. "I wish I still had that nest egg. Then all these repairs wouldn't seem so insurmountable."

He tipped up her chin with his finger. "What are you talking about, Nora? What nest egg?"

She bit her lip. "I had some savings tucked away for emergencies. But Ma got into a rough spot. I used it to keep her from losing the farm." She sniffled. "Fat lot of good it did. She just turned around and took out another loan. Only I'm not in a position to help her this time... Now I have to worry about losing this place and hers."

Kieran gulped. Sure, he'd had a tiny taste of what it was like to be poor when he left home, but what Nora was dealing with was completely different. He'd never had to worry that he'd be thrown out on the street, or worse, watch his family lose everything they'd worked for. He couldn't imagine how stressful that would be.

He made himself a silent vow. No matter what, he refused to let Nora, or her mother, lose their place. He honestly couldn't think of anyone in the realm who deserved a chance to follow their dreams more than they did. Without them, who would feed the hungry children each morning? Who would take care of young women when they were at their most vulnerable?

No. Nora and Moira were staying in Everpass. He'd make sure of it. "I'll help you, Nora. I promise, I will. Tell me what you need, and it's done."

"I can't ask that of you, Kieran." She waved at the bar. "The repairs are going to take weeks to complete, if not months. And your life is in the city."

Now didn't seem like the right time to tell her he wasn't so sure about that fact any longer. Instead, he said, "But I'm here now. And I want to help. Please let me."

Nora stared into his eyes. "I-I don't know…"

More than anything, he wished he could peek into her mind. See exactly what she was thinking. Why was she so slow to trust him? Couldn't she see how hard he was trying? Walking that fine line between offering just enough and not too much that she refused to accept his help.

Maybe if he showed her a glimpse of his secrets, she'd be ready to let him shoulder a bit of the burdens weighing her down.

Slowly, he lifted his left arm between them. He'd taken to wearing long sleeves, folding the ends so that his wrist was hidden. But with Nora watching, he tugged the fabric down, letting her look at the ugly scars he could hardly stand to see.

"Seth likes to tell everyone I lost my hand in service to the Crown. To hear him tell it, you might think it was lopped off during a duel with a traitor, or while saving a damsel in distress. But that's not what happened. Not even close."

"What really happened?" Nora barely spared his arm a glance before turning all her attention to his face, watching with attention so rapt he could scarcely bear the weight of it.

"We were on a stakeout for a band of pirates, holed up in a little alcove of an uninhabited island in the middle of the sea. At some point while sailing, I cut my palm. Just a tiny scratch, really. I couldn't even say where I got it." He sighed. "If I'd been anywhere near a village with a proper healer, then it would've been a simple enough fix. But we weren't. Then we lost the wind. And by the time we returned, the cut had become so infected there was no way to save my hand."

"Goddess… And I thought I was the one with bad luck."

He shot her a crooked grin, letting his arm fall into his lap. "You know what the worst part is?"

"What?"

"We never spotted the pirates. The mission was a colossal waste of time." He shook his head. "So, don't you see? I need this too, Nora. I need the chance to do something that actually matters. Please, won't you let me?"

He lifted his eyes, wanting her to see his sincerity again, but this time, she wasn't looking. Nora's gaze was glued to his wrist, tracing over the scarred flesh. Then she reached out and tenderly grasped his forearm. He tensed, sucking in a deep breath.

No one had dared to touch him like this since his injury. Healers, yes. Beautiful women? Nope. If he even looked like he might reach in their general direction, they bolted as fast as their pretty legs could carry them. Yet here Nora was, tenderly stroking his wrist like she wished she could regrow the flesh with the sheer force of her will.

No. He had that wrong. For the next moment, she aimed the most devastating smile he'd ever seen at him. "I like you better like this. You were too perfect before."

A startled chuckle burst out of his chest. "That right?"

"Now it feels like I might actually stand a chance." She clamped her lips closed, eyes widening like she'd said too much.

But he wasn't in the mood to let her take it back. No... suddenly, he was in an altogether different mood entirely.

Every cell in his body screamed at him to take advantage of her confession. Maybe he should've been more careful. He could've listened to the warning in the back of his mind. The one whispering that Nora was still his best friend's little sister. But for once, he couldn't be bothered to listen to reason.

He looped a hand around Nora's waist and dragged her closer.

She gasped. "Kieran, you said—"

His lips descended on hers, cutting off whatever idiotic comment of his she was about to throw back in his face. None of that mattered. Nothing mattered except for her. Her achingly soft lips. Her breathless gasps. The pounding beat of her heart as her chest pressed against his so tightly he could barely tell where he ended and she began.

Goddess... It had never felt like this. Nothing and no one would ever compare to the utter perfection of Nora melting in his arms.

His hand glided down her thigh, sinking into the buttery fabric of her skirt. He dragged it up slowly, letting anticipation build. His skin tingled as he waited for the first silky brush of skin against skin.

But then Nora pulled back, those perfect lips parting on a gasp. He nearly dived back in, desperate to taste her again. He surely would've, had she not murmured, "The door's not locked. Anyone could come in."

"I'll fix that." He hopped to his feet, fully intending to twist the deadbolt and flip the sign, but before he'd taken two steps, the dreadful thing creaked open, and a stupidly handsome man stepped inside.

"Hello." Sky-blue eyes narrowed on him instantly. "I'm looking for Nora."

"Of course you are," Kieran grumbled. It was like he'd been thrown back in time, only instead of a sexy professor, he was about to watch some tall pretty boy chat up his girl.

He stopped in place, shocked at the direction his thoughts had turned. Sure, that kiss was insane, but Nora had made no promises to him, or him to her. And he wasn't exactly the settling down type. Then again... Funny that the thought didn't feel wrong when he sat with it for a moment.

He didn't have long to linger on the revelation. Nora popped up, all smiles. "Lio. I wasn't expecting you back so soon."

Lio's gaze slid over Nora as she smoothed her dress, her cheeks rosy and her lips a bit bee-stung. And then back to him. Though Kieran couldn't see what expression he wore, it was clearly not pleasant, judging by the way Lio's jaw tightened. "I wanted to drop this off and check the fire was still fully contained, but if I'm interrupting—"

"No, you're not. Please, be my guest." Nora waved at the back door before grabbing the extinguisher from Lio. "Thank you again for all your help today."

Kieran's gut twinged as Lio strolled outside. He still couldn't help feeling guilty about not being there for Nora that afternoon.

"Hey." Nora stopped beside him. "I'm okay, really."

He forced whatever dire expression he'd been sporting to morph into a soft smile. "Sorry." And since the mood had been ruined, he decided to return to the last topic he could recall before getting lost in Nora's sweet lips. "So, are you going to let me help you?"

Nora sighed. "Yeah. I can do that."

"I'm really glad to hear that." His hand grew clammy as he glanced out the window. Not much time left if he wanted to come clean about where he'd been yesterday. "I kind of already started..."

"What? How?" She crossed her arms and lifted a brow.

"Well... I stopped by your friend's glass shop yesterday."

"You met Ali?"

"Yes. We visited with these nice farmers. They're headed to town to meet you at your book club tonight... and to offer you a contract."

Nora blinked repeatedly, seemingly struck speechless.

"Look, don't be mad. We just wanted to help, and it seems like the Barclays know their stuff. I hope this will be the solution to your supply problem, but if it's not, I'll help you find something else, I promise. Just give their offer some consideration."

She nodded blankly. "Guess I can do that."

Kieran tilted his head, not sure if she was pleased or pissed. He opened his mouth, but before he said anything else, the back door swung open and Lio stepped in.

"It looks good out there. Nothing smoldering," he announced. "I'll get out of your hair."

"Thank you." Nora spun to Kieran. "You should probably go too. I need to get the place ready for book club. Unless you're planning to join?"

"I'll pass." Frankly, he wasn't sure if he was ready to discuss the literature he suspected Nora's book club favored reading. From the looks of the cover he spotted at the Barclays', that discussion would be far too uncomfortable while the memory of her kiss was still fresh in his mind. "But I'll be back tomorrow. That all right with you?"

"Sure. See you tomorrow."

It might not be the kiss goodbye he was craving, but it was a hell of a lot better than "get out," so he'd take it.

He stepped onto Main and jogged to catch up to Lio. "Hey!"

Lio turned, gazing at him warily. "Did you need something?"

Real fun one, this guy. "I wanted to thank you for what you did for Nora." He slowed beside him and stuck out a hand. "I'm Kieran."

"Lio." He shook Kieran's right hand while his gaze trailed down to his left arm—and the wrist he'd forgotten to cover after leaving Nora's. Kieran readied himself for the inevitable questions that would come next, but Lio just stated matter-of-factly, "You should meet my friend Davos."

"Who?" His brow furrowed, and he retracted his hand hastily.

"He owns the smithy. He could set you up with a hook replacement, if you're in the market for one."

Kieran's first instinct was to tell him he wasn't interested. After all, wasn't the plan to heal his hand? With his injury healed, he could return to his old life in the city. Go back to the job he trained so hard for. The life he'd earned that a senseless accident had stolen from him.

But was that even what he wanted any longer? He had to admit, being here gave him a sense of accomplishment he'd been sorely lacking in his previous job. Working at the bar, he could see the fruits of his labor with his own eyes. And he got to put a smile on Nora's face with every repair he completed.

Besides, it would be nice not being forced to use his teeth to aid his good hand... His jaw still ached from the endless hours pulling knots taut last night.

"All right. I think I will. Where's his shop at?"

The corner of Lio's mouth quirked up in what could possibly be a smile, if one were being very generous with the description. "I'll do you better than that. How about I take you there?"

He didn't have anywhere else to be. "Lead the way."

They walked in silence as the sun sank behind the mountain, washing the streets in shadows. Clearly Lio wasn't the talkative type, and while Kieran was normally not shy about filling the silence—hell, he talked to himself half the time—it was kind of nice not mindlessly chatting for a change.

But as they approached a dark-painted building that echoed with clangs and stank of sweat and molten steel, Lio broke the silence. "I hope Davos can help you. He's made at least one that I know of, so yours won't be the first hook to come out of his forge."

A little voice piped in, full of excitement. "You're getting a hook hand? Like a pirate? That's wicked awesome!"

Kieran whipped around, hunting for the source. A girl who couldn't have been older than ten peered at them from the shadows of the store next door.

"You again." Lio dragged a hand down his face. "Give it a rest, kid. Don't you have somewhere you need to be?"

Suddenly, a familiar chime rang in Kieran's ears. Where had he heard that before?

"Echo? What are you doing out he—" Ali froze within a nearby doorway, and Kieran realized why those bells were so familiar. Her glass blowing shop sat beside the blacksmith.

Lio locked gazes with Ali and drew a deep breath through his nose. "Do me a favor and tell your kid to stop following me."

Ali's eyes narrowed. "She's not following anyone. This is *my* shop." She grabbed her daughter, quickly shunting her into Our Glass and closing her inside.

"Great. Now I know where to send her when she sneaks up on me again. I've caught her three times just this afternoon."

Kieran eased away, wondering if he should stick around for this.

"She's never seen a male nymph before. Of course she's curious."

"Not my problem," Lio replied flatly.

Ali threw up her hands and turned for her door. "Don't worry. I'll make sure she knows she's better off hanging around an imp than the likes of you."

"Ouch." Kieran chuckled nervously. "Um... I'm gonna head in. Thanks for walking me here."

With a single nod, Lio marched away, acting for all the world like that dig hadn't bothered him in the slightest.

NOT SO FAMILIAR

Nora

What a day... She stood there for far longer than she should've after Kieran left, her fingers lightly tracing her tingling lips.

Goddess, that kiss! She closed her eyes, reveling in the memory. The pure hunger in his eyes. The gentle sweep of his hand on her thigh, making her crave so much more. And his mouth, so wonderfully sinful and desperate. Desperate for *her*. She could scarcely believe that had just happened.

All too soon, another thought rose to ruin her reminiscing. What had he been thinking, meeting with suppliers on her behalf? And Ali, too. This was her bar. She should've been involved—or at the very least, consulted—well before a contract was drafted.

And of course, all the carefully crafted questions she'd meant to ask about their past had escaped her during that conversation. She'd been so hung up on her rotten day and getting back her necklace that it hadn't even occurred to her to ask... until now. At least she'd gotten a glimpse of Kieran's feelings. He wouldn't have fought so hard to help her if he didn't intend to stick around, right?

A sigh worked its way out of her chest as she finally forced herself into motion, prepping a batch of hot spiced cider. She offered a free mocktail for every book club meeting, and today would be no exception—even if half the members who planned to attend were about to surprise her with a deal she'd had no part in arranging.

Relax, Nora. They're just trying to help.

Yes, she was being emotional, but it was hard for her to cede control over anything involving Stellar Spirits. This business was her baby. But maybe it was time to get used to the fact that it took a village to be successful. Hell, how would she ever hire someone if she couldn't stand to share the work?

As she heated the cider and dumped in the necessary spices, the door scraped against tile.

"Hey, Nora. Got my sitter to come a bit early so I could too. And you won't believe who I ran into outside my shop." Ali's steps slowed, boots tapping cautiously across the floor. "You all right? Why do you look like you want to murder someone?"

She removed the bubbling pot from the heat, leaving a weighted silence hanging over the tavern. "When were you planning to tell me you hunted down new suppliers for me?"

"Um... Right now? Relax, Nor. We just handled the legwork for you. The decision is still yours."

Suppose Ali had a point. And she was grateful for the help. Not like she had a lot of time to search for new suppliers while shackled to the bar.

"You're welcome, by the way. I had to listen to that man of yours complain about the hike until my ears bled. I thought elves were supposed to be super fit? You might want to make sure you're not shacking up with a pillow princess before you seal the deal, if you know what I mean." She slipped onto a stool, smirking.

It was impossible to stay mad at Ali. Nora giggled. "Pillow princess?"

"It's what you call someone who likes to lie there and enjoy the ride." She wiggled her brows. "Don't settle for a man like that. If anyone deserves that kind of treatment, it should be you. And possibly me."

The giggle turned into a full-on laughing fit. "Okay. I'll keep that in mind."

"What are we keeping in mind?" Maalik asked, pulling out his stool.

"Nothing important." Nora scrubbed her eyes with her sleeve. She must've been laughing so hard she didn't notice the door open.

"Oh, no! It's of the utmost importance. Don't you forget it, Nora." Ali smirked again, and it was all Nora could do to keep a straight face.

Maalik rolled his eyes. "Fine, don't tell me. I probably don't want to know, anyway."

"You're probably right on that score." Nora gestured to the pot. "Would you like to try some hot cider? On the house."

Maalik eyed the brown liquid warily. "What's it taste like?"

"Here." She grabbed a mug, added a cinnamon stick, and ladled a splash inside. "Give it a try."

He sipped tentatively, only for his eyes to pop wide. "That's good." He smacked his lips.

"Glad you like it." Nora grinned and filled his glass to the brim, and a second for Ali. As she placed it before her, she said, "All right, tell me about this deal."

Ali launched into a recap of her and Kieran's trip the previous afternoon, sparing no detail. By the time the door swung open again, Nora felt a lot more comfortable with the potential contract, and almost like she'd already met the witches who might hold the answer to her supply problems.

So when the two women shuffled into the doorway, looking more than a little out of place, she rounded the bar, flashing her most welcoming grin. "Opal, Paige. Welcome to Stellar Spirits. Please come in."

They both seemed to relax at that, though Opal's shoulders were still a tad stiff beneath her patchwork cloak. "We brought our familiars along. Can they wait in your back garden?" she asked.

"Of course. Not a problem." She angled her neck, trying to sneak a peek at the animals they'd brought, but she couldn't see much with the women's skirts filling the doorway. "They can walk through the bar—unless they're too big." She suspected from Ali's story the little sausage dog, Tibbie, was Opal's familiar, but she wasn't sure what species Paige was bonded to. If it was a cow or a horse, she couldn't exactly invite them in. "There's also an alley between this building and the next."

"Oh, they'll fit just fine," Paige announced before striding inside. A dust-covered rooster strutted in on her heels, his head bobbing this way and that as he crossed the tile floor. "This way, Bok. You too, Tibbie." She turned to Nora with an apologetic grimace. "Sorry about the mess. Bok has a habit of rolling in every dust pile he sees. It's a bird thing..."

Nora rushed to reassure her. "I don't mind. That's why I installed the tile. Easy to clean."

Once Opal entered, so did the little brown dog. Tibbie lifted her nose, sniffing the air as she followed Paige toward the back door. But while Bok was content to follow his mistress, Tibbie froze before sprinting to the hole Nora had widened in the wall that afternoon. The same one where her pilfered necklace had disappeared.

Opal stiffened, her gaze narrowing on the hole.

Paige threw open the back door. "Get away from there, Tibbie. You're out back with Bok."

Tibbie tucked her tail between her legs, then abandoned the wall and waddled outside on her little legs.

"Sorry about that," Opal said. "She's always catching the scent of something."

"Not a problem." Nora smiled. "You ladies must be thirsty after the long walk into town. Can I offer you some spiced cider? On the house."

"That sounds lovely." Paige smoothed the skirt of her simple green dress as she settled on a barstool.

Opal pulled out the seat beside her, but before she sat down, shouting rent the air out back.

Goddess... What now?

All heads turned to the back door, and Nora wasted no time rounding the bar yet again.

Paige gasped. "Bok! Tibbie!" She leaped off her chair.

Before Nora made it to the garden, the incoherent shouts morphed into a voice she recognized, and she caught a flash of green skin out the window.

"Nora! What's the damn meaning of this? Why didn't you tell me? I'm gonna kill you when I find you!"

Seth... She'd forgotten to tell him about the fire, which had apparently set off one of his orc mood swings. He'd never go through with his threats. She knew that. But that wouldn't stop him from screaming until he was red-faced and sweaty.

She had to get outside and calm him down. Only, Paige put on a burst of speed and beat her out the door.

Nora yelled, "Wait! It's just my bro—" She stopped short, mouth agape as Paige's hands flew, a stream of *song* emanating from her lips. Across the yard, Seth struggled, his legs wrapped in vines that tore up from the ground to stop him in his tracks.

"Hey? Wh-what's going on?" Seth's voice grew panicked, his motions slowing until he was completely immobilized. A vine slapped him in the face before closing around his mouth, and though it didn't stop him from talking, it made the rest of his words so muffled she couldn't make heads or tails of what he was saying.

"Stop, Paige!" Nora finally shook off her surprise and found her voice. "That's my brother."

Paige's brow furrowed. "Your brother? Then why was he threatening to kill you?"

To add insult to injury, Bok joined in, using his sharp beak to peck every bit of Seth's trousers he could reach between the vines.

Seth's eyes narrowed dangerously, his gaze shooting from the rooster to Paige and back again, clouding with more anger on each pass.

"I swear, he's my brother, and he means well." Nora crossed her arms. "He just has a funny way of showing it sometimes. Can you let him go? Please?"

"If you say so." Paige started singing once more, waving her hands back and forth.

Nora's heart raced as she watched, utterly fascinated. She'd grown up with a mother who had wanted more than anything to study to be a witch, without possessing the talent or funds to procure the schooling necessary to be a success. But that didn't appear to be a problem for Paige.

Pure power crackled through the air and slipped from her tongue. As Nora watched her work, she understood the fear that lived in so many hearts where witches were concerned. She had no doubt that had Paige wanted to kill Seth instead of immobilize him, she could've.

Seth didn't seem to perceive the danger. Or perhaps he was just too riled up to keep his mouth shut. As soon as the vine retreated from his lips, he hissed, "Are you insane, Nora? Why in the realm are you hanging around with bloody witches—ow." He glared at Bok as his beak connected with flesh. "Quit that or I'm gonna wring your scrawny little neck as soon as I get these damned weeds off!"

Paige's song halted, stopping the vines' retreat while Seth could only squirm. She glared up at him, somehow managing to appear menacing, even though her petite frame was comically small compared to Seth's huge body. "Take it back or I have no problem turning you into a treehouse." She snorted. "I hear the village kids love climbing on big dumb rocks."

Seth gasped, sounding more affronted than he had any right to. "Ow! Not until you get your filthy cock away from me!"

Ali chose that moment to pop out of the back door, laughing her head off. "Wow, Seth. Filthy cock... That's priceless."

Somehow, Seth's cheeks turned even redder. Nora scrubbed a hand down her face, fighting to stay calm. That was what her brother needed. Calm...

"Nora, make this witch unhand me!" Seth yelled.

"Not until you take back what you said to Bok." Paige scooped up the rooster, stopping one problem, though she still continued to glare at her brother like she wished she could make good on her threats. "He's sensitive."

"A sensitive cock." Ali roared with laughter again. "Oh my goddess, I can't believe it!"

Every sliver of calm she'd fought to grasp evaporated like vapor. Her arms shot out, and she shouted, "Enough!" Everyone's mouth slammed closed in tandem, except for Nora's. She drew the deepest breath ever through her nose. "We're all going to calm down, and everything will go back to normal. Got it?"

They nodded furiously, eyes wide.

Nora sighed and dropped her hands.

"Wh-what was that?" Seth whispered.

At the same time, Paige blurted, "Why didn't Ali tell me you were a witch too?"

Nora blinked repeatedly, beyond confused. "What? Probably because I'm *not*."

Ali squeezed Nora's arm. "Y-you yelled 'enough,' and my mouth snapped closed mid-laugh."

"No. That must've been Paige."

Paige shook her head. "It wasn't. It was you, Nora. You might not have trained with magic yet, but that command... It was all you. I wouldn't lie about this."

Opal shuffled out of the doorway. "I agree. In fact, there's something in here you need to see." She disappeared back inside, leaving Nora reeling.

It couldn't be true... could it? Had she just used magic?

Paige nodded encouragingly. "Go. I'll set your brother free. No more arguing."

Nora spared Seth a glance, her stomach churning. It seemed the prospect of his sister being one of the beings he most despised had finally cooled his rage. He slumped against the vines, his gaze darting all over like he couldn't quite come to terms with what had just happened.

As much as she wanted to comfort him, Nora couldn't stop the pull of the unknown from dragging her feet forward.

Dazed, she marched into her bar, finding Opal and Tibbie hovering beside the hole in the wall. Maalik looked on from his trusty stool, and Nora suspected from his position, close to the open back window, and the knowing look on his face, he hadn't missed a thing that had just happened outside.

Opal cleared her throat. "There's someone here you should meet, Nora."

Brow furrowing, Nora's gaze slid across the old woman's outstretched hand. She was pointing at the hole. "I don't understand. There's no one—"

Her voice caught in her throat as the pitter-patter of clawed feet echoed in her ears, interspersed with the steady thump of Tibbie's wagging tail.

"No." She shook her head, fear rising to choke her. "If a rat comes out of there, I'm gonna scream."

Her hands quivered as the scratching grew louder. Loud enough for her to notice something off. The unseen critter's footsteps echoed strangely, almost as if it wasn't walking normally, but scrambling forward a few paces before throwing in a hop.

"If you ever call me a rat again, we're going to have a problem."

Nora cringed, her fingers pressing against her temples. "Wh-what in the—" She could almost swear she'd just heard a voice in her head. A voice that wasn't her own. "Did you hear that?"

Opal shook her head slowly. "No. But that doesn't mean you didn't."

"What?" Nora blinked repeatedly as the creature finally emerged. Her breathing sped, and she backed away, her pulse whooshing through her veins faster than ale from her tap. "It's a-a—"

"Don't say it."

She winced again, then squeaked, "A rat!"

"Meet your familiar, Nora. Isn't she adorable?" Opal beamed.

Tibbie's tail thumped steadily as she leaned down to sniff the tiny brown-furred rodent that sported an extra-long tail and ears, beady black eyes, and strange paddle-shaped back feet.

And in Nora's mind, that voice echoed yet again. *"I'm a kangaroo mouse, you silly witch. Get it right or I'll keep your amulet for myself."*

Horrifying Confessions

Nora

This isn't happening... I'm not a witch. I can't be.

Nora gaped at the little creature, but as hard as she tried, she couldn't come to terms with what she'd discovered. And she couldn't stomach the thought of asking the rodent to explain what she thought she'd just heard in her mind. Surely it was a trick. The stress of everything that'd gone wrong in the last few days must be making her imagine things.

"H-how? I-I don't understand..." She turned to Opal. "I've never used magic before. Shouldn't I have found out I have a talent for it well before this? I'm thirty, for goddess's sake."

"Hm. That is strange. Most witches who are strong enough to do what you just did without training discover their power in their teens."

Opal's lips pinched together. "Unless... Do you have something missing? It would need to be something you've always carried or worn."

Nora gasped. "I am missing something. My necklace..."

"You looking for this?" Nora winced as the rat—no, the kangaroo mouse—hopped back into the shadows. *"I'm sorry I took it, but it was time. You've stayed hidden too long."*

The mouse returned, its tiny paws wrapped around the chain holding the crescent moon pendant she'd always worn. Though her fingers itched to have it back, she couldn't bring herself to overcome her revulsion and take it.

"Ah... so your familiar took it," Opal said. "What did she say?"

"You can't hear her?" Nora's brow furrowed.

"No. Witches can only communicate with *their* familiar, not all of them."

"How did you know she's a girl?"

"Just a guess. Was I right?"

Nora gulped and nodded. The voice in her mind had sounded distinctly feminine. But there was only one way to be sure this was really happening. "How do you talk back?" she asked.

"I understand you perfectly as-is," the mouse replied.

Opal chuckled. "Talking works. With a little practice, you'll be able to communicate wordlessly as well. Try projecting your thoughts to her and see how it feels."

Summoning her courage, she focused inwardly and tried. *"Hello? Can you hear me?"*

"A quick study, I see. That bodes well, since you're so hopelessly behind."

Nora pressed a shaking hand to her chest. "It worked."

"Of course it did." Opal bent down and lifted the necklace from the mouse. "Oh... Yes. This is it. It's charmed."

"What does that mean?"

The back door slamming open delayed Opal's answer. Seth burst in, shooting a bewildered glance at the scene. "Nora? What's happening?"

She met her brother's eyes with a tentative smile. "I-I'm not entirely sure."

"Your sister has been wearing a charmed amulet that suppressed her magic," Opal explained as Ali and Paige slipped in behind him.

Seth's eyes bulged. "You really are a-a—"

"A witch. See? I wasn't lying." Paige paused, her eyes lighting up as she spotted the little rodent. "Who do we have here?"

Nora's heart pounded as Paige turned to her for introductions. "My familiar?" she squeaked out, the words sounding more like a question than an answer.

Paige giggled softly. "I mean, what's his name?"

"Her name," Opal corrected, before lifting a brow at Nora. "Go on. Ask your familiar what we should call her."

Seth paced by the door. "I don't believe this. I came here expecting a fire, but your whole damn life has turned upside down."

Paige glared at him. "Stop being so dramatic. This is a blessing."

"A blessing, my ass!"

Nora rubbed her temples. "Seth, please. I only just found out about this too."

Seth stopped pacing, his expression softening. "Sorry, Sis. I'm freaking out here. Is this really even happening?" He edged closer to Nora and angled his body like he wanted to give them some privacy, then lowered his voice and jabbed a thumb at Paige. "You sure that one isn't pulling some trick like she did with the vines?"

"Excuse me?" Paige crossed her arms. "If you plan to insult me, at least have the decency to say it to my face."

Opal's eyes narrowed on Seth. "Boy, you ought to learn a little respect. The way I see it, my daughter protected your sister when someone showed up threatening her life—despite the two only having just met. You should be thanking Paige, not flinging accusations."

Seth's head dipped. Nora worried he'd keep up the battle. She wasn't entirely sure what had caused his dislike of witches—she'd first noticed the change on one of his return visits home after he moved to the capital, though he'd never shared the details. But luckily, Opal's firm reprimand seemed to have the desired effect.

"You're right." He lifted his head and met Paige's eyes. "I'm sorry. But this... It's crazy, right, Nor?"

She couldn't help but agree. Still, with all the evidence stacking up before her, it was a little hard to ignore the possibility.

"So... her name?" Opal asked again.

Grimacing, Nora turned back to the critter. *"What's your name?"*

The mouse's shoulders lifted in a crude impression of a shrug. *"Never had one. You can give me one, if you like."*

"She doesn't have a name. Says I can choose one," Nora repeated.

Paige clapped her hands. "Ooo, how fun! Can I help?"

Nora nodded dazedly. She needed all the help she could get. Not just with the name, but with understanding how this had come to pass.

Paige tapped her chin. "How about Bean?"

"Yeah... no thanks." Nora's gut clenched as the mouse shook its head in time with the words reverberating in her mind, her gaze fixed on Paige. She could hardly believe this was happening... but it was becoming increasingly impossible to ignore that this creature was intelligent, not just responding to her, but to others too, with a keen intellect shining in her beady black eyes.

"Doty?" Paige tried again.

Another shake. *I don't like that much either.*

"What about Roo?" Paige asked.

The mouse tilted her head as if seriously considering it. *It's a little on the nose, but I guess it will do.*

Nora croaked, "Roo it is."

Seth's gaze pinged around the room before he unleashed a deep groan. "Great. Ma is gonna flip her lid when she finds out about this. It'll be like all her dreams have come true."

Nora froze. "Do you think she knew?"

"What? Of course not. She would've been screaming from the rooftops that you were a witch if she'd known."

Seth's words should've comforted her, but Nora couldn't escape the chill spreading across her skin.

"Perhaps you should speak to her," Opal suggested, a kindly gleam in her eyes.

Ali chimed in, "Paige and Opal need to visit the farm if you're planning to take them up on their offer. Why don't you all go? I'll close up for you."

Normally, she'd never dream of begging her friend to work for her. Especially when she owed her so much more than she could ever dream of repaying. But with all the revelations swirling in her head, and the need for answers driving her mad, Nora simply nodded and said, "Thank you, Ali."

Lifting her skirt, she jogged out the back door, Seth, Opal, Paige, and the strange mix of animals trailing in her wake.

"Nora!" Seth yelled. "Slow down!"

She wasn't in the mood to listen. Her boots slapped the cobblestone as she raced through town, and she hardly noticed the chill breeze. Soon, she'd reached Moira's cabin, and a sigh escaped her when she noted the formally sunken roof back in its proper place.

But she didn't stick around to admire Seth's handiwork. She didn't even wait for the others to catch up. She threw open the door and called, "Ma? Where are you?"

Moira glanced up from her spot on the living room sofa. "Nora, dear! What a surprise. Come—"

"I'm a witch, Ma," she blurted before she lost her nerve. She watched her mother carefully, desperate for any sign of deceit as the denial she would no doubt spout flew out of her lips.

Moira collected the knitting resting atop her rose-embroidered skirt and set it beside her before calmly replying, "So, you finally discovered the truth."

Nora's eyes ached so badly she was certain they'd nearly burst out of her skull. "What? Y-you... What?"

Seth and the others caught up as Nora stood there rambling, all of them piling into the tiny living room until it felt so cramped that the walls were caving in on her. Or maybe it was just what her mother had said. It was almost like she'd been expecting this... But that couldn't be true.

"I knew, dear. I've always known." Moira stood, then strode forward until she clasped Nora's shaking arms in her hands. "I've shown you the letter that was with you when you were placed on my doorstep as a baby, but what I didn't tell you—what I *couldn't* say—was that there wasn't just one letter. Your basket held a second letter, addressed to me."

Beside her, Seth gasped. "You knew? How could you keep this from Nora, Ma? Hell, how could you sit there and listen to everything I said about witches if you knew my own sister..." He palmed his forehead, his face turning crimson.

"I'm sorry. You can't imagine how hard it was for me to hold my tongue. But I had to." Moira backed up. "Let me grab the letter. Once you read it for yourselves, you'll see why I kept silent until now."

Moira disappeared into the back of the house, the banging and scraping indicating she'd headed into her bedroom.

Nora hung back, her stomach swirling with nerves. It was like her entire history—everything that she'd known, what little there was—had just been rewritten. She wasn't sure how she was supposed to react to that.

"It'll be all right." Opal patted Nora's shoulder. "You'll see."

As Moira returned to the living room, she appeared to notice the women for the first time. "Hello. Who are you?"

Seth sighed and rushed through the introductions. "Now show us the damned thing."

Moira scowled. "I know you're upset, Son, but that doesn't give you an excuse to spout your sour mood all over my house."

Paige snorted, then attempted to cover the noise with a cough, but it was clear from the glare he sent in her direction that Seth hadn't missed it. Nora barely paid them any mind. She was too busy staring at the folded letter clenched in her mother's hands.

"Here, dear. I hope this helps you see why I kept silent for so long. Once you've finished reading it, I'll answer any questions you have."

The parchment crinkled in her fingers as Nora unfolded it. She smoothed it, holding it out so that Seth could read with her.

Moira Rowen,

Out of thousands of candidates, you were chosen to care for this precious child. Raise Nora as your own. Show her all the love and kindness you have shown your son, and you shall be generously rewarded. Treat her poorly, and she will be removed from your care, and a pox placed on your house.

This child will one day grow to possess incredible power. She must always wear the amulet to suppress it. Never remove it, especially once she has reached the age of ten, or untold calamities may befall you.

Keep this letter secret until the day that Nora comes to you and acknowledges her power. Then, and only then, can you show her this letter and the book attached to it. If you disobey this rule, then she will be removed from your care.

As proof of our gratitude, you've been granted the recipe on the back of this parchment. By brewing a few simple ingredients, you can provide for yourself and your family indefinitely. Women will always have need of this tea and will pay you handsomely to supply it.

Live well, Moira, and know that we will always be watching.

Just like the other, much more familiar letter addressed to her that she'd read hundreds of times, this one wasn't signed, leaving her no clues to who penned it. But when she flipped the page over, a very familiar recipe stared up at her.

"This is how you learned to brew moon tea," Nora whispered.

"It is. When they brought you to me, I was struggling. Seth's father had just left, and I was all alone with no skills to speak of, raising a four-year-old. You saved us, Nora. Even if I hadn't fallen in love with you the moment I laid eyes on you, I would've loved you for that. You are the greatest gift I've ever been given." Seth stiffened, and Moira wasted no time before lifting on her toes and patting his cheek. "You *both* are, my loves."

Tears filled her eyes. It was all so overwhelming; she could hardly fathom it. But one fact rose above all the rest, clear and unmistakable.

She was still Moira's daughter. No matter who had sent this letter. Whatever mysterious person who would threaten Ma with one breath and offer the key to her salvation with the next was not Nora's true family—no matter if they'd birthed her or not. Moira was.

The woman who took her in and never once let her forget how deeply she was loved would always be her true mother in Nora's eyes. Sure, she wasn't perfect. Far from it, in fact. But Moira's kindness knew no bounds. Nora would always be thankful it was her doorstep she'd been dropped on.

"Don't you see, love? I had to stay silent. I couldn't bear the thought of them taking you back. Who knows if they really were watching, but I wasn't about to take any chances."

"They were watching through me." Roo's voice echoed in her ears, making Nora tense. *"I've been with you, always."*

"You know who did this?" she couldn't help asking.

"No. But I know this to be true. I can feel *it."*

Nora saved that tidbit to examine more closely later. "I get it, Ma. I think in your place, I would've done the same."

"Wait..." Seth blinked. "If you only had the one recipe, then why all"—he waved at the endless supply of bottles and jars stacked on the shelves—"of this? No wonder your potions never work."

"I wouldn't say that. Sometimes they do. When I have a little help from Nora," Moira confessed, her cheeks flushing.

Nora lifted a brow. "What? I never helped with your tonics."

"That's not entirely true." Moira's voice warbled, thick with guilt. "You see, I couldn't always make the girls who came to me pay. Sometimes they had nothing. But I couldn't turn them aside, either. And it's not like those ingredients are cheap... I had to find another way to make a little coin. So I started trying my hand at other tonics, with little success. Then one day a caller came just as I was finishing his hair growth recipe. He banged on the door, demanding to be let in. The tonic called for warm water, and I had no time to heat it. But the bathtub still hadn't been drained."

"No..." Opal's jaw dropped.

"I figured it wouldn't hurt if I used your bathwater. Water is water, right? And the fellow only had to rub the stuff on his scalp. But then… it worked! He sprouted enough hair to make all the girls in town jealous. It was a miracle. All thanks to you, dear."

"Oh my goddess…" Revulsion crawled up Nora's spine.

"Ma!" Seth shrieked. "You've been peddling Nora's bathwater?"

Moira wrung her hands. "Sometimes. But only if the recipe was meant to be rubbed on."

"Great…" Nora groaned. "Strangers haven't been drinking my bathwater, just wearing it like lotion."

Paige let out a sound somewhere between a laugh and a cough, only this time it was clear she hadn't done it on purpose.

Nora fought the urge to gag. It was horrifying to learn what her mother had done. She'd grown accustomed to Moira drawing her a bath and offering to polish her necklace while she soaked, but she'd thought nothing of it. Wasn't that something parents naturally did for their children? How could she have known Ma had ulterior motives?

Seth cleared his throat. "Um… the letter mentions a book."

Moira reached into her skirt pocket. "Here. This was attached to that letter."

Nora's hands trembled as the smooth leather cover slid across her fingertips. "What's in it?" The book was small, black, and plain except for an engraving on the cover that matched her necklace—a white crescent moon.

Moira shrugged. "I have no idea. It's locked."

Opal eased forward. "Have you ever pressed this to the cover?" She thrust out the necklace Nora had neglected to take back. Nora took it and compared the sizes. They certainly looked like a perfect match.

"No. But now that you mention it, that's not a bad idea." Moira wiggled her brows. "What do you think, love? Want to try it?"

Nora slipped the necklace into her pocket. "No. Not now, at least." She sank onto the sofa. "I need to process all of this before I'm shocked by something else."

"Of course, dear. Can I get you anything? A drink? Something to eat?"

"No thanks. Just give me a moment alone. Please?"

Paige cut in smoothly. "Actually, I'd love a tour of the garden. I hear you have a few fields sitting fallow right now?"

"Sure. Follow me." Moira flashed Nora a soft smile before leading the others away.

As everyone filed through the kitchen, then their steps retreated out the back door, Nora sighed. It was all so hard to comprehend. How could she really be a witch?

"You'll need to open that book eventually," Roo said.

Nora closed her eyes. *"I can't. Not yet."*

"I understand. Take your time. But before you decide to put that necklace back on and forget this ever happened, you should look inside."

Skittering footsteps retreated, leaving Nora completely alone.

How had Roo guessed what was running through her head? After all, if the necklace had worked for all those years, it could work again. She could cast this evening aside like it had never happened. Go back to living her life the way it was.

Was that really what she wanted? Sure, she'd always pictured her future turning out as planned, but did that mean she should push away something strange and new just because it wasn't what she'd envisioned? Perhaps she ought to give being a witch some serious consideration...

Think of all the good she could do with her magic. If that letter was to be believed, she had a lot of it. Hell, she'd stopped everyone from talking without even knowing what she was doing. With a little training, she could probably do a lot more. Could she conjure plants like Paige? Maybe even heal the sick?

Suddenly, her eyes widened and her pulse sped. She popped off the couch and raced out back. "Ma, what ailment did Edgar come to you for?" Nora stopped short, blinking furiously.

Out in the field, Opal and Paige walked beneath the moonlight, tossing down seeds and singing softly under their breath. Every spot they wandered, sprouts shot up, turning the formerly brown fields a vibrant green.

Moira spun to face her, tears in her eyes. "Nora, look! What did I tell you, dear? The goddess will provide."

Seth shook his head and crossed his arms.

"I thought I had to sign a contract," Nora said softly.

"I signed it instead, dear. Don't worry. Seth agreed to help with the harvest. Once we sell these crops, all our money troubles will be through. There's enough for your brews and then some."

Her mother wasn't even exaggerating. The two witches had covered every inch of their fields with new growth. As long as they harvested them before the first frost, they shouldn't have any worries about paying off their debts and rebuilding.

Paige and Opal finished, and as the last song silenced, they both wobbled slightly.

"Oh my. Are you all right?" Moira asked.

Nora and Seth hurried forward, offering the pair aid. Opal took Nora's arm gratefully. Paige stiffened as Seth wrapped his arm around her shoulders, but didn't appear to possess the energy to shove him off.

Moira tutted while rushing to open the door. "Come inside. I'll whip up something to eat."

Nora chuckled. "How about you let me cook, Ma? You can take care of the tea." She loved her mother to death, even after today's shocking revelations, but that didn't change the fact that Ma wasn't exactly a whiz in the kitchen.

"Of course. While the water's boiling, I'll air out your old room." Moira smiled at Paige and Opal. "You two must stay the night. Can't have our new friends breaking a leg walking through the countryside in the dark."

Seth and Paige didn't seem too pleased at that announcement, but Opal grinned crookedly. "That would be lovely. My old bones don't enjoy long walks as much as they used to."

"I know that's true." Moira giggled, sounding almost like a school-girl again.

Maybe this could be good for her... When was the last time Ma had a woman her age to talk with? Most of the villagers gave her a wide berth, shying away from anyone who possessed skill with magic. That certainly wouldn't be a problem where Opal was concerned.

Paige settled on a kitchen chair. "I'd like to help you learn to control your magic, Nora. Then you won't have to worry about using it by mistake again."

That reminds me... "Ma. What did Edgar come to you for?"

The kettle clattered as Moira dropped it on the stove a little too harshly. "Why do you want to know about that?" She waved a hand. "No matter. I wouldn't say either way. Have to respect my clients' privacy, you understand."

Goddess... She hated to bring this up with her mother of all people, but after Ma's confession, she certainly deserved the right to make her a little uncomfortable in exchange. "Was his problem in the bedroom, by any chance?"

Moira blanched. "Really, dear. Must you bring up bedroom matters here? At the table?"

"Answer the question, Ma," Seth barked.

"All right... If you must know, you guessed correctly." Moira's brow furrowed. "Why do you ask?"

Nora cringed. "He and his wife visited Stellar Spirits this afternoon. And considering what happened, I think I may have inadvertently used my magic more than once..." Suddenly, Edgar's actions in her bathroom made sense.

Opal sighed. "I'm not surprised. You've probably been causing all manner of things to change with your magic since you lost your necklace. Tends to happen the most when emotions are heightened."

If that was true... Had she caused the fire to turn into an inferno? She'd been so sure that a freak gust of wind had started the fire, but she'd been practically fuming at the time. What other calamities had she unwittingly orchestrated? She thought back to all the things that had gone wrong recently, and when she recalled the ruined paint, Nora gasped.

"What is it?" Seth tilted his head.

"I think I owe Kieran an apology." He'd been so certain he hadn't caused the spill. Yeah, he'd been the only one in the basement... but her emotions had been all over the place that morning. Could her magic have been the true cause? *Goddess, I should've never tossed him out.* And he still hunted down Ali and helped save her business. She had to straighten things out with him... and soon.

"What apology?" Seth asked.

"Mind if I fill you in later? I'll take care of it soon. Right now, I just want to eat and head home." After all the news this evening, she needed a quiet spot to sit and think everything through.

Not to mention, she'd been much wearier than usual. She'd assumed it was from all the stress she'd been under, but then she saw how much Paige and Opal were drained when they finished working out back. Now she suspected that inadvertently using magic off and on for the last couple days was the most likely culprit of her exhaustion.

Moira rubbed Nora's back. "Sure you don't want to stay the night?"

"No, I'll be all right. Besides, you have a full house." She sighed. "But I'll come back first thing to help with the harvest."

Opal cleared her throat. "You might want to put that necklace back on until Paige can teach you a few basics."

"She's right. The charm will keep your magic suppressed." Paige's nose wrinkled. "You won't be able to talk with your familiar while you're wearing it, though."

The crescent moon pendant slid over her fingers as she dipped her hand into her skirt pocket. But she didn't put it on yet. She had a few questions for her new *friend* while they walked back home. "Thanks for the advice."

After whipping up a quick stir-fry and saying her goodbyes, Nora slipped out of her mother's house into the moonlit night with the little kangaroo mouse leading the way. But it wasn't long before a thread of unease unraveled in her chest. She reached out with her thoughts. *"Um... are you going to be all right?"*

Nora winced as Roo replied, *"Why wouldn't I?"* It was going to take some getting used to, hearing a voice that wasn't her own inside her head.

"It's a long walk. And your legs are so small."

"Just because I'm small doesn't make me any less capable."

She winced. *"I get that... But earlier, you said you've always been with me. How long do your species live?"*

"Oh, I see. You think you've been saddled with a familiar who has one foot in the grave."

"Sorry... I'm pretty new at all this." That was putting it mildly.

"Don't worry. All familiars are granted long lives when they meet their charges. Unless struck by violence or an accident, they'll live as long as their witch does."

"Wow... I didn't realize."

Roo's long ears twitched. *"Speaking of things you don't know... Are you certain this wild witch is the right teacher for you? There is a school nearby dedicated to educating witches."*

"I'm not even going to ask how you know that." Nora rubbed her temples. *"I'm sure. Paige will teach me here, in Everpass—that makes her the best choice."*

"Hm... Very well. You better listen to your teacher and put your amulet back on—for now."

Nora stopped in her tracks and slid the pendant out of her pocket. *"What if I need to talk to you?"*

"Just take it off and call out for me. Promise I won't be far."

She paused with the necklace hovering in midair. *"Wait... How closely have you been watching me?"* After her mother's surprise earlier, she couldn't bear any more unwanted intrusions.

A displeased scoff echoed in her ears. *"Not that close. You can trust me, Nora. I know exactly when to make myself scarce."*

With that reassurance ringing through her ears, Nora slipped the necklace back on and resumed her walk through the empty streets of Everpass.

Two Birds, One Stone

Kieran

"Thanks for all your help, Davos. See you soon." With a jaunty wave, Kieran left the smithy, feeling more at peace than he had in—oh... maybe ever.

Moonlight shone down on him as he ambled through the quiet streets of Everpass. After spending the last few hours chatting with Davos, he was actually looking forward to seeing his prosthesis. Funny word, that, but it was better than calling it a pirate hook.

A chuckle flew off his tongue, surprising him more than anything. A few weeks ago, he'd have never pictured himself actually laughing about his injury. Yet, after chatting with Davos about all the things his prosthesis could do, watching him sketch a custom design, and having his arm measured, he'd begun to think about things in a new light.

No. That wasn't entirely true. His perspective had changed before that. And it had everything to do with a certain pretty brunette who never once made him feel less than.

He couldn't wait to see her again. Perhaps he should pop by the bar on his way home?

Shaking his head, he dismissed the idea before he'd fully grasped on to it. Nora deserved better. Yeah, he was desperate to see her, but he refused to turn into an idiot throwing rocks at her window to beg her for another kiss.

What she really deserved was a proper date. He could take her for a picnic one morning before she opened. With all the cooking she did for everyone else, she ought to be doted on for a change. And he was dying to prove to her that his cooking prowess wasn't all boasts.

Or maybe if he was really lucky, he could talk her into closing for a weekend, and take her on a trip to the capital. Considering how their first and only dance ended, he owed her a do-over. The mere thought of her twirling in his arms in another gorgeous dress brought a nostalgic smile to his face. And after, he could take her to some of his favorite haunts. Show her all the places he'd learned to love while living his old life.

Odd that he'd begun to think of it that way. He'd only meant this visit to be a means to an end. A quick reunion with his folks before he found some way to return to his job. Or barring that, setting off on an adventure all his own.

But now, all he could think about was her. Making her smile. Helping her chase her dreams. Drowning in her sweetness again and again and never ever letting her go. Yep. He'd have never guessed coming home would turn him into a smitten fool who couldn't imagine leaving, but surprise—here he was.

There was only one problem. Moira.

If Nora had been so upset when she learned he was keeping his father's ownership of Stellar Spirits a secret, she'd be devastated if she discovered he'd only agreed to help her because he was angling for a miracle cure from her mother.

But that was simple enough to fix. First thing tomorrow, he'd march over there and tell her the deal was off. Not like the chances were great she could've pulled it off, anyway.

Sure, Edgar's healing had been a success. But their situations weren't entirely the same. Moira had caught up with him the very next day and only had a few fingers to worry about. He'd been living with his loss for much longer than that. According to the healers he visited in the city, the chances of healing an injury like the one he'd faced diminished greatly with every passing day. It was why all their attempts to heal him failed, leading to his amputation.

Only now, he was starting to believe he could stand living with it—indefinitely.

Of course, he couldn't forget about Seth, either. But surely he'd understand. It wasn't like he was planning to treat Nora like some cheap fling. He wanted to stick around—forever, if she'd allow it.

He'd explain everything tomorrow. Two birds, one stone. A man-to-man chat with his best friend, and a polite "thanks, but no thanks" to his mother. Then he could concentrate on winning over the girl of his dreams.

She deserved to hear the whole truth from him personally, and not through town gossip. That was one thing he'd need to get used to all over again. He wasn't a fan of everyone in town knowing his business… unless they were whispering about Nora agreeing to be his girl. They could shout that news up and down Main for all he cared.

Then, like his thoughts had conjured her, Nora appeared, wearily trudging around the corner as he crossed onto Main. "Kieran? What are you doing out so late?"

"I might ask the same to you." He couldn't slow the grin that overtook his face. This was perfect luck! He'd already decided not to bother her so late, but now that she was right here in front of him, he might as well try his luck. "Heading home?"

"From Ma's." She rubbed the back of her shoulder, and it was impossible to miss the tension in her frame.

"Mind if I walk with you?" It was a simple enough request and not much to ask, seeing as they were only a few buildings away from Stellar Spirits, but his heart raced all the same as he awaited her answer.

"I'd like that." Nora bit her lip and resumed walking with him at her side. "In fact, I'm glad I ran into you."

"Really? Why's that?"

"I owe you an apology. I have reason to believe that you weren't responsible for the paint spill after all. I'm sorry I didn't listen when you tried telling me it wasn't your fault."

His smile softened and a tremendous weight lifted from his shoulders. "Apology accepted."

She blew out a relieved breath as they stopped in front of her shop. "That's it? Not going to chew me out?"

"Why would I want to do that?"

Her head slanted. "Don't you even want to know what really happened?"

He leaned back on his heels. "I'd rather you invite me in for a nightcap."

Nora sighed wearily. "Honestly, Kieran, I'd love to, but I don't have the energy left to mix another drink. Tonight has been... a lot."

"Book club that bad, huh?"

"The meeting didn't even end up happening, if you can imagine that."

As much as he'd been craving another kiss, he sensed Nora wasn't even remotely in the mood for romance. But that didn't mean he had to abandon her while she was clearly struggling with something.

"How about we go in, I'll mix *you* a drink, and you can tell me all about it? If you're willing to share, of course."

One of her perfect brows arched. "You mix drinks now?"

"Not as well as you, I'm sure, but I haven't poisoned myself yet."

The corner of her mouth ticked up into a crooked smile. "With a glowing review like that, how can I say no?" Her keys jingled, then the lock clicked. He followed her into the dark room, wincing slightly as she turned on the lamp beside the door.

He strolled behind the bar while his eyes adjusted to the light. When she tried to follow, he shook a finger at her. "I've got it. Grab a stool and tell me what's been troubling you."

She giggled but obeyed. "You really shouldn't encourage your customers to overshare."

He grabbed an empty glass and tossed in some ice. "That a big problem for you?"

"Yep. You'd be surprised what an earful you get even without prompting folk to chat." She smoothed her hands lovingly over the bar top. "Sitting here always loosens their lips."

"Sure that's not your drinks doing the loosening?"

"Doubt it. I've been out of spirits all week and I've still heard my fair share." Nora's curls slid across the shoulder of her black shawl, making his fingers itch to grasp the silky strands in his fist.

Speaking of spirits... That was going to make his job more difficult. He almost tossed out the ice and lifted the glass to one of Nora's taps. But he'd promised to mix her something… *Guess it's gotta be a mocktail, then.*

He dug inside her ice chest and grabbed a few bottles, giving each a sniff before deciding which to add to her glass.

Nora giggled again. "Sure you don't need a hand back there?"

"No, I've got it." He frowned as he pushed aside a jar filled with a white liquid he assumed was milk. "So what forced your book club to be canceled?"

"Goddess… You sure you want to know?"

He topped off the concoction with a bright-red liquid that smelled like the right blend of sweet and tart. "Definitely. If you need to get it off your chest, I'm happy to listen." He slipped a straw into the glass, closed his thumb over the top, and lifted it to his lips. Once he released his thumb, a trickle of tangy flavor exploded on his tongue. *Perfect.*

Nora's eyes widened as he dunked a new straw into the glass and stirred three times, then slid the cup toward her. "Okay… But first, what do you call this?"

He smirked, pulling a name from the top of his head. "Kieran's Infinite Bliss."

Nora snorted. "Are you serious?"

He leaned in, capturing her gaze. "Pretty sure I already mentioned that I'd never make you swallow anything unless it would please you."

Just like the last time he'd said it, her cheeks turned crimson. "You're awful." Still, she smirked and lifted the glass, wetting her lips before wrapping them around her straw. Her delicate throat worked before she said, "Mm… Infinite Bliss sounds about right."

Sparks of joy shot through his veins. He folded his arms on the bar top and adopted a business-like tone. "So. What's troubling you, pretty lady?"

"Is that what you think I sound like?" Nora snorted again, then set down the glass with a sigh. "Fine. I'll tell you since you keep asking, but you might want to sit down for this."

"Sounds good to me." He nodded to her glass. "Can we share?"

"Sure, your bliss is my bliss." She chuckled.

I like the sound of that.

He plopped onto the stool beside her and slipped his straw next to Nora's. Then he listened with a dropped jaw as she wove a tale full of magic, mayhem, and mysterious revelations that made his body thrum with wonder. "Wow. A lot's happened since I saw you last..." he stated after she wrapped up the story with their meeting on the road.

"Tell me about it." Nora grabbed the cup, stealing the last sip. Then she sighed heavily, all the weariness in her limbs he'd first noted on the street amplified. "You don't hate me now that you know what I am, do you?"

He couldn't shake his head fast enough. Sure, he was a little leery around folk who controlled magic. Most people who had no knack for it were, and understandably so. After the fate of the last great war was decided, based mainly on which side held the stronger witches, the common folk learned a healthy respect—and yes, often fear—of magic.

But this was Nora. He'd known her practically his entire life. He had no doubt she'd master her power and do amazing things with it. She had a heart of gold, and no magic in the world would ever change that.

"I could never hate you." He cupped her cheek, infusing his tone with complete sincerity.

She blinked sleepily. "You sure? I was so worried about Seth. You know how he is with witches."

He dragged her closer, pulling her into a hug. "I promise. Nothing will ever change how I feel about you, Nora."

Her cheek nuzzled into his chest at the same time her hand slipped down to grasp his left wrist. "I feel the same about you, too."

Kieran's heart expanded, filled with so much light and warmth it was practically vibrating. He wanted to kiss her so badly. To finish what they'd started earlier in this room, without interruptions. But Nora was boneless in his arms, so weary he sensed her slipping off to sleep as he held her.

So he choked down his urges and lifted her off the stool.

"Kieran," she muttered, a bit of her strength returning as her arms locked around his neck. "Where are you taking me?"

"To bed." He climbed the stairs to her loft bedroom. "Can't exactly leave you sleeping on a stool, now can I? I'll tuck you in and lock up. Then I'll meet you at Ma's to help with the harvest in the morning. Okay?"

She sighed. "Thank you. For everything."

He gently set her down on her bed. "It's been my pleasure."

As he turned to leave, she snagged his wrist. His gaze shot to hers, and for a fleeting moment, he prayed she'd be fully awake. That she'd beg him to stay. He would've in a heartbeat. Even if all it meant was a night spent holding her in his arms.

But it was soon clear she had no such thoughts on her mind. She blinked up at him in the dim moonlight given off by her big window, her lids so heavy she couldn't keep them fully open. "Kieran? Can I ask you one thing before you go?"

"Anything."

"I'm dying to know... What was the best thing you ever tasted?"

He kneeled and tucked her arm under the blanket. Then he brushed a wayward curl off her forehead. Nora's eyes slid closed, and her breathing evened. He wasn't sure if she was even still awake, but he told her the truth anyway.

"It was you, Nora." He pressed a chaste kiss to her achingly soft lips. "It's always been you." Then he got up and quietly strode out of the bar, locking the door behind him.

The chill night air was his only companion as he wandered through town. He wasn't sure exactly what time it was, but it had to be well after midnight. Not that the hour would matter much to his folks. They'd always loved staying out until the wee hours, and that hadn't changed in the years he'd been gone.

As he strode down the meticulously manicured lawn of his parents' house, a sigh spilled out his lips. He hated coming back here every day. He ought to put his savings to good use and buy a little cottage in town. Then he wouldn't have to wander through his parents' empty manor each night while they were off on some social visit they hadn't bothered to invite him to.

With the lights down low, he suspected he'd be in for more of the same that evening. Yet as he strolled inside, his father called out from the drawing room before he'd even eased the door closed.

"Son. We need to talk."

Kieran's palm grew moist, a learned response dredged up from his teen years that had apparently never fully disappeared. How many times had he been called in for a chat? Hundreds, probably, always when his father was most displeased. He had half a mind to slink up the stairs and pretend he hadn't heard him. But it seemed he was a glutton for punishment.

He strolled into the formal room his parents used for entertaining. But while the lushly upholstered furniture and refined décor were welcoming in the bright light of day, they took on a forbidding ambiance lit by a single lamp, which cast shadows across his father's frowning face.

"Good evening, Father. How have I wronged you today?" Sure, it was a low blow, considering he'd barely started speaking. But Kieran knew how this worked. He'd tiptoed around this dance before. It had never ended well for him.

"I'm glad you asked," Tanyth deadpanned. Kieran resisted the urge to roll his eyes. "I have some concerns about your *friend* Nora and how she's been mistreating our property."

A lot to unpack in that statement. First off, he didn't like the way his father said *friend*, like he knew Kieran's feelings for her were anything but friendly. Suppose he should've been expecting that after he almost tore Tanyth's shirt off when he thought Nora had been hurt.

Then there was his insinuation that Nora was deliberately destroying his stupid rental property. Seriously, why did he even care? Tanyth owned so many buildings that he'd be set for life even if half of them burned down.

And to blame her for what was just a series of unlucky mishaps… it made his blood boil. But he'd get nowhere with his father if he let his anger do the talking. So, he sucked a deep breath through his nose and said, "Nora isn't mistreating anything. She's just had a run of bad luck. She'll fix everything and bring more value to the property in the end. Just wait and see." Now that she knew exactly what had caused all her troubles, her luck would take a turn for the better. He was sure of it.

Tanyth's booted foot tap-tap-tapped on the polished hardwood, driving Kieran half-crazed. He plunked onto the sofa across from him, waiting for the other shoe to drop. With his father, there was always something. Some meticulously crafted scheme to come out on top, one that he was expected to play a part in, no doubt.

Only this time, Kieran wasn't particularly elated about being his father's eager little puppet. Not when it had to do with Nora.

After ages of waiting, he finally caved. "Go on, then. Spit it out. What do you want from me?"

"This isn't just about that girl's future. I have concerns about your future, too."

He laughed caustically. "Really? You have an odd way of showing it."

"What's that supposed to mean?"

"Oh, I don't know. Maybe you should try actually spending some time with me if you want me to believe you care."

Tanyth bristled. "When shall I do that? While you're slumming it, working in some bar on the wrong side of town?"

He didn't even bother arguing that Main Street was most definitely *not* the wrong side of town. "Sure. It wouldn't kill you to take an interest in my life. Spend time with my friends. Would it?"

"It would when they're beneath you."

"Beneath me?" Kieran couldn't help it then. He raised his voice just a smidge. "Did you seriously just say that the woman who wakes up at the crack of dawn to repurpose last night's meal into free breakfast for struggling village children is *beneath me*?"

Tanyth waved a manicured hand. "While charity work is certainly admirable, it doesn't change the fact that you aren't some common laborer. You served the Crown for over a decade. The people you associate with should be on your level, not below it."

"I intend to live my life the way I choose instead of worrying about your reputation. That's what this all boils down to, doesn't it?

Can't have the other elves disparaging you about your son's common friends."

"That's not it at all. I'm trying to save you from the growing pains I went through. Society doesn't look kindly on folk who choose the less-traveled path."

Goddess's sake. Could he be any more cryptic? The beginnings of a headache throbbed against his temples, making him wish more than anything his father would just speak plainly for once. "Look, I'm not in the mood to argue. Can we agree to disagree and call it a night?"

"I'm afraid not." His father's bitter words stopped Kieran from levering himself off the sofa. "I plan to rescind Ms. Rowen's rental agreement. It's well within my rights after all that bad luck you mentioned. If you don't believe me, have a gander at the fine print."

Tanyth tapped a finger on a stack of paperwork sitting on the side table. Kieran's stomach sank, but he made no move to read what he assumed was a copy of Nora's lease. Tanyth was many things, but he'd never been a liar.

"Why would you do that? To keep me from working with her?"

"In a way. But only because you deserve more." Tanyth leaned forward, capturing his gaze. "I've spoken with a few of my contacts in the capital. They're offering you a position in your old regiment."

"How did you manage that? They made it very clear I wasn't welcome after my injury." All good spies had to be capable of blending in. He couldn't exactly do that with a missing hand.

"They want you to teach new recruits."

It was everything he'd thought he'd wanted, handed to him on a platter. A chance to return to his old life in the city. All the hard work he'd suffered through to earn his position wouldn't be wasted after all. Only... "What if I don't want that life any longer?"

"But you do, Kieran. Don't throw away everything you've worked for and settle for less." Tanyth's expression softened. "Don't you see? This injury doesn't have to be the end. You can still have the job you deserve. Find a wife who suits you."

He didn't miss the true meaning of that last statement. The words his father left unsaid rang through his mind anyway. *Nora's not good enough for you.*

That couldn't be further from the truth. Why couldn't he see that? "What are you really asking me for?"

Tanyth leaned back, crossing one lean leg over the other. "I want you to accept the position I arranged for you. Commit to meeting new people while you're back in the capital. Move on with your life." He glanced sideways at the stacked papers. "And I'll forget about my plans for Ms. Rowen's lease. Everyone wins."

Kieran hung his head, completely speechless. How could he agree to this madness? It would mean giving up Nora. Leaving his best friend. Going back to a life he didn't even want any longer.

But how could he say no? Staying guaranteed he'd destroy Nora's business. More than anything, she deserved a chance to make her dreams come true. Even if he wasn't there to be part of them.

Tanyth rose from his chair. "They want you to report to headquarters at dawn in three days' time. You have until then to say your goodbyes."

"You know I'll hate you forever for this. Don't you, Father?" he hissed the last word, his chest aching like it had cracked in two.

"You may think so, but one day, you'll thank me." Boot steps tapped on the polished floor, echoing the maddening beat of Kieran's breaking heart. "Good night, Son. And farewell."

First Lesson

Nora

Nora strode through Everpass early the next morning, dressed in an old oversized tunic and one of her few pairs of black slacks. Seemed fitting, considering she was in for a long morning of harvesting. She'd gotten a later start than she'd have liked, but couldn't complain about how well rested she'd been when she'd awakened. Clearly, she'd needed it.

In hindsight, she wished she'd summoned the courage to ask Kieran to stay. He'd been so sweet last night, patiently listening to her story even when interrupted by countless yawns. And he'd never uttered a single judgmental word, which pleased her more than she cared to admit.

She couldn't wait to see him again this morning. Although a pang of anxiety struck her whenever her thoughts drifted to Seth. What would he do when faced with the reality of his little sister and best friend becoming more than friends? It was probably too much to hope for no backlash at all.

It wasn't like she'd discussed the details of the situation with Kieran. Would he be willing to come clean to Seth? She'd certainly felt like they'd turned a corner, embarking on a road that would lead to so much more. Like courting. And definitely more kissing... Or was she reading him all wrong?

Did he feel the same desire she did to have everything out in the open? If he insisted on keeping Seth in the dark, then whatever deliciousness that was brewing between them was doomed to spoil before either of them could savor a taste.

She'd lived with secrets for far too long. Now that she'd finally started unearthing the truths that had evaded her for her entire life, she couldn't stomach the thought of living in a lie of her own making.

I won't be anyone's dirty secret. Not even Kieran's.

Luckily, it was the weekend, so she didn't need to wait outside for hungry children headed to school. She'd find out soon enough what would come of all those stolen kisses. Kieran might have even beaten her to Ma's. He could be telling Seth the news right now...

The mild anxiety thrumming through her built up the longer she dawdled on the road. She traversed the last few turns at a near sprint, needing to assuage her worries. But as she hurried across her mother's front lawn and into the back, her heart finally settled into somewhat of a normal rhythm when no pained grunts or sounds of a scuffle reached her ears.

Goddess. What was I so worried about? It was almost as if she'd expected to find Kieran face down in the dirt, and Seth perched atop him, swinging like mad.

Instead, she found her brother in the garden, shirtless, his green skin coated in sweat and specks of dirt. A wheelbarrow stood beside him, half-filled with fully grown vegetables.

Paige worked in the field across from him, sheathed in a slightly too-tight familiar brown dress she'd clearly borrowed from Nora's mother, while Bok was perched atop the fence, his beak jerking this way and that each time she moved. An identical wheelbarrow—this one nearly full—sat beside her while she quietly hummed, her hands swaying hypnotically. Not a single drop of perspiration dripped from her brow.

And... no sign of Kieran. She'd beaten him there, even after sleeping in. She shook off the prickle of apprehension that struck her chest. Surely it was nothing to worry over. He was probably just eating breakfast with his parents.

"Good morning, love," Moira announced cheerfully. "Come here and sit with us for a spell. Have a drink. I'm sure you're parched after your walk."

Her mother and Opal sat in the shade on a pair of folding chairs, both of them wearing much more forgiving wrap dresses that Nora recognized from her mother's closet. A pitcher of water rested between them atop an old weather-worn card table that had lived in her mother's backyard for as long as Nora could remember.

"Good morning." Nora smiled at her mother and nodded politely to Opal. "I appreciate the offer, but I came here to help."

She stepped forward but didn't make it far before Opal said, "I wouldn't do that if I were you. You're liable to get your head chewed off."

"Huh?" She turned back with a lifted brow.

Moira giggled. "They're having a… race, I guess you'd call it."

"A pissing match, if you ask me." Opal snickered.

"Seth and Paige got into a bit of an argument over breakfast, each of them claiming to be the best at harvesting. Then they decided to put their skills to the test." Moira patted the empty chair beside her. "I wouldn't interrupt them until they wear themselves out."

Opal nodded sagely, and Tibbie shadowed the motion, her cute brown head bobbing up and down in tandem from her spot between Opal's feet. "She's right. Besides, now's the perfect time for your first lesson in magic."

Nora settled on the chair tentatively. "I thought Paige was going to be my teacher?"

"And who do you think taught her?" Opal asked, more than a hint of snark in her tone.

"I'm guessing it was you."

"Damn right it was. I taught that girl everything she knows. But I'm too old to be traipsing in and out of town for your lessons. Still, might as well put me to use while you have me around."

Moira grabbed a wooden cup off a stack and filled it. "Oh, I'm excited! I always dreamed about attending Maudwin in my youth. But it wasn't meant to be."

Opal's gaze softened. "It's not too late to learn a few new tricks. Even folk with no magic skills to speak of can be taught a thing or two. Just takes much more study and practice than those of us who are naturally inclined to it."

Nora's stomach clenched as she grabbed the cup her Ma handed her. "And I'm one of the natural-born ones?"

Opal leaned back in her chair. "You are. Some folk wake up one day bursting with potential. No one's sure why some have it and not others, though it tends to run in families. If I have the right of it—and I usually do—then you've always been one of us. It was just impossible to discover with that charmed necklace of yours keeping your magic suppressed."

Her hand lifted to her neck, where the opal crescent hung. "Guess I should take this off, then?"

Opal tilted her head. "No way to test your skills if you don't."

As Nora pinched open the latch, Opal launched into a long speech about the history of magic that she hardly paid any mind to. She'd never been one to learn best by listening to lectures. It wasn't until she got hands on that the knowledge sunk in.

Paige called out across the field, "Send her over here. Looks like I have plenty of time to teach while the lesser harvester catches up."

Seth shot her a glare cold enough it would surely make most men quake in their boots. But Paige's smile only widened as she sang softly, using magic to push her overflowing wheelbarrow forward.

Moira chuckled. "Go on, love."

"Yes." Thankfully, Opal didn't appear too mad about her history lesson being interrupted. "Paige will show you what she's doing. Let's see if you can do it too."

"Hey, that's cheating!" Seth scowled. "If Nora starts helping you, then you forfeit."

Paige rolled her eyes. "Please. We'll work over here." She strolled away from the field she was in and toward an untouched row of corn. "Come on, Nora."

"Okay..." She hopped to her feet, marveling at how the corn towered over her. This time yesterday, the field had been completely empty. How wild was that? "What do you want me to do?"

"Let's see if you can move things with magic. I'm willing to bet that you can. It's something most witches master relatively easily."

Nora's pulse raced. "Sure… but how do I do it?"

"For me, and Ma too, it helps us to sing and move about while picturing what we want to happen in our mind. The words don't really matter. Just the intention behind them."

"So it's not like learning a spell? I don't have to memorize anything?"

"Goddess, no. At least, not the way we do it. I'm not sure if that's something they teach you in that fancy school. Me and Ma are self-taught, like all the Barclays who came before us." She chuckled, and a teasing gleam lit her eyes. "Honestly, you can sing anything. Watch this."

Paige started humming wordlessly, her arms swaying upward. The closest stalk of corn swayed with her. Then she opened her mouth and sang, "My mother once told me, beware of he who has brawn without a lick of sense in his head. Eyes may delight in what you see, but when the girls come calling, you'll wish you'd left him for dead." As the last word rolled off her lips, the corn stalk lifted easily from the ground. Paige hummed again, keeping it up until the stalk landed softly in an empty wheelbarrow.

"You hear this dreck, Nor?" Seth scoffed as he ripped a carrot out of the dirt harshly. "Witch thinks she's a damn minstrel. I have half a mind to pay her… to leave."

Nora giggled. "I don't know. I kind of liked it."

Paige nudged her arm. "Go on. You try."

She couldn't be expected to do that right now… But what if she could?

Only one way to find out.

"Okay. Here goes nothing." Nora hummed softly, letting her body go loose and fluid. She swayed to the beat of her own tune while staring at the corn. Finally, the stalk moved a bare inch. "Was that me? Did I do that?"

Paige chuckled nervously. "Pretty sure that was the wind."

"Oh." Nora's heart sank.

"Don't give up. We're just getting started." Paige patted her shoulder.

"Try making something grow instead," Opal shouted from her chair.

"Good idea, Ma." Paige lowered her voice. "Most witches are naturally more talented in one area than others. Me and Ma are great at growing things, but there are lots of other things we struggle with."

Nora cocked her head. "Really? Like what?"

"Healing, for one. Most of the elemental stuff. I couldn't start a fire if my life depended on it. Ma is pretty good at summoning rain, but I can only make it drizzle, and even that drains me."

"Drains you?" Seth piped in again, evidently unable to keep from eavesdropping. "What does that mean? Is this dangerous?"

Nora held up a hand. "Seth, please."

Paige's voice turned grave. "No, he's right. Magic *can* be dangerous."

"Nope." Seth threw up his hands. "Then Nora's not doing it."

Paige shot him a glare, daggers in her eyes. "Let me finish." She spun back to Nora, her gaze softening. "It can be dangerous. But it's even *more* dangerous to live your life without learning your limits. Then, when you need to use magic—maybe to save your life or the life of someone you love—you'll know how far you can tax yourself. As long as you don't wear yourself out too badly, it's simple enough to recharge with a little rest."

"And if she wears herself out too badly? What then?" Seth demanded, his arms crossed.

"I'll be there to make sure that doesn't happen."

He clearly wasn't about to let Paige off with that half-answer. "What happens, Paige?"

She might be mistaken, but Nora was almost positive she caught Paige shiver before she sucked in a deep breath and straightened her shoulders. "In some extreme cases—mostly with untrained witches, mind you—using too much magic can be fatal."

"Fatal..." Seth paled. "Nora, call this foolishness off. Please."

Nora's stomach wobbled. But she couldn't let fear stop her. Not while she'd barely scratched the surface of what she was capable of. "Seth, I'll be fine. Don't forget"—she dug into her pocket and pulled out her necklace—"I still have this. I can slap on my necklace and whatever I'm doing will stop, easy as that."

Seth didn't look convinced. But he'd come around. He just needed some time to adjust.

"Well, now that we've settled that, why don't you try making something grow?" Paige hovered over the hole in the ground where she'd just extracted the corn stalk. She plucked a single kernel off the corn stalk beside it and dropped it into the dirt. "Picture the seed sprouting roots. Give it a reason to grow." With that, her lovely voice turned melodic and more humming filled the air. She swayed on her feet, arms waving, her eyes closing until they were half-lidded.

It was hard tearing her eyes off the mesmerizing sight as power crackled around them. But she had a hunch she couldn't resist testing.

So while Paige's spell wove around them, coaxing a new stalk out of the ground, Nora glanced at her brother. While she'd been just as enthralled with Paige as she was with the plant inching upward, his gaze was firmly locked on the signing beauty, his jaw clenched tightly, but his eyes lit with wonder.

Oh... That was *very* interesting, indeed. She turned back, hiding a smile behind her hands as Paige stopped with the plant only halfway grown.

"Go on, Nora. You try. It should be easy since I already got it started."

Nora nodded and attempted to copy Paige's movements. But no matter how she swayed or what pitch she hummed, the plant remained exactly the same.

She wasn't sure how long she stood there, stubbornly trying, but it was long enough that her throat and arms ached when she finally quit. Seth had long ago returned to his task, and his wheelbarrow was almost as full as Paige's had been when she'd called Nora over. Ma and Opal had disappeared inside, working on lunch, no doubt.

"It's no use." She lowered her head.

"Don't worry. I bet we just haven't found your specialty yet. Once you narrow down what you're really good at, everything else will fall into place."

Paige's words gave her hope, but she doubted it would be that easy. For one, how was she supposed to discover what she was good at? There were so many types of magic out there. She might try different things for ages at this rate.

"Ah, shit!" A string of curses far fouler than his first oath spilled out of Seth's lips.

"What's wrong?" She hurried to his side when she spotted him cradling his hand against his bare chest. "Are you okay?"

He grimaced. "Damn wheelbarrow bit me." He flashed her his palm, showing off a nasty diagonal gash that covered the entire width, from thumb to pinky. "It's not so bad."

"Not so bad?" Paige blinked repeatedly, looking woozy. "T-that's... That's awful."

Seth's grimace shifted to a smirk. "Oh, look at that. Little Miss Perfect can't handle a little blood."

Nora swallowed the urge to roll her eyes. "I'll run inside. Grab some bandages."

"Wait." Paige straightened. "Now's the perfect time to test if you're a healer."

"While he's bleeding like that?" What if she was destined to fail again? Seth might end up like Kieran, cursed with an infection that caused him to lose his entire hand. "No. Let me grab some bandages. We'll try something else to test my healing skills." Or lack thereof.

But Seth snagged her elbow as she moved to run into the house. "Nora... wait. I think she's onto something. I mean, what else have you been helping Ma with all these years? All her tonics are meant to cure something."

Nora's heart sped. Could he be right?

"Fine." She drew a steadying breath and hummed. She swayed and danced and hummed some more. But after ages of trying, she gave up with a defeated sigh. "I tried. Can I get the bandages now?"

She couldn't stem the wave of disappointment that rose with the failure. For a second, she'd almost believed he was right. After all, if she'd been the one responsible for that bald man's hair tonic working, why couldn't she heal flesh too? But it seemed she was just as useless at healing as she was at moving and growing things.

Would she ever find her talent?

"Darn. I thought that would work." Paige nodded at the door. "You better get the supplies."

But as she turned to leave, Seth called out, "Wait! I have an idea. Ma stole your bathwater to make her tonics work, right? What if you need water?"

Nora's brow pinched. "I don't see how that will help..."

Paige gasped. "Actually, it might. Singing and dancing work for me and Ma, but there's no guarantee it will work for you." She waved at the pitcher left out on the card table. "Let's try it."

Seth preened. "See? I'm not just a pretty face." He tapped the top of his head with his forefinger. "There are plenty of brains in this handsome head, too."

Paige conceded, "I suppose a few of the rocks rattling around in there have a sharp edge."

Nora left them trading insults and jogged for the pitcher. By the time she returned, they were both glaring so fiercely she hopped between them, sure they were about two seconds away from tearing each other apart.

"Okay. What do I do?"

Paige shrugged. "I'm not entirely sure. This isn't part of my process."

"Dunk your finger into the water and think about healing." Seth shrugged. "Can't hurt to try."

The cool water moistened her finger. Nora closed her eyes and wished for Seth's palm to heal. Then her eyes popped open, and she poured a bit of water on her brother's hand.

Seth hissed. They all stared at his bloody palm… but nothing happened.

Nora's shoulders slumped.

"Try speaking this time," Paige suggested. "Maybe you need to vocalize."

"Huh… I do like to sing in the tub." A tiny bud of hope bloomed as she dipped her finger again. "Heal, Seth. Heal," she sang. "Please, just bloody heal."

Seth snickered. "Nice tune, Nor."

She dumped the water a little more forcibly than before. A strange tingle spread, starting in her feet and working its way up through her chest. The same tingle she recalled feeling once before, when she poured a mug of ale for Edgar and told him she wished whatever problems he was facing would work out.

"Hey! That stings." Seth scowled, but only for a second. Then his gaze shot to his hand, and his jaw dropped. "My goddess... It's healing. You did it, Nor!"

Nora stared in shock as the bloody gash healed before her eyes. "Wow. I really did it."

Paige beamed. "See? I told you this would happen. You're officially a witch, Nora. A healer."

As the most profound sense of wonder she'd ever experienced washed over her, making her chest expand, footsteps crunched around the side of the house. A few seconds later, the one person she'd been dying to see all day emerged.

"Kieran, you're here." But... something was wrong. The mood shifted, all the elation evaporating as she took in his slumped posture and severe expression.

"Hey, Nora. Can we talk?"

SORRY

Kieran

R acing thoughts bombarded him from every direction. Kieran had stayed up all night, plagued with worries.

Was he doing the right thing? In so many ways, the decision he'd finally settled on before sunrise still felt wrong. Viscerally, unequivocally wrong, on so many levels. But he couldn't see any way around it.

Even more so now. He'd rounded the corner into Moira's backyard, and there she was. Stunning as always—but he'd seemed to have caught her at a particularly momentous instant. Her eyes had been lit with pride, her expression full of wonder.

Goddess, why is she so perfect? So utterly beautiful, inside and out. He'd basked in the glow of the stolen moment during the split second before she'd spotted him. But like all good things—at least where he was concerned—it couldn't last.

She'd turned to him, and he must've looked as bad as he felt. One glimpse was enough to dim the light radiating around her. Nora's voice reached him, a beam of brilliance cutting through fog. "Kieran, you're here."

He forced out words he had no desire to say, "Hey, Nora. Can we talk?"

Tension pooled in the air, thick and cloying. He could scarcely stand it.

"Oh. Sure." Nora stepped forward, her head tilted, gazing softly at him like she knew something was off and she was hoping to be the one to fix it. She dug into her pocket, slipped the crescent moon pendant out, and latched it around her neck as she walked.

His stomach twisted, wrenching more with each step she took. Each crunch of grass battered his ears as he worked up the courage to speak.

He'd been unable to tear his eyes off her since turning that corner, so when another voice rose, Kieran flinched.

"What the hell's going on?" Seth stood in a field, shirtless and drenched in sweat. Beside him, Paige looked on, both of them staring at him like he'd grown two heads. And from the looks of it, neither one had any intention of giving him privacy for this conversation.

Great. Two birds, one stone. That was what he'd wanted originally, wasn't it? It wasn't exactly how he'd pictured today playing out, but apparently he'd gotten his wish.

Nora stopped in front of him, and he pushed aside the dread of losing his best friend. A week ago, he couldn't imagine anything worse than letting Seth down, the one loyal friend he'd relied on for decades.

But as he met Nora's whiskey eyes, he realized cutting ties with her would be even more dreadful.

She was everything he'd been missing. A woman who saw him as more than some lauded spy. One who couldn't care less about his reputation. Who treated him as her friend and trusted him enough to let him into her life. She didn't give a damn about his shortcomings. Never once made him feel less than.

With Nora by his side, he'd actually begun to believe that an ordinary life could be full of the adventure he craved. Because she wasn't ordinary at all. It wasn't just her drinks; everything about her was extraordinary.

But he had to face the facts. *She's not meant for you.*

Seth had seen it. His father too. It was time he stopped living in a fantasy world where he got to ride off into the sunset with the girl of his dreams. His life wasn't some grand tale, fantastic enough to be woven into a tapestry children hung on their walls.

Or maybe it was. Only he wasn't the hero. He was the villain.

Before he lost his nerve, he blurted, "I can't help you finish your repairs. I'm really sorry."

"You can't? But why?" Nora's gaze darted across his face before falling to the ground.

Seth barreled forward, his brow creased and his voice thick with confusion. "Hey, what's going on, man? I thought I could count on you?"

Kieran didn't even spare him a glance. Not while Nora stood there, so damn beautiful, even while her heart was breaking.

"Yeah, I thought so too." Nora hugged her arms around her middle. "You promised."

His chest burned, a terrible heat blazing within his ribs. Somehow, he managed to ignore it. To spit the next words out even as they soured his tongue. "My father pulled some strings. I've been offered a job in the capital as an instructor in my old regiment. I leave today."

A single sniffle filled the silence before cutting off harshly. "Congratulations," Nora stated flatly.

And because fate was clearly not on his side as of late, Seth definitely noticed that his precious sister was far more upset than she ought to be in this situation. His head turned on a swivel, alternating between a vicious glare when it fell on him and dawning horror when it landed on Nora.

"No, this is all wrong. You never wanted to teach." Seth dragged a hand through his hair before jerking his arm harshly between them both. "And what the hell is *this*?"

Paige grabbed Seth's arm. "Maybe we should go inside—"

Seth shook off her hold. "Stay out of this. I'm not going anywhere."

Paige's eyes flashed, but she held her tongue.

Seth's icy stare sliced through Kieran's skin and burrowed into his marrow. "One thing. When I never asked you for anything—ever. Why couldn't you just listen? She's my sister! What the hell happened?" By the time the last word rang out, Seth was practically screaming.

The back door slammed open, but Kieran didn't bother to turn. Adding more witnesses to his misery seemed fitting.

He had to say something. He owed Seth that much. Nora too. But every word that flashed through his mind sounded like a lame excuse that would only cause more pain.

Through it all, Nora huddled there, trembling slightly, seemingly too shocked to speak.

Not Seth. With every passing second, Seth *seethed*. His face reddened, hands balling into fists at his side, his chest heaving like he'd just run up the mountain pass.

A tremendous sigh escaped him. "Like I said, I'm really sorry."

He saw the hit coming but made no move to dodge Seth's fist. It would've been simple enough to accomplish. Seth was far stronger than him, but Kieran had always been nimbler.

Crack.

He welcomed the agony that radiated through his cheek. Then the burst of pain that followed as he slammed into the ground. It was far less than he deserved. But even as a groan spilled out of his chest, all the physical pain couldn't compare in the slightest to the agony radiating from within.

Two birds. One dreadful stone foisted on him and set loose to wound the two people he loved most in the entire realm.

An enormous shadow fell over him as he sprawled in the dirt. Seth lunged for him, but Nora's voice cut through the air like a blade wrapped in silk, sharp and cold but filled with so much compassion it stole the air out of his lungs.

"Seth, no! Stop him, Paige. Please!"

A vine tore out of the ground, wrapping around Seth's waist and jerking him away just before his fist connected with flesh for the second blow.

"Let me go, you damn witch!" Seth hissed. "Dirty prick screwed my—"

"No, he didn't." Nora squared off in front of Seth, her arms crossed, red-rimmed eyes flashing with anger—and pain. "It was nothing. Obviously."

The dismissal in her tone stung far more than Seth's strike. Kieran rolled into a seated position, trying to ignore how much his head swam. Was it from the blow? Or just a side effect of his life imploding before his eyes?

Honestly, did it really even matter in the end?

"Like hell it was nothing. Look at you, Nor." Seth's voice cracked. "I'll kill him!"

"No, you won't." Nora straightened her shoulders and spun, pinning him with a glare laced with so much venom he could scarcely stand it. "Kieran's leaving."

"Nora—" He reached out with his good hand. Not sure what for... Maybe his mind was still rattled from the blow. Or perhaps his body hadn't caught up with reality yet. Either way, when her lip curled into a sneer instead of her leaning down to take it, his heart wrenched.

"Go, Kieran. Just *leave*." Nora turned her back on him, and Paige pulled her into her arms.

He stood in a daze, wanting nothing more than to grant her wish. It was the least he could do after ruining everything else.

Seth struggled against the vine holding him back. "Yeah, you better go! Good riddance."

The words slammed into his back, leaving agony in their wake, like he'd been pelted with a thousand stones.

Goddess, what have I done?

It was for the best, wasn't it? Sure, Nora would be upset for a while. And Seth would probably never forgive him. But it was better than him sticking around and watching her dreams get torn away from her.

If she lost one lease, no one would give her another. Especially not when news spread about her newfound powers. It was hard enough being a female business owner, but with all the prejudice surrounding witches, she'd have two strikes against her. Then to add a default into the mix... Nora would never recover.

No. He would play his father's game, ensuring that Nora stayed right where she was. He might have crushed her spirits temporarily by leaving, but he wouldn't be the reason her dreams didn't pan out.

Still, he wouldn't forget the promise he'd made. Even if he wasn't around to witness her and Moira's business thrive, he would keep his word.

So as Kieran trudged back to the house he refused to think of as *home* with his snake of a father present, he took a detour. There was one place he needed to visit before he left Everpass—for good.

I hope one day she'll be happy. Even if it's not with me.

That's All

Nora

P aige wrapped her in a soft embrace while her brother fumed, curses rolling off his tongue in an unending wave. Nora stood there, feeling completely numb.

Did that just really happen?

Where was the man who had so sweetly tucked her into bed a few hours ago? The man who'd stayed up all night tying knots by the dozen—just in case she ever needed an escape. Or how about the passionate one who'd held her like he never wanted to let go while kissing her like he couldn't wait to tear off her clothes?

Was it all a lie? Another fleeting adventure he pretended to enjoy while he waited for his real life to come calling? A bit of fun on the side? And all the while, she was stupidly falling for him.

Goddess, she was such a fool. She'd been worried he'd only want her as some dirty little secret... Well, the joke was on her. He didn't want her *at all*.

Moira and Opal closed in, and suddenly she was wrapped in not one but three sets of arms. In the shelter of all that love, the first tear slid out of the corner of her eye.

"What happened?" someone asked. With the haze surrounding her, she couldn't even say who was speaking.

"Kieran's leaving. Nora's upset. I think they have feelings for each other."

"I'll kill him. Let me go!" That voice, at least, was unmistakable. Seth.

The dam holding back her tears burst in the face of his rage. She'd just cost her brother his best friend. And for what? A few stolen kisses and a broken heart?

"I-I'm a t-terrible s-sister," she wailed.

Gasps surrounded her.

"Don't say that."

"Of course you aren't, dear."

Seth called out again, but his voice had lost its hard edge. "I mean it this time. Let me down. Please."

Shuffling sounded, then more pressure landed on her shoulders. When she chanced a peek up from the cradle of her hands, her brother stared down at her, the biggest spoon of all, his arms so massive he held all four of them in his embrace. "I'm not mad at you. I swear. Everything's gonna be all right. Please don't cry."

Seth could sure get angry, but deep down, he was a big softie. And she was so grateful to have him in her life.

She blinked back her tears. "I'm sorry. I didn't mean to fall to pieces like that." Her chin wobbled. "And I never wanted to tear you and Kieran apart."

"Oh, little sis." Seth's face puddled with sympathy at the same moment he squeezed, like he thought he could pulverize all her pain if he hugged her tightly enough. Unfortunately, he seemed to forget that she wasn't the only one locked in his arms.

"Enough, you big oaf! You're liable to snap Ma like a twig," Paige insisted, her voice pinched.

Seth backed off with a soft, "Sorry," which caused all the women to break away as well.

Opal shot Paige a glare. "I'm not that fragile yet, I'll have you know."

"Relax, Ma. It got him off, didn't it?"

Seth's eyes narrowed, but he didn't rise to the bait. He grabbed Nora's hand and tenderly stroked the back of her wrist. "Tell me what happened. What did Kieran do? Was what you said earlier true? He didn't—"

She squeezed his hand. "We kissed. That's all. But I…"

"You thought he fancied you, hm?" Opal prompted.

"Yeah. But I guess I was wrong."

Seth squeezed back, hard enough to make her wince. "Fuck him. I mean it, Nor. I told him to steer clear of flirting with you, but he just couldn't resist. Damn entitled elves. You're better off without him."

Sure, she'd met her share of stuck-up elves—elegant men and beautiful ladies like Tamora who wouldn't bother giving her the time of day, even while she stood right in front of them. But Kieran wasn't like that. At least, he never used to be.

Had his time in the city changed him? No… If it had, surely he'd have acted differently from the start. But he'd never once treated her like she was beneath him the way Tamora had. Even as he stood there breaking her heart, he didn't make any claims about her lack of station.

He hadn't offered much of an excuse at all. No conversation about the future. No what ifs or maybes. Not a whisper of an invitation to come visit.

Seth was right... If he'd drop her so fast, giving up on the possibility of a relationship growing between them, then he wasn't worth her time. She could go back to concentrating on her business. On making her dreams come true.

She'd lived through Kieran's rejection before. She could do it again. *But why does it hurt so much worse this time?*

She buried the thought down deep and met her brother's eyes. "You're right. I'm done with him. It's over."

Seth grinned. "That's the spirit."

Nora sighed heavily. "I need a drink. Who's with me?"

Seth slung an arm around her shoulders. "To Stellar Spirits."

"Wait... The harvest." She was supposed to be helping...

Paige stepped closer. "We've got this. Go on."

Opal nodded. "Yes, we'll take care of things here. Go have your drink, dear."

"Thank you." At least she could count herself lucky on that score. Kieran might be gone, but he'd brought two wonderful women into her life.

Her mother ducked in their path. "Come back when you close up, love. I don't want you to be alone tonight."

"Don't worry, Ma. I'll keep her company." Seth squeezed her shoulders.

"You don't have to do that." Her refusal sounded lame, even to her own ears.

"Course I do. We're family." Seth steered her into the front yard, and even though her heart still felt like it was shattered into a million shards of ice, her chest warmed a smidge.

She might not have love, but she had a family who treasured her. Friends who truly cared. She'd get through this unscathed.

And yeah, a traitorous voice might have screamed in the back of her mind that Kieran had none of that. The thought should have calmed the rage boiling in her gut that wanted him to suffer for what he'd done. But... it didn't.

Because she couldn't stop wondering if she'd just watched the best chance at love she'd ever had walk away...

WHAT'S BEST

Kieran

Three months later...

He tugged his cloak collar higher, the icy chill stinging his cheeks. You'd hardly know it from looking at the recruits in front of him. Bare arms and foreheads glistened with sweat. Piles of furs and cloaks lay discarded on the field's sidelines, a testament to the grueling exercises he'd forced them to complete.

"That's it for today. Dismissed," he announced.

A chorus of exhausted groans punctuated with a few delighted whoops echoed around him. The young men and women scooped up their cloaks as they hurried to leave. It was late afternoon, just before winter break. Clearly they were all eager to spend time with their family and friends.

With a sigh, he strolled off the field, not bothering to duck into the stately manor that housed his office. The red brick building was empty. All the other instructors had taken it easy that afternoon and left early, right along with their students.

Maybe it was cruel to keep his class late, but it wasn't like he had anywhere else to be...

Deep down, he saw what he was doing—taking out his frustration at the mess his life had become on the recruits with every punishing exercise—and he hated it with every fiber of his being. Yet, he couldn't seem to stop himself.

In the few short months he'd been teaching, Kieran had built a reputation as the hardest bastard to please. He knew the students groaned when they saw his name pop up on their class rotation. That most of them loathed him more than they'd ever admit in his presence.

And when he looked in the mirror, he couldn't help seeing his father's face staring back at him. An intimidating presence who would never be satisfied no matter how hard his recruits tried. Always pushing, needling, to make sure they were the best.

It was like when he'd left Everpass he'd left the old Kieran behind too. All the best parts of himself were gone, tossed off like a mantle that had grown too heavy to bear. There were no acts of kindness. No more playful words between friends.

Hell, he didn't even have any friends. Just a silent, empty villa he sat in every night. Completely alone.

Might as well return to it. He marched down the bustling streets, his expression so menacing that folk parted before him easily. He ignored them all. Especially the few whose gazes drifted to his missing hand, then rose in pity.

He was used to it now. Their stares. The "I'm sorrys" they flung around without really meaning it. With each one, he couldn't stop craving something different. The simple acceptance he'd tossed aside for a reason that didn't seem to matter anymore.

No. It mattered. Nora deserved to keep everything she'd worked so hard for. He couldn't forget that.

Truth was, he couldn't forget her, no matter how hard he tried.

"Hello, darling."

The familiar voice stopped him in his tracks just before he stepped onto his front porch. "Mother?"

Courtney sat on a worn bench rocker, wrapped in furs, gloved hands perched atop a cloth bundle that rested in her lap.

A memory assailed him of the day they'd gotten that rocker. Seth had spotted it on the street and *had* to have it. He'd tried to persuade him against it. It had been one loose screw away from falling apart, set out as rubbish, and far too heavy for them to cart through the streets.

But Seth had swayed him, the brightest grin on his face as he promised to repair it. Kieran just had to help him drag it back. And like always, Seth had been true to his word. Now it was sound, the wood painted in a coat of bright-blue paint that had dulled slightly over the years.

A nostalgic smile tugged at the corner of his mouth as he sat beside his mother. Then he brushed off the past and turned his full attention to his surprise visitor. "What are you doing here?"

"Can't a mother visit her only son?" She patted his leg. "It's been too long."

He nodded to the bundle. "That for me?"

She handed it over easily. "I stopped by the smithy like you asked."

Kieran's chest pinched. "Thank you." He'd asked her to pick up his prosthesis, fully expecting her to send the package by runner once she'd collected it. Hell, he assumed she wouldn't bother going to the smithy at all, just instruct Edgar to do it. "You didn't have to bring it all this way."

"I know. But I wanted to. I've missed you, Kieran."

His throat tightened, clogged with so many things he wanted to say. But all that popped out was, "Are you hungry? There's a place I like just down the road…"

"I'm starving." Courtney beamed, rising to her feet. "Do you want to try that on before we go?"

He shook his head. There'd be time for that later. He didn't want the newness of his prosthesis distracting him while they ate. He was a fiend, slavering over a tiny taste of the thing he craved most. An update from home. Maybe if he was lucky, his mother would slip in a brief mention of *her*.

He opened the door long enough to set the bundle on a side table, then locked up again.

His mother tapped his shoulder and lifted a brow until he cocked an elbow. Then Courtney slipped her dainty hand through the crook of his arm and held on tight for balance.

The move brought another memory flashing. His mother had done the same thing countless times, always in the winter when the paths froze. As a human, she wasn't half as nimble as elves were on the ice. Nine times out of ten, it was his father whom she leaned on. But every time she'd chosen him to be her guide, Kieran had swelled with pride.

Looking back on it now, he couldn't escape the trickle of unease in his gut. He'd always longed for the open, honest declarations of love Moira showered her children with.

What if he'd been ignoring the more subtle signs around him? Yeah, his father was a lost cause, but his mother had come all this way when she didn't need to. She'd *missed* him. That had to mean something... didn't it?

"So what's the best item on the menu where we're headed?" She clung to him, taking small, careful steps. "You know what? Why don't you order for me? It can be a surprise."

"Sure. I can do that."

They walked in silence to the small cafe. Kieran pushed the door open and ushered his mother to his usual table, a corner booth beside the window.

More memories rose. Countless meals shared with his best friend—once they could finally afford to splurge on more than noodles. So much laughter. A sound completely missing from his life now.

The server came and went, taking their order and leaving them in a quiet bubble. He cleared his throat. "How are things back home?"

"Oh, you know how it is. Always another party to attend. Your father's keeping me busy." She chuckled softly.

"No surprise there," he said flatly.

Courtney's lips pinched as she scrutinized him. "I hear your friend Seth has plans to settle down. He's stopped by some of your father's vacant properties. Farms out in the countryside, mostly."

He brightened at that news, a ghost of a smile crossing his face. "That sounds about right." Just as Nora had predicted.

"His sister is doing well, too. I've visited her tavern a time or two."

His heart thudded heavily in his chest. Half from the mere mention of Nora and half with surprise. "You have?"

Courtney nodded primly. "It's very impressive what she's accomplished with that old run-down potion shop. And those drinks of hers... delicious. Now I know why Chef can't stop raving about her weekly visits."

He was saved from having to answer when the server returned with their food. He'd ordered them both chicken pot pie. But the meal he normally savored tasted like flavorless mush on his tongue.

"How have you been, darling?" Courtney asked softly.

"Fine."

"Really?" She tilted her head. "I've heard differently."

His brows shot into his hairline. "You've heard?"

"Did you think your father is the only one with contacts in the capital?" Courtney speared a chunk of chicken with her fork. "I have friends too. And I haven't liked what they've been telling me."

He rocked back in his chair, shocked to his core. His mother kept tabs on him? He wasn't sure if he should be flattered or repulsed. "What did they have to say?"

"That you're not yourself. You don't go out. You just work, work, work." She set down her fork. "If this job isn't what you expected, there's no shame in quitting. Why don't you come back home?"

Kieran scoffed. "Tell that to Tanyth."

His mother reared back like he'd slapped her. "Kieran. That's your father. Have some respect."

He shoved a bite of tasteless pot pie into his mouth.

Courtney leaned forward. "Your father wants what's best for you. That's why he secured you this position. You gave it a shot, but clearly it's not right for you. He'll understand that if you decide to come home."

He swallowed thickly, then gulped his water when the lump lodged in his throat. Did she really not know? "I can't go back. And Father will *not* understand."

"Don't say that. He will. I know he—"

"I wouldn't be here if he hadn't forced me to come. He threatened me. He threatened Nora." His jaw clenched, red-hot lava boiling his veins.

"What?" A gasp spilled out of Courtney's lips as her eyes widened, the show of surprise far too real to be anything but genuine. "No... He wouldn't."

"Yes, he did," Kieran hissed.

Courtney blinked dazedly before her eyes narrowed. "Tell me everything."

So he did. He repeated every word he could recall from the dreadful conversation that changed everything, which ended up being nearly verbatim, since that night was permanently seared into his brain. Through it all, his mother sat and listened with no outward sign of emotion until he wrapped up with his father's parting words.

"Can you believe he actually thought I'd thank him one day?" Kieran sneered. "What a joke."

Her eyes watered. "Oh, darling. I think I know why he did this stupid, idiotic thing."

Shock speared him. Was she actually taking his side? "Care to enlighten me?"

She dabbed her lashes with a napkin. "It doesn't make it right. And mind you, this is just a theory, but believe me, once I go home, I will get the truth out of him. Mark my words."

Her fierce declaration coaxed out another tiny grin. "Go on."

"Your father was engaged to an elf before we met. After we fell in love, many things changed for him. I think that's what he meant when he warned you about choosing the less-traveled path." She sighed. "He was trying to save you from enduring what he did when he chose to love me."

"I don't understand..."

"His father cut him off. He lost his first job, and the elvish community he'd grown up in here in Fairvale shunned him. We had to start over in Everpass." She reached across the table, grabbing his hand. "I should've told you this long ago, but it still hurts. He gave up so much for me."

He squeezed her hand, eliciting a sniffle.

"I know we've always encouraged you to settle down with an elf. You see... we found out just after you were born that your grandfather wrote you into his will. But he had a requirement before you inherited it. It was his dying wish. His entire estate has been held in a trust until the day you wed. Either it all goes to you or his favorite charity."

He pulled his hand back. "Are you serious?"

"We never wanted to pressure you, but I suppose the constant suggestions became a bit much in the end. It seemed harmless enough when you'd never shown a serious interest in anyone to keep nudging you in that direction. But now..." She shook her head sadly. "I swear, I didn't know he'd take it this far. More than anything, we both just want you to be happy."

Kieran rubbed his temples. "I wish you'd told me. I don't give a damn about the money." He had more than enough as it was. His father did, too.

"I suspected as much. For what it's worth, the charity is wonderful. I've donated to it myself in the past." She sighed. "Honestly, I don't think it was about the money. Not to Tanyth. He's always wanted what's best for you. To give you the life you deserve."

His brows pinched together. "But why? Why do I always have to be the best? Why isn't it enough to just be me?"

She said they hadn't wanted to pressure him, and maybe that was true regarding the inheritance, but he'd lived under constant pressure to be *the best* his whole life. And frankly, he was sick of it.

At least now, his father's actions made a bit more sense. He'd been chasing perfection, wanting to give him the future he thought he deserved. The one that'd been stolen from him when his grandfather cut ties.

Still, that didn't make it right. And he wasn't ready to forgive his father for what he'd done. He might not ever be. Especially after he'd dragged Nora into this mess.

"Oh, darling. I-I didn't realize you felt that way." Her lip wobbled, voice thick. "You *are* enough just the way you are. I'm so sorry we made you feel like you weren't."

"It's all right. Please don't cry." Goddess, he could hardly believe his mother was here right now, on the verge of tears, for *him*. If nothing else came out of this, at least he finally knew that she cared. The evidence was right there in front of his eyes.

She swiped at her cheeks harshly. "No. It's not all right. Far from it, in fact." She straightened in her chair, the spark he'd noted earlier returning with a vengeance. "But I promise you, it will be. I'll speak with your father. The threats he made to Nora were unconscionable, and I'll make sure that he knows it." She snagged his hand again, squeezing fiercely. "Nothing is going to happen to her tavern. I guarantee it."

"You'd do that for me?"

"Of course I would, sweetheart. I'd do anything for you." A watery giggle spilled out of her lips. "Besides, I wasn't kidding about being fond of her drinks. And I've been hearing good things about their book club."

Oh no. "Mother... You're joking. Right?"

She giggled again, and Kieran choked down a groan.

Then her expression flattened, the humor draining from her in an instant. "Listen, darling. I know that was a lot to take in. But please, just know that we only want what's bes—" She shook her head. "No. Screw the best. Find your *happiness*, Kieran."

Her words rang in his ears long after they paid the bill and she set off. It was good advice. But would he ever know true happiness again?

Without the threat hanging over Nora's lease, nothing was stopping him from going back. He could beg Nora for forgiveness. Find some way to make amends.

Still, so much time had passed… What if she'd moved on? If her bar was doing so well, did that mean she had time to date? What if she'd already found someone else? Someone better than him. Someone whole.

Warring thoughts plagued him. He had half a mind to march into Stellar Spirits that instant. But every time he rose to fetch his boots, he sank right back down.

He'd only end up hurting her again. Just look at their history. He'd done it at the masquerade. Then again, in her mother's backyard. He'd left her standing there with so much pain swimming in her eyes.

He had the right of it when he left. Nora was better off without him.

She's not meant for me. She never will be.

Just Like That

Nora

"That's perfect, Tini." Nora grinned, watching as her new barmaid poured a freshly shaken cocktail into a martini glass. "Don't forget the garnish."

"This one gets a lime, right?" Her hand hovered over the garnish tray as she waited for Nora's confirmation, her bright-blue dress contrasting nicely with the lime slices.

"Sure does. You're doing a great job."

A blinding smile lit Tini's face, and the ice around Nora's heart momentarily thawed.

The young woman had come a long way since she'd hired her just over two weeks ago. Nora still hadn't worked out exactly what had made her so sad she'd bawled her eyes out, but Tini smiled a lot more now. Especially after mastering a tricky recipe.

She could hardly believe she had the funds to hire help at all, after the disastrous run of bad luck she'd endured. But thankfully, the harvest had provided more than enough for her to brew replacements to almost all her liquors and cordials.

With her expanded menu, she'd attracted more clientele. Word about Stellar Spirits had somehow reached the neighboring town that housed Maudwin University, which had helped immensely; she suspected a certain professor might have something to do with that, though she hadn't thought to ask when she wrote to him, declining his job offer. The barstools were full most evenings. And on the weekends, the place was so packed she could scarcely weave between bodies to collect empties.

She'd welcomed the long days and hard work over the last few months. Anything to keep her mind off a certain someone who lingered there, no matter how often she tried to force him out.

Some days, her heart ached, but she truly wished him the best. She hoped his job was fulfilling. That he'd found new friends and all the happiness in the capital that he couldn't seem to discover in Everpass.

Others, she cursed his name while images bombarded her—Kieran whirling a pretty young lady around the dance floor. Him whispering in her ear that they could have lots of fun off their feet. Then dragging her into a shadowed alcove and kissing her senseless.

Nora shoved thoughts of Kieran aside yet again. He'd made his choice, and it didn't include her.

"Ah hem…" The voice in her mind only elicited a minor flinch, there and gone in an instant. *"They'll be closing soon. Stop dawdling."*

"Thanks for the reminder." She shot a glance at her shelves. Roo lounged in a nest built out of an old milk crate and blankets. It was

still a little strange, having another voice pop into her head at random, but it hadn't been long before she'd begun thinking of the mouse as a friend.

She'd gotten some odd looks at first when customers spotted the nest wedged in between the bottles; Roo prized the high vantage, where she could keep an eye on everything. But before long, the regulars had accepted her. Now, they said "hi" and "bye" each visit, and often declared she was "the cutest thing ever," which made Roo's little ears twitch and her chin lift.

"Tini, can you handle things by yourself for a few?"

Panic flashed in her expressive blue eyes. "Alone? Already?"

"Yes, I trust you." It was early, with only a few patrons who'd already been served their meals. So far, Nora had always been close by while Tini worked her shift, but this would be the perfect time for a solo test run. And with Roo there, she'd be alerted at once if Tini got swamped and needed her help. Nora shrugged her coat on atop her favorite black dress. "Relax, Tini. You're ready. Besides, I'm just popping to the bank and back. I won't be gone long."

"Oh. Okay. See you soon."

A pang of anxiety hit her as she strolled through the door. Her fingers itched to rip it open and duck back inside. To go back to running the show like she always had.

But then the first blast of frigid afternoon air chilled her lungs. She breathed deep, loving that she could actually enjoy it for once without worrying about closing up, disappointing her regulars, and losing out on sales.

This was what she'd been dreaming about for so long. Success. And her next step would ensure that she'd never be in the position where it might be ripped away from her ever again.

The coin purse was heavy in her hands as she entered the bank. The place smelled dimly of metal and dust and was so quiet she couldn't miss the thundering beat of her pulse. She smiled at the teller, an elf in a pink dress with blonde curls framing her pale heart-shaped face. The badge on her chest dubbed her Kayla.

She placed the bag on the counter with a loud clunk. "I'd like to open a new account."

"Name, please," Kayla replied in a monotone, bored and just polite enough, while not entirely friendly.

"Nora Rowen." She leaned on the counter as Kayla dug through a bank of file cabinets behind her.

Kayla paused, a file in her hands. "Confirm your birthdate and address for me."

Nora rattled off the answers, then said, "I need a new account, please. I closed my last account six months ago."

"Hm. You sure about that?" Kayla brought the file back. "Our records say otherwise."

Nora's eyes widened. "They do?"

"Yep. Do you still want a second account?" She grabbed the purse, dumping out the contents. "Or should I add this to your existing account?"

Weird. She must've left a few coins in it without realizing. "What's the balance on the existing account?"

Kayla told her the total, and Nora nearly passed out. "What? That can't be right..." It was more than her old nest egg—a lot more.

"Oh, it is." Kayla lifted a brow, her gaze darting across the file. "We don't make mistakes. So... Second account, or no?"

"Kayla," a man yelled from somewhere in the back, "where are the figures I asked you to drop on my desk?"

Cringing, Kayla lowered her voice. "Excuse me for a moment." She darted into the back, leaving Nora's coins half-stacked into piles on the counter.

She had to know... Nora grabbed the file, flipping it around. Then she gasped. "Kieran." His signature sat there, plain as day, on a transfer request.

Footsteps echoed, and she flipped the file back just as Kayla burst into the room. "Sorry about that." The coins clattered as she returned to stacking. "So should I open that new account? There's not much sense having two. There's a startup fee."

"Yes." Nora blinked, utterly confused. "No." She sucked in a deep breath. "Sorry. I guess... just add it to the existing one."

"Okay..." Kayla frowned, staring at Nora like she was half-mad. "Are you sure?"

"Yes, I'm sure." She'd figure out what to do about the funds Kieran had deposited into her account after she left and shook off her shock.

Why did he do it? Was he assuaging his guilt for bailing on the repairs? He hadn't reached out once since he'd left. Not a single letter or visit. And now this.

She needed to understand why. But she couldn't fathom the thought of approaching him after his rejection.

There was only one person she could think of besides Kieran who might have the answer...

The next day, she strolled into Ma's back garden while tugging a knee length, navy-blue cloak tightly closed around her. A light layer of frost decorated the empty fields, slowly dissipating as the morning sun rose. "Hey, big bro."

Seth was sprawled on a bench beside the old card table, his breath escaping in puffs of mist as he rocked. "Little sis." He wore clothes far too thin for the weather, an off-white long-sleeved tunic and black trousers, though she wasn't surprised. Seth had always run hot, which likely explained why he tore off his shirt every chance he got.

Nora did a double take. "Nice rocker. You just buy it?"

"Nope." He slid over, making room. She plopped down beside him. "I've had this baby for a few years." His smile faded around the edges, his eyes going unfocused, like his thoughts were suddenly far away.

She squeezed his knee. "You all right?"

"Yeah. Why wouldn't I be?" He brightened, but just like each time she'd seen him in the last few months—which was nearly every day, since he'd insisted on helping at Stellar Spirits—something was off.

Guess that's what happens when you lose your best friend...

There was no mistaking Seth missed him. How could he not? They'd spent a decade as roommates, living and working side by side. Then one day, it just stopped.

All thanks to her.

But she couldn't allow guilt to drown her. She'd come here for a reason. "Hey, Seth?"

"Hm?" He shifted to face her. "You need me to come in early today?"

"No. I wanted to ask you something..." She swallowed. "Do you have any idea why Kieran would transfer an insane amount of coin into my bank account?"

Seth drew back, eyes narrowing. "Are you joking?"

She shook her head. "Found out yesterday when I went in to open a new account."

He scrubbed a hand down his face. "How much are we talking about?"

She leaned over and whispered the total in his ear.

"Goddess's sake, Nor!" He blanched. "You sure it was just a kiss?"

"Hey!" She punched his arm—hard, her face burning. "I don't like what you're implying."

"All right. I believe you." He lifted his hands in surrender before rubbing the spot where she'd hit him. "I have no clue why he'd do that. It's kind of strange, if you ask me. Kieran's always been stingy with his coin."

"Really?" She hadn't gotten that impression. He'd only been there two days before offering to bail her out—not that she'd taken him up on his offer. And he'd been so generous with Oliver.

"Yep. He's never been one for lavish gifts. And if a lady looked like that was all she was after, he'd lose interest real fast."

Nora's heart twinged.

"Sorry, Sis." He winced. "Too soon?"

"It's fine."

"No, I shouldn't be jabbering about his conquests." He scooped up her hand, swallowing her entire glove in one of his massive fists. "I hate that he broke your heart."

"You're sweet, Seth. But really, I'm okay." She plastered on a wobbly smile. "You know, I don't mind if you two go back to being friends." It would kill her to see him, for a while at least. But she'd get over it. Her brother didn't deserve to lose someone so important over a silly crush that didn't work out in the end.

Seth frowned. "I mind, Nor. He broke my trust. He wasn't supposed to go after you."

She almost punched him again. "And who gave you the right to choose the men who court me?"

"It wasn't like that." He dropped her hand. "I was just looking out for you."

"I appreciate the thought. But seriously, cut it out. I'm a grown woman. You don't need to scare off all my suitors like I'm some fresh-faced teen who'll throw herself at the first pretty boy who bats his lashes in her direction."

"Fair enough." He chuckled. Silence fell between them, broken by the rhythmic creak of the rocker. "Can I ask you something?"

"Sure."

"The two of you... Was it just a bit of fun... or was it serious?"

She sighed. "It was serious for me. For him? Who knows?"

"I never saw Kieran act serious about anyone." Seth pursed his lips. "Then again, he sure never sent a fortune to any girl in the capital."

Nora's stomach wobbled. What did it all mean? Was she different from all the other girls he pursued, then dropped?

No. She couldn't be. If he'd cared for her at all, he would've stayed. He wouldn't have broken his promise to help her, jumped to take the first job thrown in his lap, and left without a backward glance.

"You know what doesn't make sense *at all*?"

She glanced at her brother. "What?"

"The instructor job. Kieran hated every second he spent at headquarters. He lived for going out in the field. I can't understand why he'd take that position."

"Hm. That is strange." Kieran had always craved adventure. It seemed out of character for him to accept a position that would force him to do the same thing day in and day out.

"Now he's giving you money. And sending me furniture."

Her nose wrinkled. "Huh?"

Seth knocked on the back of the bench. "This came from his villa. He had it delivered last week with no note or explanation." He scratched his stubbled chin. "I don't know… Just seems bizarre."

Hope swelled in her chest. Maybe Kieran hadn't completely vanished from their lives after all…

"Eh. What do I know?" He stood, staring at the rocker as it swayed. "He was probably just sick of having something I plucked off the street on his porch."

And just like that, the hope withered to dust.

She needed to stop looking for something that wasn't there. Kieran was done with her. That was all there was to it.

Hours later, Nora was mindlessly wiping the spotless bar when a blast of frigid air threw open the door—with no customers. After shivering for far too long, she jerked her head at Seth, silently urging him to close it.

Just as he lurched up from the floor, abandoning his current project—sound-proofing the bathroom—the scritch scratch of clawed feet rang out.

Paige hurried in behind Bok. "Sorry about that. A gust of wind blew Bok halfway down the street! Looks like a storm is brewing." She tugged the door closed and unwound a long, knitted scarf from her neck.

Seth stiffened, then turned, heading back to the bathroom.

"Paige. I'm glad you're here." In the last few months, Paige had stayed true to her word, helping Nora learn to control her magic. She hardly had to rely on her necklace anymore, though she still kept it close by just in case. But today, she wasn't excited about testing her skills. Nora ducked under the bar and lifted a heavy coin purse in her hands. "I have the rest of the coin we owe you."

Paige grinned, pocketing the purse before shucking off her cloak, revealing a teal long-sleeved dress that made the golden highlights in her hair more prominent. "Thanks. I don't have the collateral on me. Do you mind if I bring it on my next visit?"

"Huh?" Nora's nose wrinkled. "I didn't give you any collateral."

"I know, but Kieran did." Paige slid onto a stool.

Seth popped out of the bathroom. "He did?"

"Yeah. He gave us a bunch of jewelry when he and Ali visited the farm. We wouldn't have taken the risk with our seeds otherwise." Paige lifted a brow. "No one told you?"

Nora shook her head.

"Wait... You didn't know about this?" Seth asked.

"Ma signed the contract, remember?" Her heart pounded. "Guess I should've read the fine print."

Paige rested an elbow on the bar. "You haven't reconnected since he left?"

"No." Nora pressed a hand to her chest. She thought she'd buried the last of her feelings, but now...

"Oh." Paige frowned. "Suppose I can hire a runner to send his jewelry to Fairvale."

Seth spoke up. "Or you could bring it to him, Nor."

Nora froze. "What?"

He rounded the bar, taking her shoulders in a soft hold. "You still care about him, don't you?"

Nora's eyes burned. She blinked hard, forcing the tears to subside. "Of course I do, but he made it perfectly clear where he wants to be."

"Look at this place, Nor. Look at what you've created." Seth rubbed her arms softly. "It's amazing."

She glanced at her tavern, her heart warming. She'd built it from the ground up, not quitting even when it seemed crazy. Even when she was out of funds and everything was burning down around her—figuratively *and* literally.

"You've never had a problem going after what you want with your business. Why are you so afraid to do the same when it comes to love?" His voice softened. "Did I... Is it because of me?" Her pulse sped, but before she opened her mouth to refute him, Seth barreled on. "Earlier, you said Kieran and I should be friends again. Well, now it's my turn. Don't throw away someone you truly care about to spare my feelings."

"No. That's not it at all." Sure, that had been one thing holding her back in the beginning. But she hadn't been worried for ages about what Seth would think. "Kieran doesn't want me. I won't waltz into Fairvale and hand him my heart when I know he'll just toss it aside."

"Are you sure about that? I've known Kieran a long time, and I can honestly say he's never done anything like this. And not just once, Nor. That has to mean something, don't you think?"

"Sure, he helped Nora. But that doesn't excuse what he did." Paige's eyes narrowed. "You ask me, he should be the one fighting to win her back, not the other way around."

Seth glared across the bar. "Did we ask for your opinion?"

Nora peeled out of Seth's hold. "No. She's right. Kieran knows where to find me. I'm not going anywhere." She grabbed the rag and went back to wiping, her spine stiffening.

Should she set her pride aside and make the trek to Fairvale? Bringing the jewelry would be the perfect excuse. She could demand to know why he left. Why he'd take a job that didn't suit him. Why he kept inserting himself into her life with his coin but refused to stick around and actually be there for her.

No. Paige had it right. She'd done nothing wrong.

If Kieran wanted her, he had to prove it. And the next time they met, she wouldn't be the one down on her knees.

Clearing the Funk

Kieran

Winter break had come and gone. Kieran had watched it pass him by, doing nothing to celebrate. Tomorrow classes were scheduled to resume, and he'd be back to the grind, heading into work each day. He should be there now, getting his supplies sorted and his course planned, yet he'd stayed put, delaying the task until it became unavoidable.

At least the routine would give him something to do other than sit alone with his thoughts, though he couldn't say he was excited about it. He wasn't cut out to be a teacher. Maybe he should just leave. Head in and quit, then disappear. Only he knew if he left, there was only one place his feet would yearn to take him...

A knock on the door interrupted his miserable thoughts. He certainly wasn't expecting anyone. "It's open," he yelled from the sofa when he couldn't summon the energy to get up.

Footsteps thumped down the hall. "Can't say I like what you've done with the place." Seth stopped in the middle of the room, his upper lip curled as he scanned the mess.

The normally neat blue-and-green sitting room was far different from when Seth saw it last. Paper to-go containers littered the floor. Curdled milk and week-old juice lingered in nearly every mug he owned. Piles of laundry were stacked haphazardly along the walls—only some of which were clean.

Kieran had grown accustomed to the stench that accompanied it all, but Seth clearly wasn't enjoying it. He coughed into his fist, shoving a box aside with his boot as he inched further inside.

"You come to play maid?" Kieran drawled.

"Nope." Seth shoved a hand into his cloak pocket. "Here."

"Oof." Kieran's stomach jolted as something heavy jabbed him in the gut. He picked up the pouch, using his hook to jerk open the drawstring. Metal and gems stared up at him from within. "What's this?"

"Your collateral."

"Oh." A tiny spark of warmth flashed in his chest. "Nora got it back already? That was fast."

"Yep." Seth grabbed an armchair, tilting it forward and spilling the mess perched on it to the floor. He dropped it with a thump, hung his cloak on the back, then sat down heavily on it. "We alone?" He peered over Kieran's shoulder, a brow lifted and his jaw clenched, like he expected some scantily clad woman to traipse out of the bedroom.

"Does it look like I'm up for entertaining?"

Seth snorted. "Point taken."

What was Seth doing here? Kieran's pulse kicked up, rattling in his chest like it couldn't quite recall how to beat fast but wanted to attempt the feat anyway. He lifted the pouch. "Well, thanks for this." He dumped it on the floor, not caring in the slightest where it landed.

The dull drumming of Seth's fingertips against the arm of his chair reverberated through the room. "So that's it? I come to see you after months, and that's all you have to say to me?"

"What do you want me to say?"

"How about an apology? You promised me you wouldn't treat my sister like some meaningless fling."

Kieran chuckled humorlessly. "Nora has never been meaningless to me."

"Really? Because that's not what she thinks."

Kieran reared back, his head thumping onto the top of the sofa. That was the last thing he wanted her to think. How could she not realize that she meant *everything* to him?

Seth kicked a filthy mug, setting it spinning just like the acid in his gut. "I mean, why wouldn't she when you'd rather wallow in your own filth and take a job you can't stand than stick around and help her?"

Yet, even without his help, she'd managed to get back on her feet. Seth wouldn't be returning his collateral otherwise. Nora would find someone new. Someone who'd never made her feel like she was nothing to them.

"She's better off without me," he stated flatly.

Seth leaned forward, balancing his elbows on his knees. "I wish that were true."

"What?" His head jerked up, his gaze connecting with Seth's.

"Truth is, she's fine. Better than fine, really. Her business is taking off. She's bounced back from all the bad luck… But she's not the same. And it's your fault."

Kieran forced a tight smile. "You gonna hit me again?"

Seth growled, "No, you idiot. I'm trying to talk some sense into you." He shook his head, letting his gaze travel across the mess. "What are you doing here, Kieran? This isn't you. That damn job isn't you either."

"It doesn't matter."

"Yes, it does. Tell me. Please, brother."

He could handle Seth's anger. He'd even welcome the pain if he decided to finish what he started in his mother's garden. But his kindness? Having his friend back—the same one who'd always listened when they were kids without a single word of judgment—that was more than he could stand.

A lone tear rolled down his cheek. "I had to come here. My father—" He rubbed his face with his sleeve.

"I'm not going anywhere. Take your time." Seth leaned back, his face filled with compassion that Kieran didn't deserve. But he wasn't going to waste it.

The story spilled out of him in a rush. He started with the masquerade ball and that stolen kiss. Then he jumped ahead to when they'd returned to Everpass and he'd fallen for Nora more with each passing day. He told him about the promise he made to help her no matter what. How he'd been planning to tell Moira he didn't want her potion any longer and then come clean to Seth about everything. Until his father dropped his ultimatum and he had no choice but to leave.

Seth sat silently through it all, his face an unreadable mask. "Okay... so let me get this straight. You've been secretly into my sister for a decade?"

"Pretty much."

"And your dad is a total prick."

"Can't argue with that."

Seth's lips twisted. "But your mom promised to set things straight."

He nodded. "She did."

"And that was after you deposited the coin." Seth's brow furrowed. "Why exactly did you do that?"

Kieran sighed. "If either of them got in hot water with their lenders, the bank is the first place they'd go looking. I figured setting them up with some funds was the least I could do."

"Wait... them?"

"Nora and Moira."

Seth gaped. "You transferred money into Ma's account, too?"

"Yeah."

A startled laugh spilled out of his chest. "You're serious?"

Kieran leaned back. "Yep."

"Hell..." Seth's eyes turned glossy. "Now I'm sorry I punched you."

"Don't be. I deserved it."

"I love you, man, but you're about to get hit again."

Kieran turned his cheek. "Be my guest."

"Why do you do this to yourself? Something goes wrong, and you just... accept it, like it was bound to happen." Seth crossed his arms. "You did it when you lost your hand, and now you're doing it again with Nora."

He wasn't wrong... "I honestly don't know."

"Your father was hard on you growing up. I get that. But you can't keep listening to his voice in your head telling you that you aren't enough. You're a good man, Kieran."

His heart warmed, and yet... "Not good enough for Nora, though, right?"

"No, that's not right." Seth dragged a hand down his face. "Nora already chewed me out for butting in on her business. And I promised I'd stop."

Kieran glanced up. "Bet that stung."

"It did… but I can see her point. And hell, man. You're already like a brother to me. Might as well make it official."

"You mean that?"

"Course I do." Seth thumped his fist into his palm. "But you know what's coming if you hurt her."

Kieran shot him a lopsided grin as an echo of pain reverberated in his jaw. "Yeah, I hear you." But then his smile slipped.

He had Seth's blessing. And it seemed like they were back on track to picking up their friendship where they'd left off. But he wasn't sure if Nora would be so understanding.

Seth stood, then clamped a hand on his shoulder. "You deserve to be happy, brother. And so does Nora. So pull your head out of your ass and go fix this." His gaze caught on Kieran's prosthesis. "I don't know if she told you, but Nora's the reason Ma's tonics worked. Maybe she can heal you."

"She told me. But I don't care about that any longer." He lifted the hook, which had been the one source of brightness in his current funk. It fit perfectly, thanks to Davos's expert craftsmanship, and it hadn't taken him long to adjust to using it, though he'd been careful not to wear it too long to avoid soreness.

Even if that weren't the case, he had no plans to beg Nora to heal him. With all the time that had passed, his injury was likely impossible to heal. And more importantly, he didn't want her assuming that was why he'd come back for her, because that couldn't be further from the truth. Losing her had left a far greater mark on him than losing his hand. If he could just find some way to convince her to give him another chance, he'd be the happiest man in the realm, missing hand and all.

"All right, then." Seth grinned. "What are you waiting for?"

Kieran lurched up from the couch, sending crumbs flying. "You're right! I'm—"

"Whoa, on second thought, better wash up first." Seth's face pinched as he took in the rumpled clothes Kieran hadn't bothered to change out of in days. "Nora might be into you, but she's not desperate."

The first heartfelt smile he'd worn in months flashed on Kieran's face. "Thanks, brother. I don't know what I'd do without you."

"Yeah, I know... You can thank me by removing your stench from my nostrils."

Escaping the Storm

Kieran

The sun had barely risen the next morning when Kieran left for Everpass. He'd dropped off his resignation letter at headquarters the night before—after taking the bath he so desperately needed—so there was nothing to slow him.

Seth had stayed behind, volunteering to clean up the villa like the amazing friend he was. Kieran wasn't sure yet what he'd do with his old place. Sell it, perhaps. Or maybe he'd hang on to it. It would be nice to have somewhere to stay when he swept Nora away to the capital for dinner and dancing.

Now that he'd given himself permission to go after his happiness, he was determined to make that dream a reality. Nora would surely take some convincing, but he wasn't afraid to put in the work. No matter what, he'd make her see that they belonged together. Not just for now, but always.

By midmorning, he'd trekked through the first of three tunnels on his route. The Savurios Mountains stretched between Fairvale and Everpass. The white-capped peaks glistened overhead, silent witnesses to his journey on the deserted pass.

In days of old, he'd have never attempted this trek in winter. Scaling the mountains turned the trip into a grueling week-long hike. Luckily, after the last great war, the tunnels had been dug. Dozens of witches had worked in tandem with trolls to blast through even the toughest rock. Now the hike only lasted a few hours.

Of course, the tunnels weren't his favorite place to be. His pulse pounded with each step, that old irrational fear of dark underground places plaguing him. Lamps hung on the walls at even intervals, yet the light magic couldn't erase the shadows completely.

Normally, Seth made the trip easier. He'd crack jokes, easing Kieran's anxiety. Today, he only had himself to rely on. He locked Nora's face in his mind. It would all be worth it as soon as he saw her.

Would he arrive before Stellar Spirits opened? He hastened his steps, hopeful that he'd manage it. But as Kieran emerged from the second tunnel, his heart sank. Gray clouds dominated the sky ahead, no doubt full of snow—or worse, sleet.

"Damn winter weather," he muttered. The wind picked up, and he tugged his cloak more firmly around his neck. At least he hadn't neglected to dress appropriately for the weather. His cloak was waterproof. His boots too. No matter what the skies rained down on him, he'd suffer through it to get to her.

Would she listen when he tried to explain? Seth hadn't taken much convincing once he'd shared his side of things, but Nora had more reason to hold a grudge. He'd betrayed her trust. He'd abandoned her without a single word of explanation. She'd be well within her rights to refuse to see him altogether.

Shadowy thoughts pressed down on him as the skies continued to darken. And as he approached the halfway point between the next tunnel and the last, the first drop of ice fell from the sky. The wind whipped between the mountains, increasing in ferocity with each step he took toward the storm.

"Perfect. Just perfect." He trudged forward, refusing to let it stop him. Even so, he suspected he was in for a long, miserable march. But then, like a ray of sunshine cutting through the gloom, the most beautiful sight appeared before him. "Nora?"

She'd just rounded a corner, her long brown hair wrapped in a soaked scarf. Her head jerked up, and she froze as the sound of his voice reached her. Well, she attempted to freeze. Her body didn't appear inclined to listen. Shivers wracked her frame, which was no surprise, seeing as she'd come from the direction of the storm, which was spitting sleet in a diagonal sheet.

He raced forward, his heart in his throat, but his need to warm her shoved all his fears down like they'd never existed. "What are you doing out here, in *that*?" Her cloak was long and blue, and completely soaked, clearly not waterproof like his own. He shucked his cloak off hastily, wrapping it around her shoulders.

She scowled. "Are you crazy? You'll freeze."

"I'll be fine." He dragged the fabric closed, fastening the buttons. Cold seeped into his bones, the thick sweater that remained doing little to ward off the icy wind and freezing rain. Then he grabbed her elbow, carting her back around the bend. "Come on. We need to make it to the next tunnel and take shelter."

Nora dug in her heels. "Kieran, stop. I'm going to Fairvale."

He lifted a brow. "Fine." They were halfway between tunnels. They could shelter in the one he'd left just as easily as the one that lay ahead. He turned back, blinking the sleet out of his eyes as the first shiver assaulted him.

"Wait." Nora squinted into the storm. "I know somewhere closer." Her wet glove slapped against his leather one. "Come on." She dragged him off the path, into the trees.

"Where are we going?" he yelled. The storm made it difficult to hear her shouted reply.

"It's close. Trust me."

Howling wind dogged their steps, laced with needles of ice. Kieran's sweater grew heavy, the trees' naked branches providing little protection from the onslaught. He'd never ventured off the main route before. Frankly, he wasn't sure what good it would do them. As far as he knew, no one lived up here. At least, not since the tunnels were built.

Nora slowed, her trembling lower lip caught between her teeth. Was she lost? If she hadn't asked him to trust her, he would've tugged her back and demanded they change course.

But then her face brightened. "Here!" She hurried forward, then paused, dragging her boot across a flat rock set into the damp soil, dislodging the pine needles and old leaves that had partially hidden it.

She only lingered there for a second before hurrying forward and repeating the action. "We're on the right track," she yelled. "C'mon."

They followed the overgrown stepping stones on a meandering path through the trees. He wanted to ask how she'd found them, who had built them, and about a dozen more questions, but with the storm whipping around them, he left the thoughts unsaid. There'd be time for that once they found shelter.

Luckily, the path didn't stretch far. Soon, the trees thinned and the stones stopped before the sheer side of a gigantic mountain. But unlike the rest of the mountains on his route, this one housed an enormous wooden door.

Nora headed straight for it. She grabbed the knob and tugged, but the door didn't budge.

"Need some help?" he yelled over her shoulder.

He expected her to put up a fuss, like when he'd offered to force open her windows, but she merely moved aside, her shoulders slumping. He took a turn with the knob, and after considerable effort, the old door creaked open. Dark stairs lurked behind it, sloping down into the earth.

"Let's go." Nora stepped forward eagerly.

"Wait." His boots were rooted in place. "What's down there?"

She spun toward him, her face softening as she searched his expression. "Nothing to fear. I promise. Trust me." She stuck out her hand expectantly.

He wanted to take it, but with the darkness staring back at him, he couldn't force himself to move. Prickles spread up his arms and legs, his chest tightening and breath speeding beyond his control.

A cold wet cloth landed on his face so unexpectedly it forced his gaze away from the black hole and to Nora's warm golden-brown eyes. She cradled his cheeks with her gloves. "Kieran, it's safe. I swear." She trembled, evidently beyond cold, even with his cloak. But she didn't take another step within their shelter, just stood there, waiting for him to get a handle on his fear long enough to follow her.

"O-okay." He reached for her, intending to stick his hand inside his cloak pocket. "We need fire." He always kept matches with him when traveling, though he'd surely have a hard time finding dry kindling...

"No need." Nora's gloves slid off his face, and she grabbed his hand. "Come on."

He nearly dug in his heels again, but as Nora turned back, she mumbled something under her breath and lifted a hand. A bright light formed in the shape of a globe, hovering in the palm of her hand, instantly chasing away the worst of the shadows.

"Nora, that's amazing!"

She managed a grin, even with her teeth chattering. "Let's get inside."

With the light magic illuminating the stairs, his feet finally became unglued. The first couple steps were the hardest, but by the third, the tightness in his chest loosened. Until Nora peeked over her shoulder and said, "Shut the door."

And enclose them in the dark?

"It's freezing out there."

Of course it was. And Nora was clearly not even close to being warm. They had to get inside and start a fire.

He dragged the door closed. The wind cut off, warming the space instantly, though not enough to stop their shivers.

"Thanks. Come on." Nora hastened her descent, and he hurried after her and the light.

At least now he could finally talk without shouting. "What is this place?"

"An old relic from before the tunnels were built. Used to be an inn run by a family of trolls."

"Ah, I see." Trolls were well known for preferring their homes underground. "How did you know about it?"

"Seth brought me here to escape a rainstorm once, on our way back from Fairvale." The stairwell ended, letting out into a short hall that led to another gigantic door. "Not sure how he discovered it, but I'm glad for it now."

She strode to the door and pushed it open easily. They emerged into a massive hall that he suspected was once the inn's great room. Cobwebs and dust cluttered the space, the lone orb of light barely denting the gloom.

Kieran's breathing sped as his gaze lingered over the dark corners.

"Oh, good." Nora approached an old, dust-covered lamp hanging on the wall. "I'm glad they left these." She lifted the ball of light beside the glass. Soft humming echoed in the vast room, and the lamp began to glow.

"Wow. How did you learn how to do that?"

"Paige taught me." She strode to a second lamp and repeated her actions. "It was one of the first magics I tried to master. It's lucky I have a knack for it." She skipped the third lamp, her boots crunching in broken glass that lay below the shattered globe.

"Why is that?"

She paused at the next lamp and shot him a small smile. "So I could pay back Ali for all her help, of course."

With each lamp she lit, a little more of his anxiety eased. By the time she'd circled the room, the chamber was awash with a soft glow that still left the abandoned inn feeling dreary, but blessedly chased away most of the shadows.

Unfortunately, the lamps were one of the only things the previous owners left behind. Where tables and chairs had surely once sat, only empty floor remained. A long bar rested along one wall, with no stools in front of it, which appeared to have been carved out of the same stone that comprised the floor and walls.

His heart lifted as his gaze trailed to the far corner. "Don't suppose you have a knack for fire magic, too?" An enormous hearth still stood, along with a small stack of logs that he suspected some other traveler in a similar predicament was kind enough to leave behind.

"'Friad not."

At least he could make himself useful there. "I'll take care of it. You should get out of those wet clothes." He walked toward Nora, needing his matches.

She backed up until she hit the wall. "Where do you think you're going?" Her breath hitched, eyes widening.

He stopped in front of her, leaving a pace between them. "You have my matches. They're in the right pocket of my cloak."

"Oh." She chuckled nervously before pulling them out. "Here."

As her icy fingers slid across his, he frowned. "I'm not kidding about the clothes. You'll never warm up if you stay in them."

Her eyes flashed. "Are you insane? I'm not doing that."

"Nora…" He stepped closer, brushing the wet edge of her scarf away from her face. "You're soaked." Goddess… That was a poor choice of words. Desire flashed down his spine as he imagined saying those words for a different reason.

She swatted his hand away. "I'm fine," she insisted, but her chattering teeth told another story.

He sighed and turned for the fireplace. "For what it's worth, I'm not suggesting you traipse around in the nude. You can wear my cloak while your clothes dry."

A scoff echoed in his ears.

Deciding to take his own advice, he peeled his wet sweater off. He shivered in just his thin undershirt, but once the fire was going, he'd warm up swiftly. "I promise I won't look." He crouched before the fireplace, giving the task his full attention. "I'll be over here… starting the fire. Perfect time to stop being so damned stubborn."

As he began stacking the logs, he kept an ear open for sounds in the room. His skin prickled with each silent moment that passed. Would she listen to reason? Even with a fire, it would be ages before her clothes dried if she insisted on wearing them.

How long could he stand there watching her shiver while the solution was so simple? Not long, that was for sure. If she truly needed privacy to feel comfortable, then he'd give it to her. He'd just resigned himself to hunting for another room in the spooky dark inn when a pair of thumps sounded behind him.

He peeked over his shoulder, catching a glimpse of Nora's boots on the floor before she shrieked, "Hey, you promised! No looking."

He spun back so fast he was surprised his neck didn't crack. "I won't." Pulse thumping, he finished stacking the logs, trying not to hyperventilate as fabric rustled and wet articles slapped onto the floor.

He hardly kept the first match steady long enough to light it. Thank the goddess the logs were dry. As the fire burst to life, crackling and giving off enough warmth to stop the worst of his shudders, footsteps padded beside him.

"Is it safe to look yet?" he asked softly, keeping his gaze trained on the fire.

Nora drew in an audible breath. "Yes."

He spun slowly, utterly entranced by Nora's shapely frame sheathed in his cloak. Her ankles and toes peeked out the bottom, the only part of her visible except for her hands and head. Still, he couldn't escape the knowledge that she was bare beneath. In *his* cloak. He might never wash it again...

"Kieran... We need to talk."

RUINED

Nora

Nora huddled beside the fire, finally warm enough that the worst of her trembling subsided. But another war raged within her, the dueling desires chilling her even worse than the storm had.

What was Kieran doing here? And how could he just sit there, acting like nothing was wrong? How could he look at her, his gaze practically burning with longing after he'd abandoned her so easily?

So yeah. They needed to talk. He was lucky she wasn't already screaming.

She wanted to stay angry, but he made it close to impossible. Like the first moment she'd spotted him on the path. She'd frozen in place, so wrapped up in her head that she had no clue what to say. Then she'd practically swooned after he'd torn off his cloak and wrapped it around her.

And, as always, he was sinfully handsome. The only man who'd ever made her heart beat out of control while she remained comfortable in his presence. Then there was the fire in his eyes as he stared at her, even though she probably looked like a drowned rat.

Speaking of, she was glad she'd left Roo behind to keep an eye on Stellar Spirits. The last thing she needed right now was a ticked-off familiar chittering in her ear. If only she'd listened to Roo this morning when she advised waiting for the storm to blow over, maybe she wouldn't be in this mess to begin with...

Kieran rose from his crouched position, standing beside her. "You're right. We should talk. Do you want to go first?"

She crossed her arms, grateful for the oversized cloak that was miraculously warm and dry while all her clothes were decidedly *not*. And yeah, she'd felt a thousand times better after shucking off the sodden layers. But that didn't mean she wanted to spend the next few hours being ogled by a man who'd rejected her—repeatedly. "What I'd like first is for you to stop looking at me like *that*."

A crooked grin crossed his face. "Like what?"

"Like you're imagining what I'm wearing beneath this." She plucked at the collar, not missing the way his eyes tracked the motion.

His expression softened. "Can you blame me? I missed you." He reached for her, but before his hand connected with her shoulder, she backed up, putting some much-needed space between them. "Wait. I'm sorry. Come back to the fire. I'll behave. Promise."

She returned to the spot she'd just been in, studying him closely.

Kieran smiled sheepishly and rocked back on his heels. "See? I know when to keep my word."

"Do you really? Too bad you couldn't remember that the day you left." He'd promised to help her. How was she supposed to forgive him for that?

"Guess I deserve that." He rubbed the back of his neck. "For what it's worth, I had my reasons for leaving."

"Were you ever planning to share them with me?"

"That's what I was doing out on the pass today. I was coming to tell you everything."

"You were?"

His fingers twitched, but this time, he stuffed them into his pocket. "I was. You deserve to know the truth, Nora. I should've told you everything from the beginning."

"So tell me now."

His chest rose and fell sharply as he sucked in a deep breath. Then, with his gaze trained on the fire, he began, "When we met on the road the night before I left, I'd already decided to come clean about everything. I was planning to talk to Seth that morning. And then your mother."

"My mother?" Her brow furrowed. "Why did you need to talk to her?"

"She was the one who asked us to help you. Remember?"

"Yeah..."

"Well, what you don't know is that she offered me a cure for my help." He held up his arm, which currently sported a hook that she'd noticed but hadn't bothered to ask about yet. The metal gleamed in the firelight and appeared to be well-crafted, though she couldn't appreciate it as his words sank in, chilling her bones.

Was that the only reason he'd helped her? If Kieran hadn't lost his hand and then been bribed by her mother, he'd have never even sought her out. All that time, she'd been pining for him, but she wasn't even a whisper in the back of his mind… was she?

"That morning, I was planning to tell Moira I didn't want her cure."

Her gaze shot back to his face.

"I'd just met with Davos and commissioned this." He lifted the hook slightly before dropping his arm at his side. "That's where I was coming from when I spotted you on Main."

"Why didn't you tell me then?" Of course, it was the same night she learned she was a witch. She had dominated the conversation, hadn't she?

"It didn't come up. Then you fell asleep on me…" He shrugged. "It didn't seem that important at the time. Especially since I was planning to set everything right the next day. Not just with your mother. I was going to talk to Seth, too. About us."

"Well, I'm sorry I ruined your plans. If you'd apologized to Seth for kissing me before you broke the news about your new job, you would've saved yourself some pain."

His brow furrowed. "No. That wasn't it at all." He turned away from the fire, his gaze burning again, the longing she couldn't stand cutting even more sharply. "It was never about the job. And I wasn't planning to leave. Not until I got home and my father called me into his study."

She blinked. "That's when he offered you the job."

"Offered isn't how I'd put it… More like coerced."

Her stomach churned. "How?"

"He wanted me back in my old position. At the time, I thought it was just to keep his reputation sparkling, but now I know his motives weren't so black and white… But that's neither here nor there." He waved a hand, like he knew he was getting off topic. "I told him no.

That I wanted to stay. But... then he gave me an ultimatum I couldn't bear to refuse."

Nora's heart rattled like a broken cork stuck in an empty wine bottle. "What was it?"

His head dropped. "He said if I didn't go, he'd revoke your lease."

"Oh, goddess." Tears threatened, forming in the corners of her eyes. "You're serious?"

Kieran lifted his tortured gaze to meet hers. "I couldn't be the reason you lost your dream, Nora. I'm sorry."

She pressed shaky fingers to her chest. "How could he? That's... horrid."

"You should know, the deal is off now. My mother stepped in. Your lease isn't at risk anymore because of me. But if you want nothing to do with me now... I understand."

He thought she was horrified because of the lease? That wasn't even close. "I'm not worried about that..." She grabbed his hand and squeezed. "I'm appalled at what he did to *you*. I always knew your family was difficult to handle, but this..."

He squeezed back, filling his lungs with a deep breath. "I know."

They stood there for a time, silently holding hands in front of the fire as Nora digested his words. She had Kieran pegged all wrong. She'd been so worried he'd left because he didn't care enough about her to stay, but this proved that he *did* care. Why else would he upend his life, cut off his best friend, and take a job he couldn't stand, just to protect her dreams?

But as she thought back on his confession, there was one question she had to ask. "If your father hadn't demanded that of you, what would you have said to Seth?"

He turned to face her. "Probably the same thing I told him when he came to talk some sense into me yesterday."

She cocked a brow. "Which was?"

He let go of her hand and squared his shoulders before meeting her eyes. "That I know I've been a bit of a scoundrel with the women I've courted in the past—"

She interjected with a scoff.

"—but it was because those ladies meant nothing to me. There's only ever been one woman who held my heart hostage and refused to let it go." He reached out tentatively, stroking her arm just above the elbow. "She caught it in her net when she was just a girl and she begged me to throw back the poor fish I'd landed." His fingers drifted up to her shoulder as he stared into her eyes. "Then she wrapped it in silk, the night I stole a dance from the most gorgeous stranger I'd ever laid eyes on. Her name was burned into my soul after the kiss I could never forget, no matter how hard I tried."

He does remember. A tear slid down her cheek.

He gently cradled her face, swiping the warm droplet away. "I was an idiot for letting her go. But... then we met again. And with every sharp word out of her mouth and every glimpse I stole of her generous heart, I knew I would be the realm's greatest fool if I didn't do everything in my power to make her mine."

Nora's pulse raced, her heart so damn full it ached. "You mean that?"

"I do. Truly, I do. And I swear if you give me another chance, I'll never forget it." He stepped closer, resting his forehead against hers. "Can I ask you something, Nora?"

She nodded, not trusting her voice not to crack.

"Why were you going to Fairvale?" He pulled back, staring down at her so intensely she knew he was dying for her to say it was for him.

"Someone once told me I shouldn't hold so tightly to my pride." She blinked back her tears. "I thought, maybe if I followed his advice, I might find the courage to go after the thing I want most."

His Adam's apple bobbed. "Your job? Are you expanding?"

"No." She flung her arms around his neck and dragged him closer. "It's you, you idiot."

The most stunning smile she'd ever seen flashed across his face. "Thank the goddess. I'm so glad to hear that, Nora. Because for me, it's always been you." Then his lips descended, the soft kiss he gifted her setting off a chain of memories.

He'd said that before... hadn't he? She'd forgotten it until now, likely due to being exhausted and half-asleep, but with his lips tenderly sliding against hers, the memory flashed, bright and vibrant.

He'd tucked her in so chivalrously after carrying her up to bed from the bar. Even now, he was so gentle, holding her softly and kissing her sweetly, careful not to push things too far, even though she felt the evidence of his desire pressed against her.

But she wasn't in the mood for chivalry any longer. She pulled away and peered up at him, her eyes half-lidded and full of desire. "Kieran, I want you."

Another grin flashed. "Yes, you said that already." His head dipped, lips pursed for what would no doubt be another sweet kiss.

Her palm landed flat on his chest. "No. I want you—now."

His eyes widened, his tone turning equal parts excited and incredulous. "Really?"

"Yes, really." They'd been skirting around intimacy for far too long. Frankly, she couldn't wait to know what it would feel like to be connected to him—fully connected in both body and mind. If his lovemaking was anything like his kisses, then she didn't want to wait another second to experience it.

"You're sure? Even… here?" He gestured to the dreary old inn.

"We're all alone. In front of a roaring fire. It's kind of romantic, wouldn't you say?" She reached for his shirt, dipping her fingers beneath the bottom hem.

Kieran grasped her hand, his voice wavering. "And you're sure you don't mind… about this?" He lifted the hook between them, meeting her gaze.

Nora traced the metal with the tip of a finger. "I don't mind at all."

The breath of relief he released shot straight through her chest, took hold of her heart, and clasped it in a vise. She cradled his face with her palm, wishing she could erase every shadow of doubt she glimpsed in his eyes. Keiran was wonderful—just the way he was.

"Honestly, Kieran, I think it's great." She backed away slightly, treating him to a lingering gaze that started at the hook, then trailed up his toned arm and chiseled chest, before ending on his devastatingly handsome face. "And there's no denying you wear it well." His lips twitched with the beginnings of a smile. "But if it bothers you, I can try to heal you. I don't know if I'll be successful or not, but—"

"No. If I've learned anything through all this, it's that chasing perfection is never the answer. And knowing you accept me even though I'm not perfect makes me so damn certain we're made for each other."

A tiny laugh bubbled out of her chest. "I think so too."

He smirked. "Besides, this thing has its uses."

"Really?" She smiled up at him, inching closer. "And what might they be—" Her question cut off on a gasp as the buttons on his cloak skittered across the floor. "Kieran!" She gaped down just in time to spot his hook tearing off the last button. "You ruined your cloak!"

"Did I?" His gaze turned positively feral as it dropped, eating up every inch of her skin peeking between the gaping fabric. "You're going to have a hard time convincing me I didn't just improve the design."

Then he tipped up her chin and planted a searing kiss on her lips—one that wasn't sweet in the slightest. This kiss was desperate, urgent, and full of so much passion she felt it in her bones.

Drugging kisses turned to questing touches. Nora reveled in the moment, in *him*, and when he stripped off the cloak and lay down upon it before the fire, she stretched out beside him without a single speck of hesitation.

Her heart raced as they moved as one while the dancing flames reflected in Kieran's eyes. It wasn't just about pleasure, though there was that in spades. It was seeing him come undone—for *her*. Hearing her name on his lips and uttering his in return. Knowing that whatever life threw at them next, they'd face it—together.

By the time they were through, the buttons weren't the only thing that had been ruined. Nora was lost, body and soul, to the only man she'd ever wanted. The one man who saw all the parts of her and claimed her as his. The perfectly imperfect man whom she never thought she'd be lucky enough to capture, who'd been ensnared in the same tangled web of longing and lost chances just as tightly as she was.

Yes, she was well and truly ruined. And she couldn't be happier about it.

A Different Adventure

Kieran

Two weeks later...

"Better eat that on the go," Kieran urged. "You don't want to be late for class."

Oliver snagged the paper to-go box, barely waiting a second to tear open the lid. Steam curled in the chill air, along with a delectable aroma laden with savory and salty notes that made Kieran's stomach rumble.

"Wow, this looks good." Oliver ripped off a glove, then scooped out a few sweet potato fries and stuffed them in his mouth. "Iss wealy gooft," he mumbled around a bite.

Kieran chuckled. "I'll pass on your compliments to the chef." He retreated to the picnic bench, sitting atop it beside a dwindling pile of boxes.

With a wave, Oliver wandered off, sheathed in a long black cloak dotted with dozens of buttons that looked extremely familiar. Kieran had acquired a new cloak of his own—one that fastened with ingenious magnetic snaps he'd purchased from Davos. Much better for him, considering what happened to the last...

Oliver's compliments would have to wait. He'd begun helping Nora in the mornings, wanting to spare her the cold. He'd roll out of bed—*their* bed now—creep downstairs, and heat up the leftovers Nora had prepped for the village children. Most days, like today, he left her sleeping, knowing exactly how she'd show her appreciation for the extra shuteye when they closed for the night.

A smirk danced on his lips as memories rose. He wasn't sure which was more delicious... the scent wafting from the boxes beside him, or the pictures swimming in his mind. Ah, who was he kidding? Everything about Nora was positively delectable.

He'd been riding a high since that day in the mountains. It was almost too good to be true. He never imagined that losing his hand would lead to the best thing that ever happened to him. But he was so lucky it had, and nothing was going to put a damper on the fantastic mood that living with the girl of his dreams inspired.

"Kieran?"

Well... almost nothing.

He frowned, his gaze jerking toward the back fence as the familiar voice reached his ears. "Father. What are you doing here?"

Tanyth strolled through the gate without waiting to be invited in. Every inch the polished businessman, even first thing in the morning, he wore a tailored peacoat, the rich navy fabric highlighting his icy blue eyes. "I heard you were back in town. I came to say hello. And to bring you this."

He lifted a folder, piquing Kieran's curiosity. But before he gave in to the feeling and demanded to know what was inside, he had to ask, "Just hello, is it? Not here to read me the riot act for disobeying your orders and leaving that job you were so desperate for me to take?"

Tanyth stopped beside him. "May I sit?"

Kieran was amazed his jaw didn't land in the snowy grass at his feet. "When did you start asking for my permission for anything?"

"I've been trying something new." He adjusted his perfectly cuffed sleeve. "Lots of new things, in fact."

"Oh? Do tell." Kieran lounged back and gestured to the table beside him.

Tanyth's lips pursed as he examined the old picnic table. Kieran could guess what was running through his mind; that he had no intention of sullying his fine coat on the dirty wood. But his father surprised him again when he climbed up and perched there with the boxes between them.

"Oh... I must say, whatever's in there smells wonderful."

"What are you doing here, Father?"

Tanyth reached into the folder and pulled out a crisp sheet of parchment. "I've come to apologize for how dreadfully I handled matters when you were here last. Your mother helped me see the error of my ways. It was wrong of me to let my issues with my father affect my relationship with you. I see that now. I hope this will go a long way toward setting things right."

Kieran plucked the page from his father's hand. "Is this what I think it is?"

"If you've deduced that it's the deed to the building we're currently sitting outside of... then yes."

He gaped at the deed—which outlined the ownership of Stellar Spirits being awarded to him—then lifted his gaze to Tanyth's. "Why would you give me this?"

"I should've never threatened your friend's livelihood. I realize that now. This is my way of showing you it will never happen again."

It was a nice gesture. Perhaps the nicest his father had ever offered him. And yet... "I can't accept this. This business is Nora's. She's worked her ass off to make it successful. If anyone deserves to own Stellar Spirits, it's her. Not me."

He glanced down at the parchment, wondering if he'd just made another idiotic mistake. It wouldn't be his first... but if he knew anything about Nora, he knew she wouldn't want this. The woman whose pride refused to let her take a handout even when it would save her from ruin didn't want success handed to her on a silver platter. She wanted to earn it. And he planned to help her every step of the way.

"Can I ask what you intend to do now that you're out of work?" Tanyth asked softly. "I thought perhaps this could be the start of you following in the family business."

"I'm sorry, Father, but your job? It's not for me. I'll help Nora here, of course. But... I've been seriously considering joining the fire brigade."

"Huh... I can't say I'm pleased to hear that, but if it will make you happy, then you should."

Wow. His jaw slackened. But he didn't let the shock immobilize him. Instead, he handed the parchment back. "You should take this. I don't want it. And honestly, Father? I'm not ready to accept your apology either. Not after what you did to Nora."

"I'm not surprised." Tanyth shifted, clutching the folder in a white-knuckled grip and clearing his throat. "What I did was unacceptable and you're an honorable man, no thanks to me. I'm proud of you, Son—not only for everything you've accomplished, but for just being you. I'm sorry it's taken me this long to say it. For what it's worth, I don't need you to forgive me now. Although, I hope you will, in time. And I vow to keep doing what's right, so perhaps one day I'll deserve your forgiveness."

Kieran's chest burned. "I'm glad to hear that." Maybe there was hope for his father after all…

Tanyth took the deed back, a small smile painting his lips. "I suspected you might not want this. That's why I drafted another."

As he pulled a second page from the folder, the back door swung open. "Kieran, are you out here?" Nora emerged, wearing a sleepy grin that vanished as her gaze fell on Tanyth. "Oh…"

"Miss Rowen. I'm pleased you're here. This is for you." Tanyth hopped off the table, his elvish ancestry allowing him to fluidly cross the garden in a few quick steps. Before Kieran shook off his surprise, the page was clutched in Nora's hands.

As her gaze darted across the deed, his gut churned. What was Tanyth up to? Nora didn't want a handout. She was liable to tear that paper to pieces out of spite…

But then she lifted a hand to her lips, hiding her expression. "Is this for real?"

Kieran hurried to her side. Was she happy? Horrified? He honestly couldn't say.

"It is," Tanyth announced proudly. "I'm afraid I've stretched myself too thin with all my properties as of late. And considering how much success you've had at this location, I thought you might be interested in changing the terms of our agreement."

"What is it?" Kieran asked, leaning over her shoulder but unable to read much with the parchment shaking in Nora's grip.

She turned to him with glossy eyes. "He's offering me a rent-to-own deal. Once I make enough payments, the ownership of Stellar Spirits will change... to me."

"I have no doubt you'll fulfill the terms swiftly." Tanyth rocked back on his heels, smiling pleasantly.

How had his father gleaned that Nora would turn up her nose at the same offer that he'd made to him, but this would be like a dream come true? He had to concede that his family wasn't as awful as he suspected. Just maybe, they truly cared for him, albeit in a different way than he'd always envisioned.

Nora fluttered the deed in front of her chest. "Thank you, Mr. Dornelis. I'm so grateful for this opportunity."

"You deserve it, my dear. And please, call me Tanyth."

"Tanyth. Thank you so much." She beamed up at him, then nodded at the door. "Would you like to come in? I'll find something to sign this with. Oh, and I'd love to make you a drink." She tilted her head, eyes pinched as she scrutinized him. "You look like a bourbon man... Can I tempt you with a sour mash that just finished aging?"

Kieran's chest pinched, his father's declaration on the night he sent him away returning to haunt him. Would he dare lower himself enough to be seen drinking at a bar on the "wrong side of town"?

But it appeared today was a day for surprises.

Tanyth fell in step with Nora, flashing a delighted grin. "That sounds wonderful. And you're quite right. I do enjoy a good bourbon."

As Kieran scooped up the remaining boxes, his fantastic mood snapped back into place.

Well... I wanted a life full of adventure. Looks like I got my wish.

Sure, the adventures weren't exactly the same as he pictured. He never guessed he'd be watching his father slum it, joining the fire brigade, or facing his fears only to find everything he'd been missing. But that was what made living in Everpass so much fun. And he wouldn't have it any other way.

Before he went inside, two familiar faces popped up at the fence. "Seth, Ma. What brings you two here this morning?"

Seth led his mother into the yard, his steps careful with his mother clutching his arm, both of them decked out in cloaks, scarves, and the fluffy hats he knew for a fact Seth hated to wear but always donned when Moira urged him to.

"Does a mother need an excuse to pop in on her daughter?" Moira quirked a grin.

"We're here for breakfast," Seth explained. "Ma burned the last of the eggs."

Moira swatted his arm and scowled. "Kieran didn't need to know that."

Kieran chuckled as he handed Seth a to-go box. "This ought to tide you over until Nora whips up something fresh." He knew Nora would insist on it when she spotted them. Besides, a child's portion of leftovers would never appease Seth's hearty appetite. "She's inside, and you'll never guess who's in there with her."

Seth lifted a brow. "Easy enough to find out." He bounded for the door as he tore into the container.

"Hold up, Ma." Kieran's soft request made Moira linger behind.

"Yes, love?"

"I haven't had a chance to catch up with you since I got back." He toed at the snow with his boot. "I just thought you should know, I'm not expecting that healing tonic you promised me."

"Well, that's good." Moira flashed a smug grin. "Seeing as how I never intended to give you one."

His stomach flip-flopped. "You didn't?"

"If I recall, the only claim I made was that I knew exactly what you needed, and that if you helped Nora, you'd find it." She patted his shoulder. "It was never about your injury. I knew from the start that the goddess had plans for you and my girl. Why else do you think I let Seth catch me wandering around, chanting at the moon?" She winked. "Had to get you two alone so you could see what you were really missing."

"Moira... you're quite the cunning witch, aren't you?"

She preened at the compliment. Then she leaned in and whispered, "Do me a favor. Don't go filling Seth in on what I just told you. Goddess knows he ought to be the next one settling down. His doddering old mother might need to make another appearance or two to set that boy of mine straight."

Uh oh... Sounded like Seth had some meddling in his future. *But who am I to stand in the way of what the goddess wants?*

He mimed locking his lips with a key. "Don't worry, Ma. My lips are sealed."

Infinitely Sweet

Nora

Three Weeks Later...

"Thanks again for hosting. I'm so excited for this one!" Andra clutched a new paperback against her chest, a huge grin lighting her face. "See you at the next meeting!" The plump redhead's green dress twirled as she ducked out Stellar Spirit's door, along with half a dozen regulars who'd begun attending their book club meetings.

"Bye, ladies!" Nora called out, swiping their coins off the bar as Tini grabbed their empties.

Ali sipped a mug of cider from her stool beside Maalik. "I have to hand it to you, Mal. The picks lately have been a huge hit." Since swapping from the pure filth Ali liked to read to romances that were more action and adventure oriented, they'd attracted lots of new members.

Maalik chugged from his mug before replying, "Still wish you'd find more men to join. If I have to listen to one more lady swooning over the love scenes when they ought to be dissecting the battles—"

Ali patted his back. "I'll work on it. There has to be a few men in this town who appreciate the written word."

The front door opened, letting in a gust of chill wind and Tini's brother, Lio. He strode to the bar without unbuttoning his long black cloak.

Tini brightened. "My shift doesn't end for a quarter hour. You here for a drink?"

Ali spun on her stool, a crooked grin on her face. "Lio. Thought I told you book club started an hour ago? Don't worry." She tossed him a paperback. "I saved you a copy of our next pick."

Lio caught it easily, his tall, burly frame making the book look smaller than it was. As he lifted it to eye level and examined the scantily clad couple embracing on the cover, a muscle in his jaw twitched. "I'm not here for a drink. Or... this." He set the book down on the bar and turned to Nora. "Is Kieran around?"

"Sure, just let me grab him." Nora's purple dress brushed against her ankles as she strode across the floor, then threw open the door to the loft. She ducked inside, stopping on the bottom stair, and yelled up, "Hey, Kieran, get down here! You have a visitor."

His boots echoed on the stairs as he made his way down to her. "Hey, love." He pulled her into his arms and planted a quick peck on her lips that made her stomach flutter. "Please tell me it's not my mother... If I have to hear her thoughts on your books one more time, I'll gouge out my eardrums."

She giggled while smoothing her hands over his black tunic. "She left already, so you can relax. Come on."

Kieran's smile faded as he spotted Lio waiting for him beside the bar. "Lio. What a surprise."

Nora's pulse raced. It had surprised no one in Everpass when the old fire brigade chief retired and named Lio as his successor. As a water nymph, he was naturally suited to the position, not to mention he'd proven himself to be a hard worker to boot.

Kieran had shared how impressed he was with Lio after his interview last week. Since then, he'd been anxiously waiting to learn if he'd landed a spot on the crew.

Nora couldn't help worrying a little, too. Sure, she knew Kieran was extremely capable, lost hand or not, but that didn't mean the rest of the realm would think the same...

Lio's stone-like expression lifted as he gifted Kieran a rare smile. "Hope you don't mind. I was planning to walk Tini home, so figured I'd speak with you while I was here."

"Efficient. I like it." Kieran chuckled softly. "Should we grab a table in the back and have a chat?"

The rest of the room probably didn't notice anything off, but Nora picked up on the subtle signs of Kieran's anxiety. His grin was a touch pinched, his spine slightly stiff as he led Lio away.

Please, please be good news...

"Don't fret." She hadn't meant to project her thoughts, but that didn't stop Roo from chiming in. *"He'd have to be a fool to reject a former spy for the Crown. And that one there is no fool."*

"I hope you're right."

Nora split a glance between Roo, perched comfortably in her nest, and Lio. She hadn't gotten to know Lio well, even with his little sister working for her. Fact was, no one in town had. He kept to himself habitually, only visiting with Davos, the town blacksmith. But Roo had an uncanny knack for judging people correctly.

She slid back behind the bar. "Before you leave, do you mind doing a quick inventory in the basement?" she asked Tini.

"No, not at all." Tini left with a grin on her face and a spring in her step.

Once the basement door banged closed, Nora leaned over the bar. "What's going on with you two?" She nodded at the back table, lifting a brow.

Ali's bob floated around her ears as she shook her head. "Nothing at all."

"Uh-huh." Nora pursed her lips. "When did you invite Lio to book club?"

Ali waved a hand. "It's not like I hunted him down and begged him to come. He was in the smithy when I was inviting Davos, and it would've been rude not to extend the invite to him, too."

Davos was the most introverted guy in town—which wasn't surprising, seeing as he was the only one of his kind in Everpass—but that didn't stop Ali from befriending him. She was always urging him to get out of his shop, unsuccessfully for the most part. But that was beside the point.

"Admit it." Nora lowered her voice. "You have a thing for the hot new nymph in town."

"Do not," Ali sputtered, crossing her arms.

Maalik added, "Would be a good match."

Ali's eyes flashed as she turned to him. "Just because we're the same race doesn't magically make us right for each other."

"Not because of that." Maalik spun his mug. "I've been paying attention to those books, and you two are the perfect example of grumpy and sunshine."

Nora burst into laughter. "Oh my goddess. He's right!"

Ali shushed her. "Listen, it's not happening. Not ever. I don't want to get into it now, but there's a few things about nymphs that you aren't aware of. Just… trust me when I tell you that Lio is *way* out of my league."

Her heart fell. "Really?"

"Yeah. But it's fine. I'm happy with my books and my friends." Ali shot Maalik a cheeky grin before bumping shoulders with him. "Who needs dead weight dragging you down when you have these babies, am I right?" She tapped her knuckles on her paperback.

Maalik's only answer was a long pull on his mug.

Ali leaned over the bar, lowering her voice. "Besides… I get the feeling that stick in the mud is not a fan of kids. You know I'd never bring a man into Echo's life who didn't love her unconditionally."

"You're right." Nora sighed. "Guess it's not meant to be."

Maybe she was just seeing romance everywhere now that she'd found a love of her own. But she couldn't help it. She wanted Ali to find her match. She might claim to be happy with her books, but for someone who was so obsessed with romance, she had to be secretly craving it in her life, not just in her fiction.

"Speaking of Echo…" Ali frowned. "I may have my hands full more than usual. Thought I ought to mention it since I probably won't be by as often after work."

Nora blanched. "Oh no. Is everything all right?"

"I hope so. She's been getting sick a lot this winter. And she's been acting out at school. I thought it was just due to the weather change… but now I'm not so sure."

"Please let me know if I can do anything." Nora reached across the bar, grabbing Ali's hand. "I'm still learning my limits with healing, but if I can help, I'm happy to try."

Ali smiled softly. "I appreciate that, Nor. But I suspect this is something magic can't fix. I need to spend more time with her and figure out exactly what's going on. It'll mean closing up early and losing some sales, but I have to think of Echo first. I'm all she's got."

The last thing she wanted was to see Ali's business suffer. Still, she was right. If Echo needed her, Ali would never ignore that. She'd burn the world to the ground to make sure her daughter was living her best life. It was what made her such an incredible mother, and Nora would always admire that about her.

The cellar door creaked open at the same moment Kieran and Lio stood, shaking hands over their table. Nora's heart raced as the men converged on the bar.

Before they arrived, Tini thrust out the inventory list. "Here's everything. Do you need anything else?"

"No, Tini. This is perfect. Good work today. I'll see you in two days for your next shift." Nora stuffed the book under the bar while Tini threw on her coat and said her goodbyes. As soon as the front door banged closed behind Lio, she blurted, "Out with it. What did he say?"

Kieran inhaled deeply, his face unreadable. "You're looking at the newest member of the fire brigade."

"Congratulations!" Nora raced to his side, threw her arms around his neck, and planted a kiss on his lips. "You deserve this, Kieran. I'm so proud of you."

"Thank you for pushing me to try out. I'm so lucky I have you." Kieran gazed down at her, a look of pure adoration on his face.

She sighed, dragging him down for another lingering kiss that had her toes curling in her boots.

"Eh hem." Maalik's stool scraped the floor. "Sounds like my cue to leave."

Ali said, "Me too."

Nora peeled herself off of Kieran. "No. Wait!" Everyone froze as Nora darted back behind the bar. "There's something I've been avoiding for far too long. I need you both here for moral support."

Maalik dropped back onto his stool. "All right. I'm intrigued. What is it?"

Nora bent down, opening a cabinet she'd kept locked since the night she learned about her heritage. The black book emblazoned with a crescent moon thumped as she plunked it atop the bar. "I'm finally ready to see what's inside."

Roo perked up, her ears twitching as she hopped to the edge of her nest. *"I'm glad you're finally ready. Bring me closer, please."*

Ali whistled. "So this is the mysterious book that your birth family left on your mother's doorstep?"

Nora flattened her palm beside Roo, a wash of pride rolling over her when she didn't cringe in the slightest as the little critter climbed on her hand. She'd gotten so used to her familiar now that she could hardly recall what had frightened her so badly when they'd met. "Yep, that's it." She deposited Roo on the bar top.

When she first got the book, she never imagined it would take her so long to open it. But after Kieran left, she'd been too out of sorts to consider it. And then she'd been so busy getting Stellar Spirits running smoothly. But now that her life had settled into a normal rhythm, she was finally ready to discover what secrets it held.

Kieran traced a finger over the cover, lingering on the crescent moon. "Do you have the necklace?"

"I do." Swallowing, Nora dug into her dress pocket. "Let's hope this works."

The white pendant was cool against her fingertips as she lowered it to the cover. Everyone leaned in, holding a shared breath. The moon sank into the embossed mark—a perfect fit.

Nora blew out a shaky breath. She'd been expecting something to happen when she fitted the necklace onto the cover. A flash of light, or maybe a click, as an unseen lock opened. But so far... nothing.

"What are you waiting for?" Roo asked. *"Open it."*

She tentatively reached for it... and it pulled open smoothly, like it had never been locked.

"I can't stand it!" Ali exclaimed. "What does it say?"

Nora opened it to a random page in the middle. She frowned and flipped the page. Then another. "It's... empty."

"What? No." Maalik scowled. "That's ridiculous."

She stood the book up and flipped it around so they could all see. "It is. Look." She flicked through the pages, each one as blank as the last.

"Well... That's a letdown," Ali muttered. She brightened. "Maybe you're meant to fill it?"

Her heart sank. "I suppose." All this time she'd been so sure the book would hold untold secrets that would bring new meaning to her life. But now, she couldn't chase away her disappointment.

Kieran's brow creased. "Wait... Go back to the very beginning."

She shrugged and flipped to the front cover. Then she gasped as she spotted ink scrawled on the first page. "There is something!"

"Go on. Read it," Kieran urged.

Nora took a deep breath and read aloud.

Nora,

It is my greatest wish that this book reaches you at the right time in your life. For reasons I cannot expand upon, you had to be raised by a stranger. I have every confidence that the family we selected will give you a wonderful life. But now that you've discovered your power, you must know that you are not alone.

This book is charmed, allowing you to communicate with the woman who owns its twin. Everything that you write within it will be written in the pages of her book, and likewise, her words will appear in yours. When you're ready, introduce yourself to your sister.

Silence fell as she read the last word of the unsigned note, which was written in the same script as the letters her mother had shown her.

"Oh my goddess…" Nora's eyes filled with tears. "A sister. I have a sister!"

"Are you going to write to her now?" Maalik asked.

Nora shook her head. "Not yet. I have to think of what to say." And more importantly, how to break the news to her mother and Seth. Her stomach twinged. She didn't want to disappoint them—they'd always be her family. But… she had a sister too. If she didn't at least attempt to talk to her, then she'd always wonder… what if?

Ali gasped. "Maybe she already wrote to you. Flip the page!"

With shaking fingers, she slowly turned the page. "Drat. No such luck."

"This is good news." Kieran wrapped an arm around her shoulders. "Now you have all the time you want to craft the perfect introduction."

"You're right." Nora's lips curved into a lopsided smile. "I can't believe I have a sister. I wonder what she's like. Do you think she'll want to meet me?"

"She'd be a fool not to." Kieran grinned.

Roo yawned. *"I agree. And I'm here for you if you need advice about what to say."*

"Thank you, Roo." She held out her hand again, then gave her sleepy familiar a lift back to her nest.

Ali sighed. "I'm happy for you, Nor. But I really ought to be getting home. I just hope I have some good news about my little family soon."

Maalik chuckled. "Listen to you. Acting like an ornery preteen is the worst thing ever. Puh-lease."

Ali popped a hip. "Oh yeah? That's rich coming from a successful banker. I bet you don't have a care in the world."

Maalik scoffed. "You'd be surprised."

"Try me." Ali lifted a brow.

"How about being stuck with the most useless power in the realm?" Maalik shot back. "Not all of us can be witches or summon fire at the snap of their fingers."

Nora slammed the book shut, instantly intrigued. Maalik never talked about his abilities or his heritage. She was dying to know what he could do.

Apparently, Ali was wondering the same thing. She smirked and, in the most goading tone imaginable, stated, "Boo hoo. I'm Maalik. I cry myself to sleep each night on my piles of coin because my hidden power is *so* lame."

His face reddened, and he reached for his mug. "It *is* lame. Tell me… what good is this?" He set the mug in front of him and gingerly tapped it with the tip of his finger. The glass shuddered and started vibrating, barely moving on the bar top. "All proper trolls can imbue an object with enough quake to break through the toughest rock in the realm. But not me. All I can manage is this pitiful shaking." He sighed heavily. "There. Now you know it. My secret shame." He hung his head.

Ali stared at the pulsating mug blankly for a moment, and then her expression morphed, her face breaking out in a look of pure… delight? "Maalik… You are a genius! I can use this… Oh my goddess, this is going to be *glorious*! How would you like a side gig?"

Nora's jaw dropped. "Um… What? I'm lost."

"Don't worry. You'll see." Ali threw an arm around Maalik's shoulders and led him out of the bar, whispering excitedly in his ear.

Kieran crossed to the window and flipped the Open sign to Closed.

"Do you have any clue what Ali was talking about?" Nora asked.

"Not a one. But I'm sure you'll be the first to know."

That was true… She just hoped whatever scheme Ali was cooking up with Maalik went well. At least it had shaken off a bit of the funk that Echo had unleashed in Ali's life lately.

"You ready for bed?" Kieran asked.

As Nora met his gaze across the bar, she couldn't stop the smile that overtook her. Months ago, she was crying on the floor, so certain that she'd just watched her dreams implode at the hands of an ill-tempered orc and mouthy imp. But now, she couldn't be more thankful for that disaster. Almost losing everything showed her exactly what was most important. Yeah, success was great, but having someone special to share it with… that made life infinitely sweeter.

"I'm ready." She wiggled her brows and backed up slowly, heading for the stairs. "Race you up there?"

"What do I get if I win?"

"You won't!" She took off with a squeal, but it wasn't loud enough for her to miss Kieran's reply.

"You're wrong about that, Nor. I've already won."

Nora's Mocktails

Hot Spiced Cider

Half gallon of apple cider

One cinnamon stick

Half teaspoon of whole cloves

Pinch of ground nutmeg

Directions: Add ingredients into a saucepan and heat on the stove. Remove large seasonings before serving. Garnish with cinnamon stick (optional).

Dirty Twist:

Create as above. Before serving, add to each glass:

Half ounce dark rum

One ounce butterscotch schnapps

Stir well. Enjoy responsibly.

Honey Lemonade

Three cups water

One cup lemon juice

Half cup honey

Directions: Mix water and lemon juice in a large pitcher. Add honey and stir well until combined (for faster mixing, use a blender). Serve over ice.

Dirty Twist:

Create as above. Before serving, add to each glass:

One and a half ounces of lemon vodka

Stir well. Enjoy responsibly.

Interested in discovering the recipe for Kieran's Infinite Bliss? It's available free to newsletter subscribers with the bonus short story

Mayhem and Masquerades—which features the ball where Kieran and Nora first kissed, told from Kieran's POV.

Download it at www.amberlwerner.com

Also By

The Palisade Trilogy

Shadows That Bind Us — Palisade Trilogy 1

Muses That Align Us — Palisade Trilogy 2

Lines That Drew Us — Palisade Trilogy 3

Palisade Trilogy – Omnibus Books 1-3 : an epic fantasy adventure

Sign up for my newsletter for a free standalone prequel novella that tells the story of how the Palisade was built centuries ago.

Fates That Entwine Us

You'll find the link on my website amberlwerner.com

Standalone Short Story

Somewhere In Between

The Blood Song Trilogy

The Odyssey Ring – A Blood Song Trilogy Prequel

Bloodfeather Lullaby — Blood Song Trilogy 1

Bloodfeather Heartsong — Blood Song Trilogy 2

Bloodfeather Symphony — Blood Song Trilogy 3

Fairvale Cozy Fantasy Romances

Magic and Mocktails

Upcoming Novels:

Sparking the Vibe – coming soon!

Ruling the Roost

Serenades and Steel

About the Author

Amber L. Werner loves to write about magic, monsters and mythical creatures. She lives in Norristown, PA with her husband and two children. The Palisade Trilogy is her debut series.

Follow her Facebook page Amber L. Werner
Or Instagram amberlwerner

Sign up for her newsletter and receive a free novella.
Find it here amberlwerner.com

www.ingramcontent.com/pod-product-compliance
Lightning Source LLC
Chambersburg PA
CBHW020738310726
48969CB00002B/317